Chimichanga™

Written and illustrated
by
Eric Powell

With colors
by
Dave Stewart

DARK HORSE BOOKS

Editor SCOTT ALLIE
Assistant Editor DANIEL CHABON
Designer JUSTIN COUCH
Publisher MIKE RICHARDSON

Mike Richardson *President and Publisher* · **Neil Hankerson** *Executive Vice President* · **Tom Weddle** *Chief Financial Officer* · **Randy Stradley** *Vice President of Publishing* · **Michael Martens** *Vice President of Book Trade Sales* · **Anita Nelson** *Vice President of Business Affairs* · **Micha Hershman** *Vice President of Marketing* · **David Scroggy** *Vice President of Product Development* · **Dale LaFountain** *Vice President of Information Technology* · **Darlene Vogel** *Senior Director of Print, Design, and Production* · **Ken Lizzi** *General Counsel* · **Davey Estrada** *Editorial Director* · **Scott Allie** *Senior Managing Editor* · **Chris Warner** *Senior Books Editor* · **Diana Schutz** *Executive Editor* · **Cary Grazzini** *Director of Print and Development* · **Lia Ribacchi** *Art Director* · **Cara Niece** *Director of Scheduling*

Published by
DARK HORSE BOOKS
A division of Dark Horse Comics, Inc.
10956 SE Main Street
Milwaukie, OR 97222

First edition: September 2011
ISBN 978-1-59582-755-5

1 3 5 7 9 10 8 6 4 2
Printed by 1010 Printing International, Ltd., Guangdong Province, China.

Chimichanga™ & © 2011. All rights reserved. Dark Horse Books® and the Dark Horse logo are registered trademarks of Dark Horse Comics, Inc. All rights reserved. No portion of this publication may be reproduced or transmitted, in any form or by any means, without the express written permission of Dark Horse Comics, Inc. Names, characters, places, and incidents featured in this publication either are the product of the author's imagination or are used fictitiously. Any resemblance to actual persons (living, dead, or undead), events, institutions, or locales, without satiric intent, is coincidental.

This book collects the *Chimichanga* comic-book series #1–#3, previously published by Albatross Exploding Funny Books.

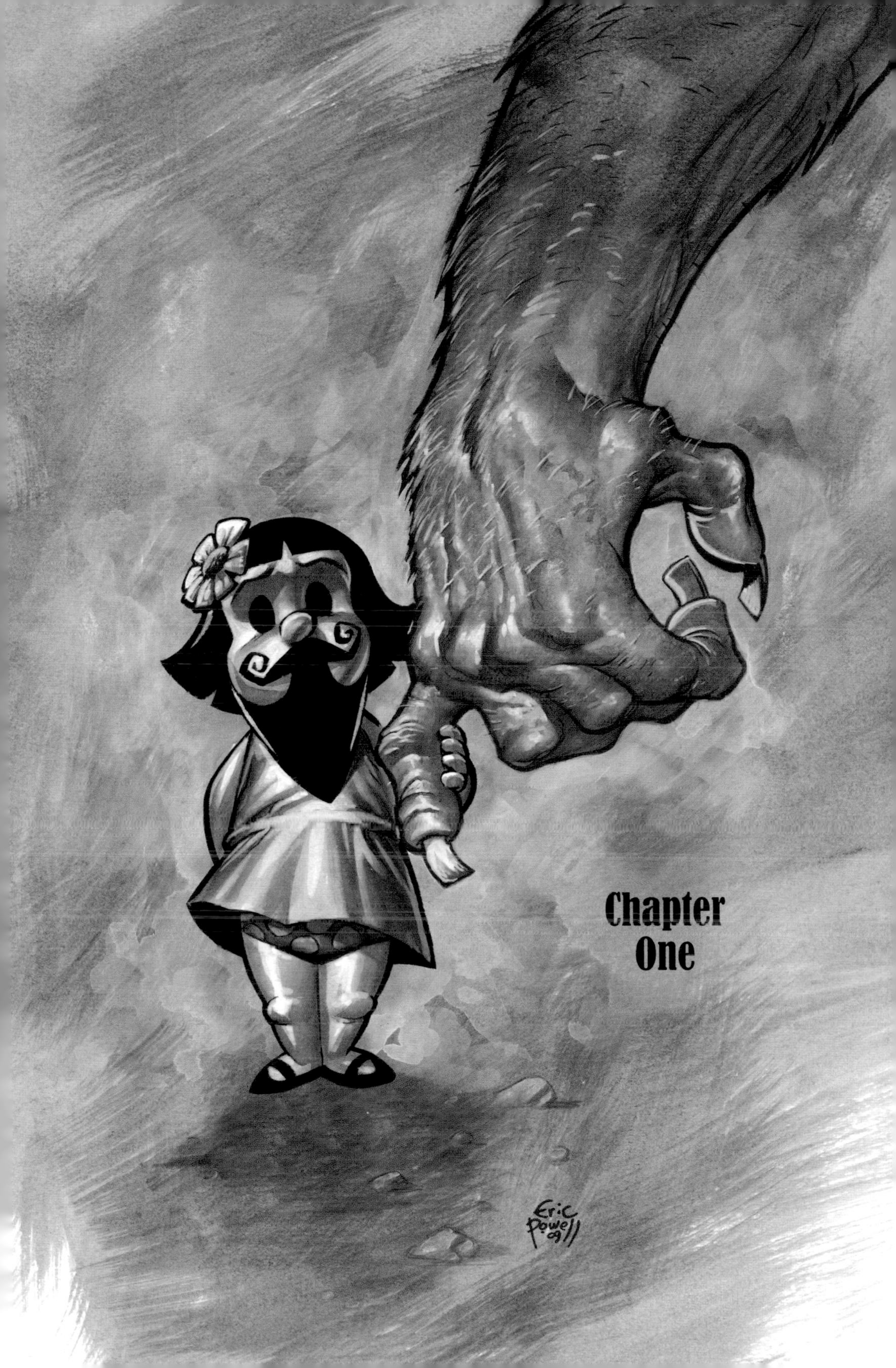
Eric Powell 09

Chapter One

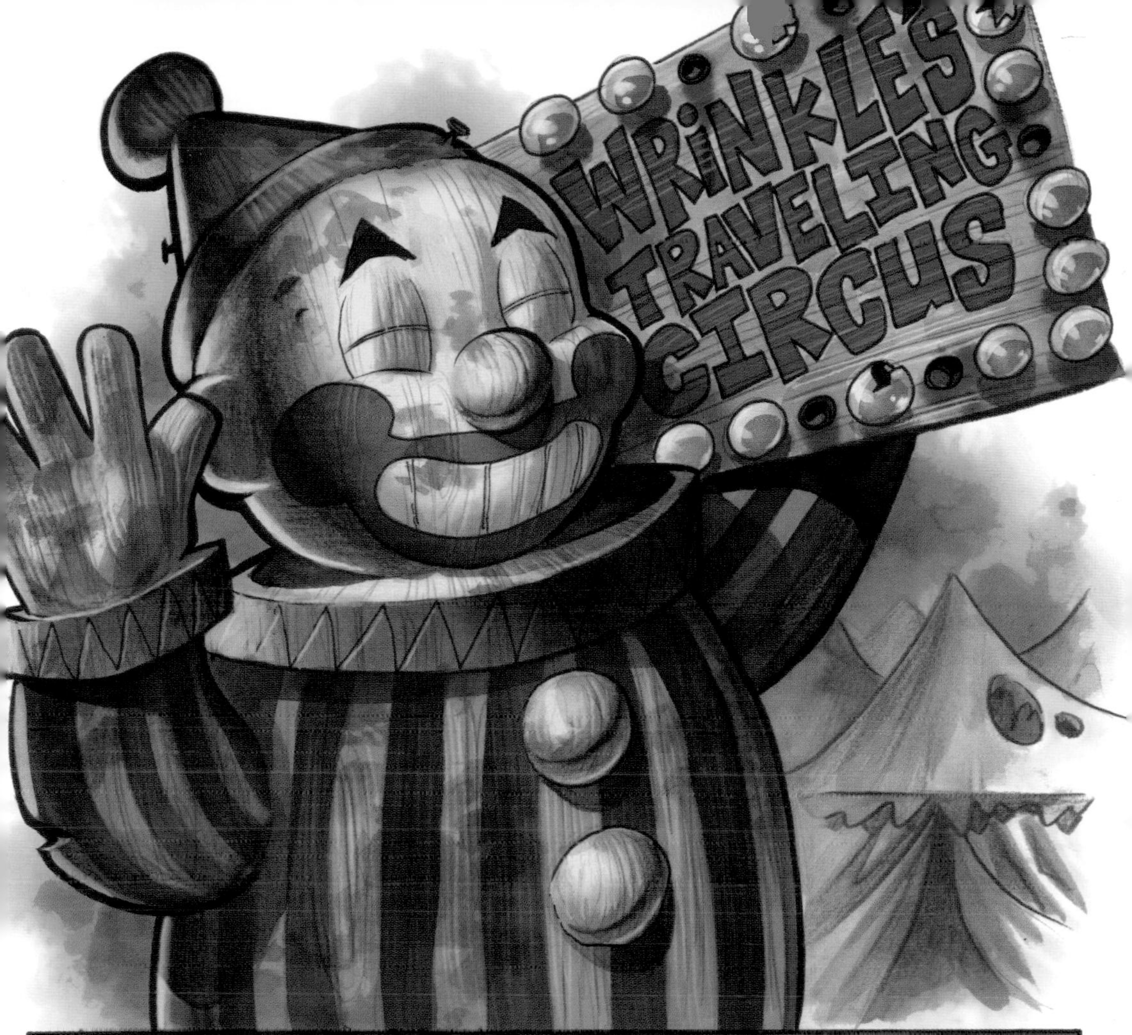
WRiNKLE'S TRAVELING CIRCUS

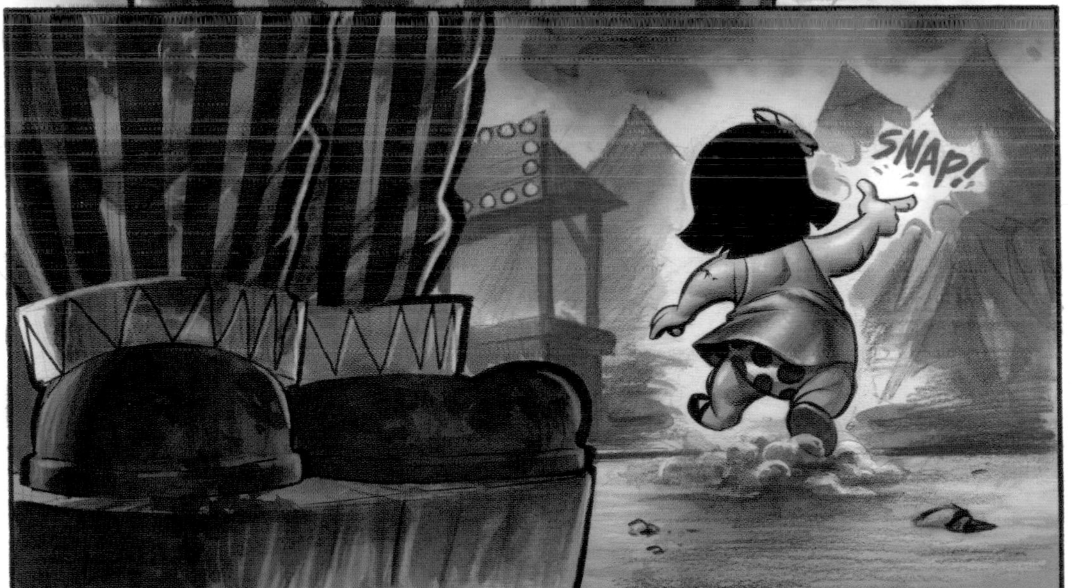
SNAP!

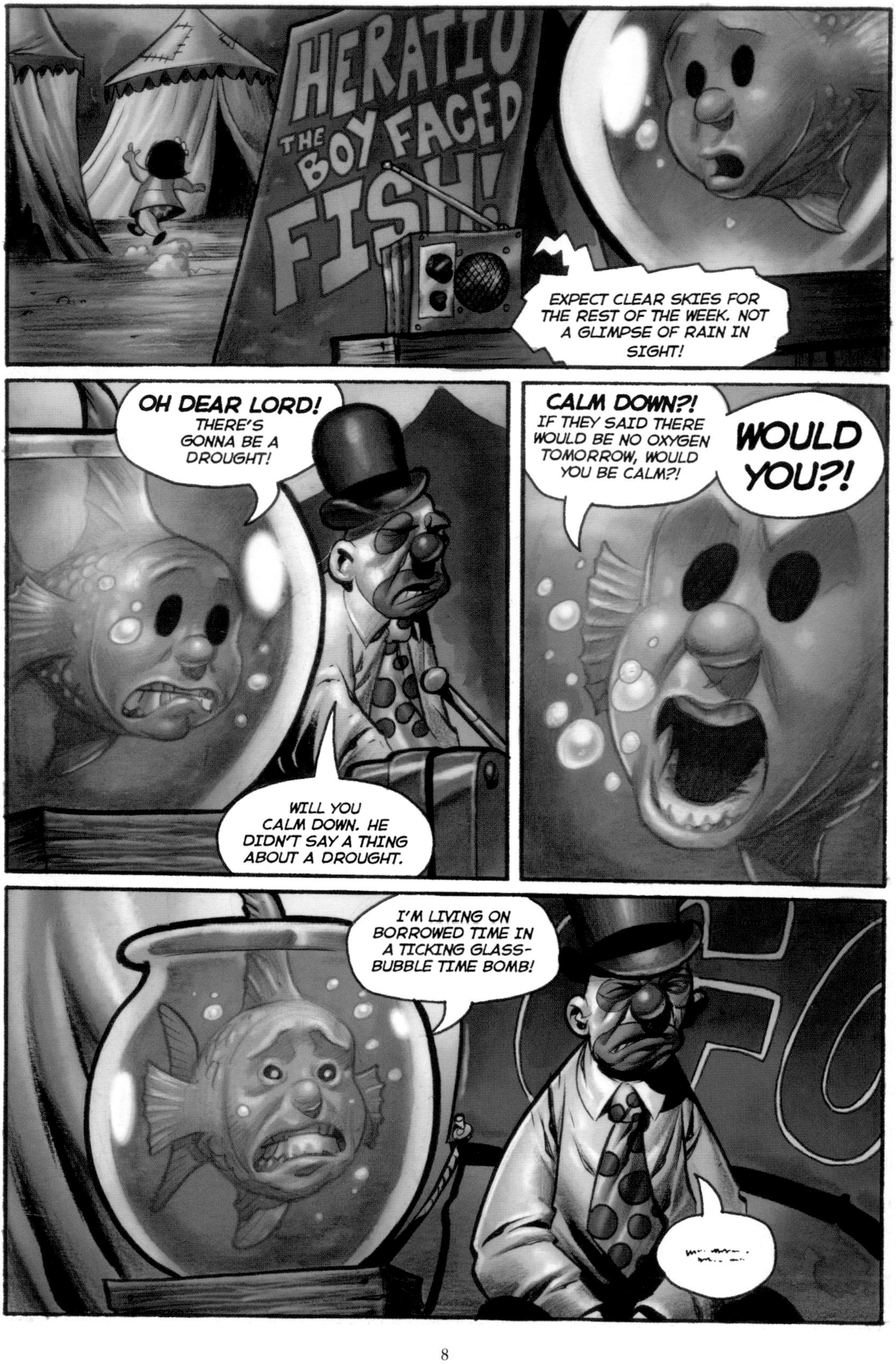
HERATIO THE BOY FACED FISH!
EXPECT CLEAR SKIES FOR THE REST OF THE WEEK. NOT A GLIMPSE OF RAIN IN SIGHT!
OH DEAR LORD! THERE'S GONNA BE A DROUGHT!
WILL YOU CALM DOWN. HE DIDN'T SAY A THING ABOUT A DROUGHT.
CALM DOWN?! IF THEY SAID THERE WOULD BE NO OXYGEN TOMORROW, WOULD YOU BE CALM?!
WOULD YOU?!
I'M LIVING ON BORROWED TIME IN A TICKING GLASS-BUBBLE TIME BOMB!

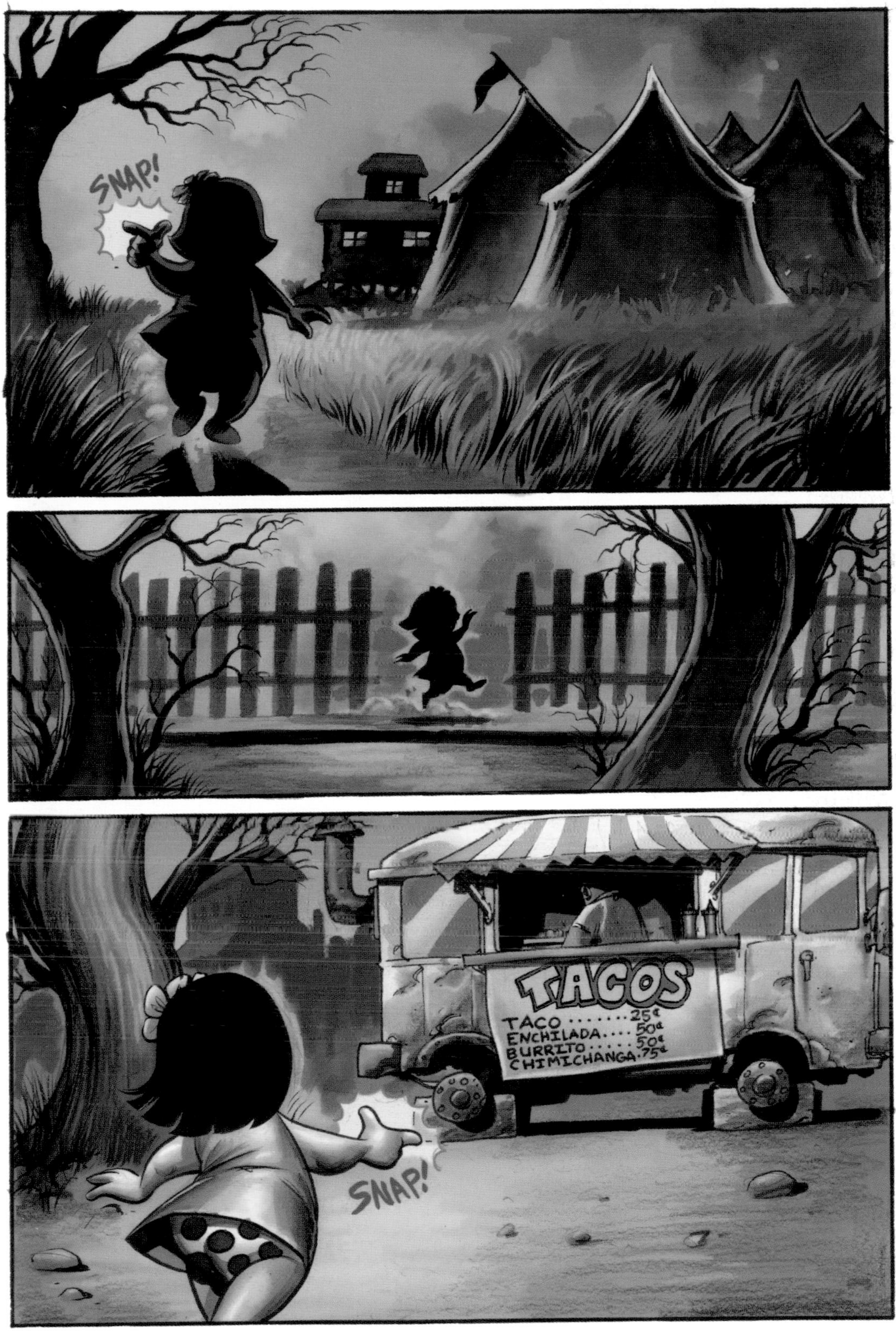
SNAP!
TACOS
TACO ....25¢
ENCHILADA....50¢
BURRITO......50¢
CHIMICHANGA.75¢
SNAP!

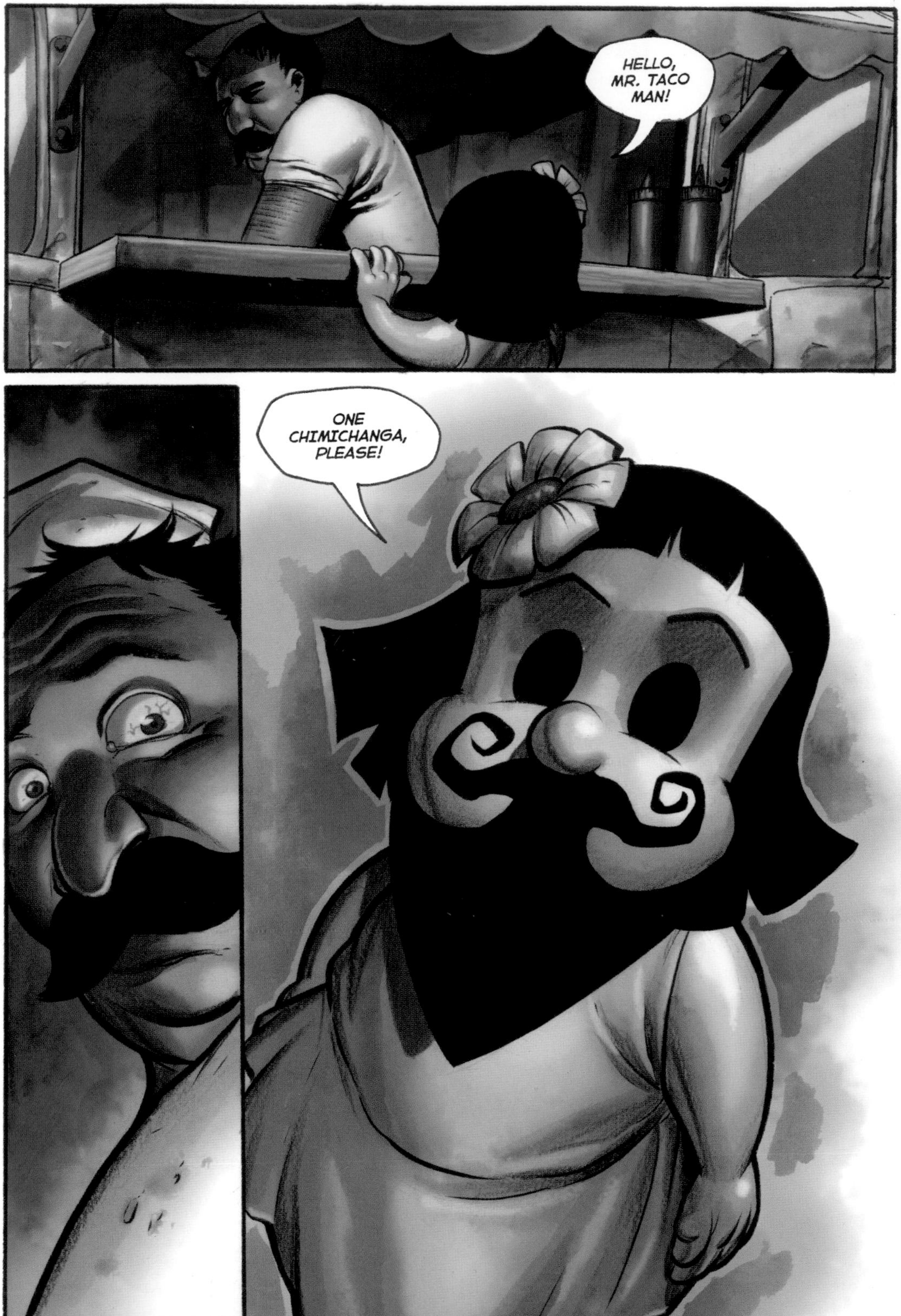
HELLO, MR. TACO MAN!
ONE CHIMICHANGA, PLEASE!

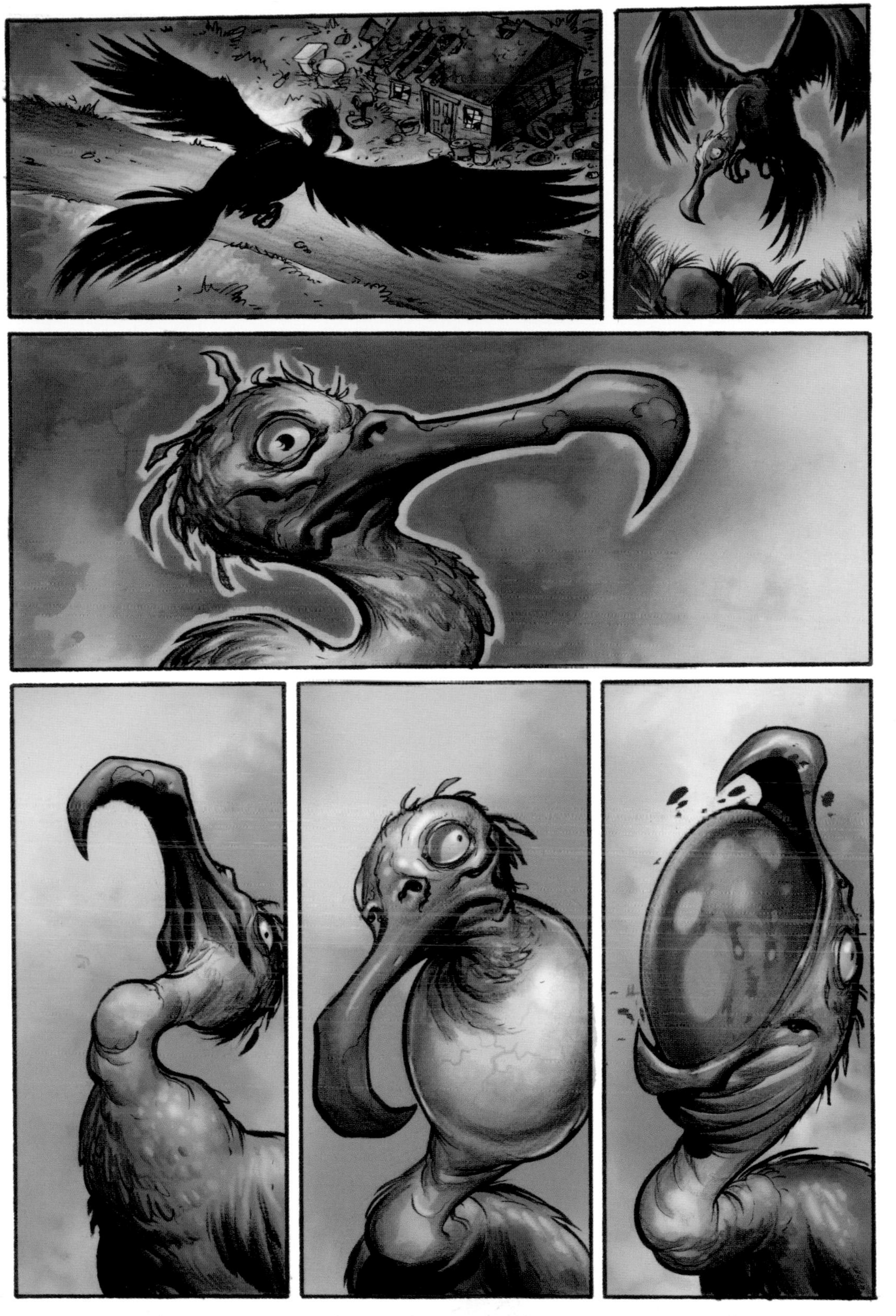

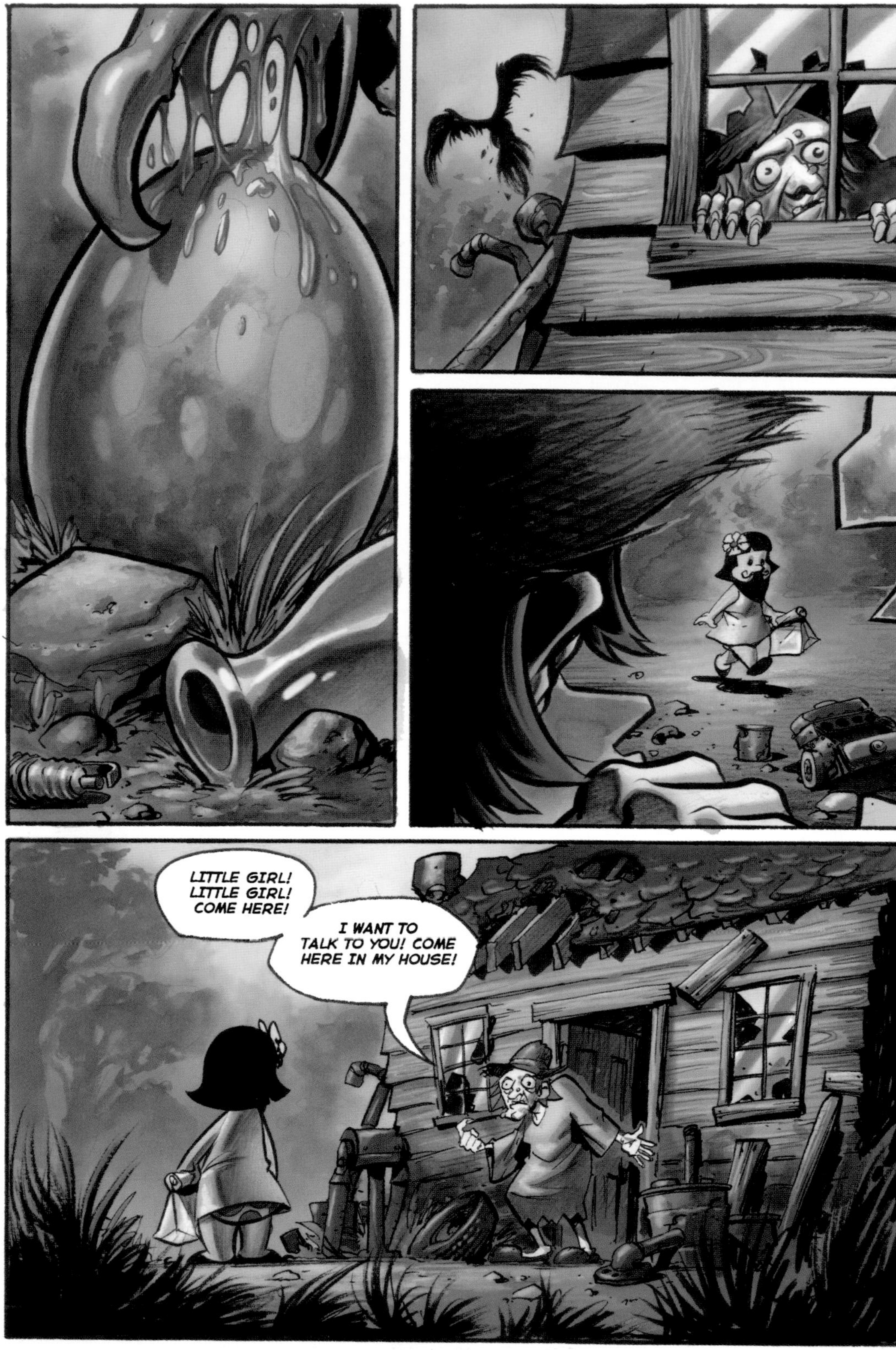
LITTLE GIRL! LITTLE GIRL! COME HERE!
I WANT TO TALK TO YOU! COME HERE IN MY HOUSE!

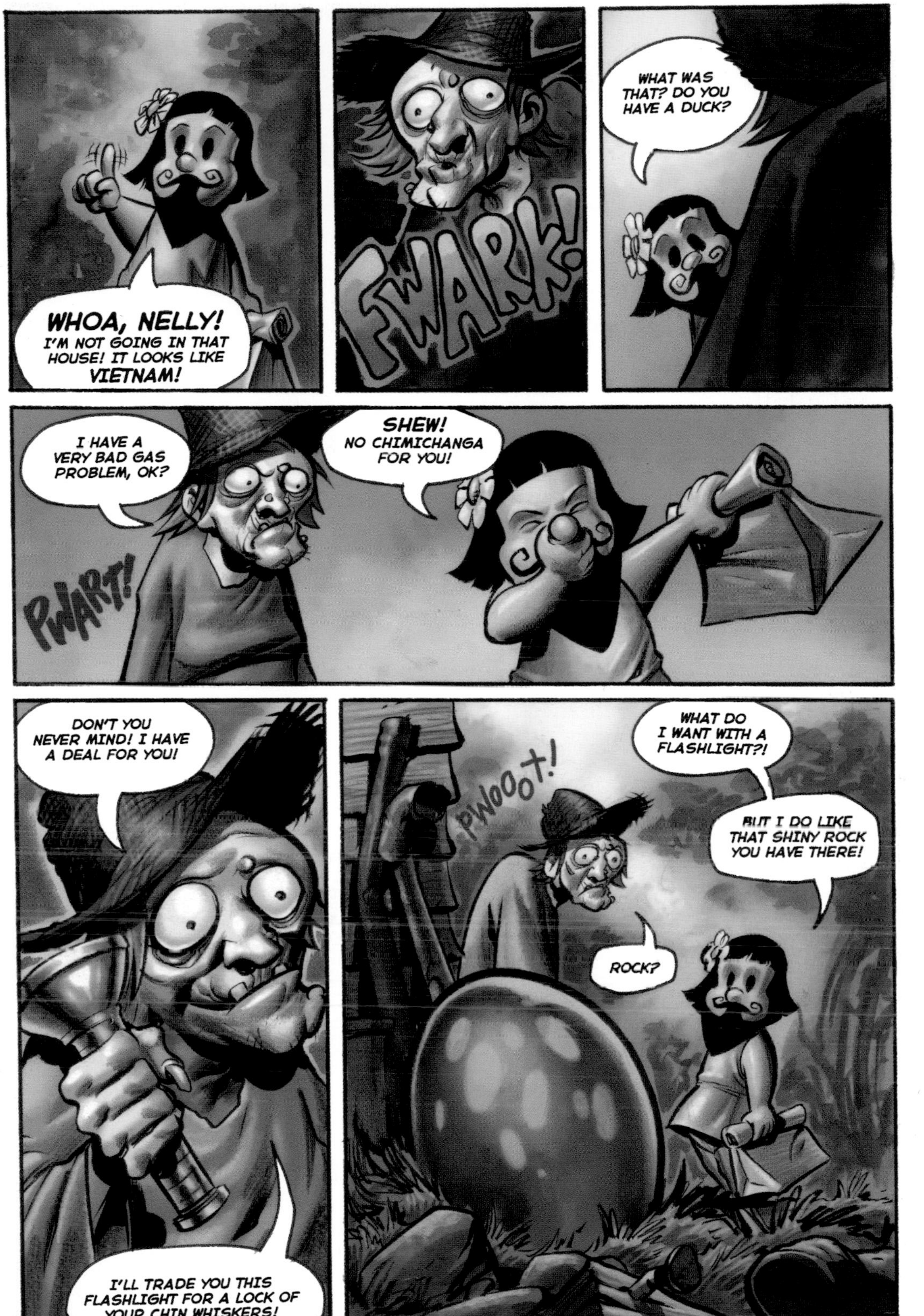
WHOA, NELLY! I'M NOT GOING IN THAT HOUSE! IT LOOKS LIKE VIETNAM!
FWARK!
WHAT WAS THAT? DO YOU HAVE A DUCK?
I HAVE A VERY BAD GAS PROBLEM, OK?
PWART!
SHEW! NO CHIMICHANGA FOR YOU!
DON'T YOU NEVER MIND! I HAVE A DEAL FOR YOU!
I'LL TRADE YOU THIS FLASHLIGHT FOR A LOCK OF YOUR CHIN WHISKERS!
PWOOOT!
WHAT DO I WANT WITH A FLASHLIGHT?!
BUT I DO LIKE THAT SHINY ROCK YOU HAVE THERE!
ROCK?

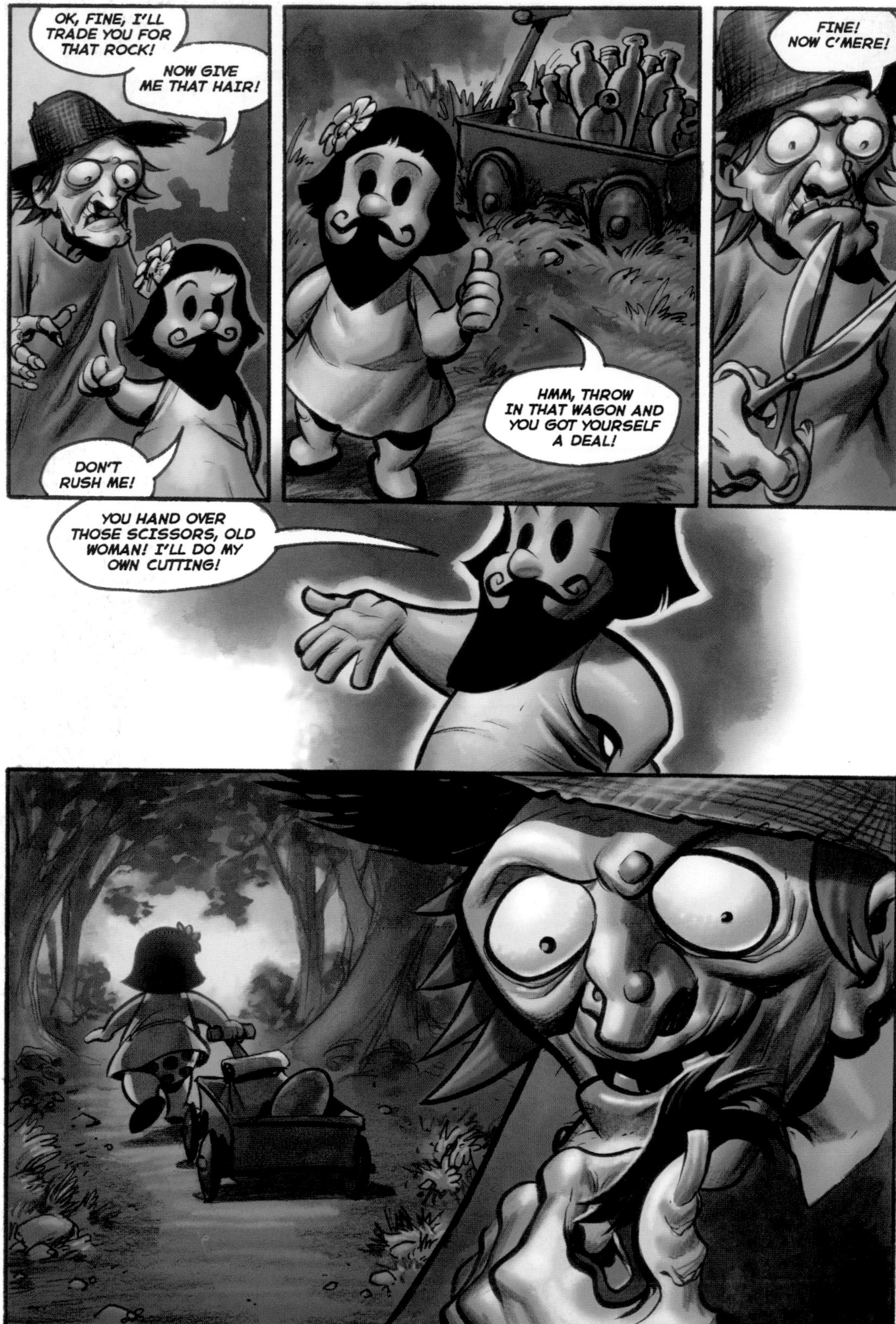
OK, FINE, I'LL TRADE YOU FOR THAT ROCK!
NOW GIVE ME THAT HAIR!
DON'T RUSH ME!
HMM, THROW IN THAT WAGON AND YOU GOT YOURSELF A DEAL!
FINE! NOW C'MERE!
YOU HAND OVER THOSE SCISSORS, OLD WOMAN! I'LL DO MY OWN CUTTING!

SQUEEP!

FINALLY! THE LAST COMPONENT OF MY POTION!

HAIR FROM THE CHIN OF A BEARDED WOMAN!

ONCE I DRINK THIS, I WILL BE ALL POWERFUL! THE WORLD WILL FINALLY KNEEL AT THE FEET OF DAGMAR THE WITCH!

HA! HA! HA!

BWRAP!

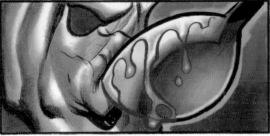

HEY... I DON'T FEEL ANY DIFFERENT... NOTHING HAPPENED!

WHAT A GYP!

THAT'S THE LAST TIME I LISTEN TO YOU!

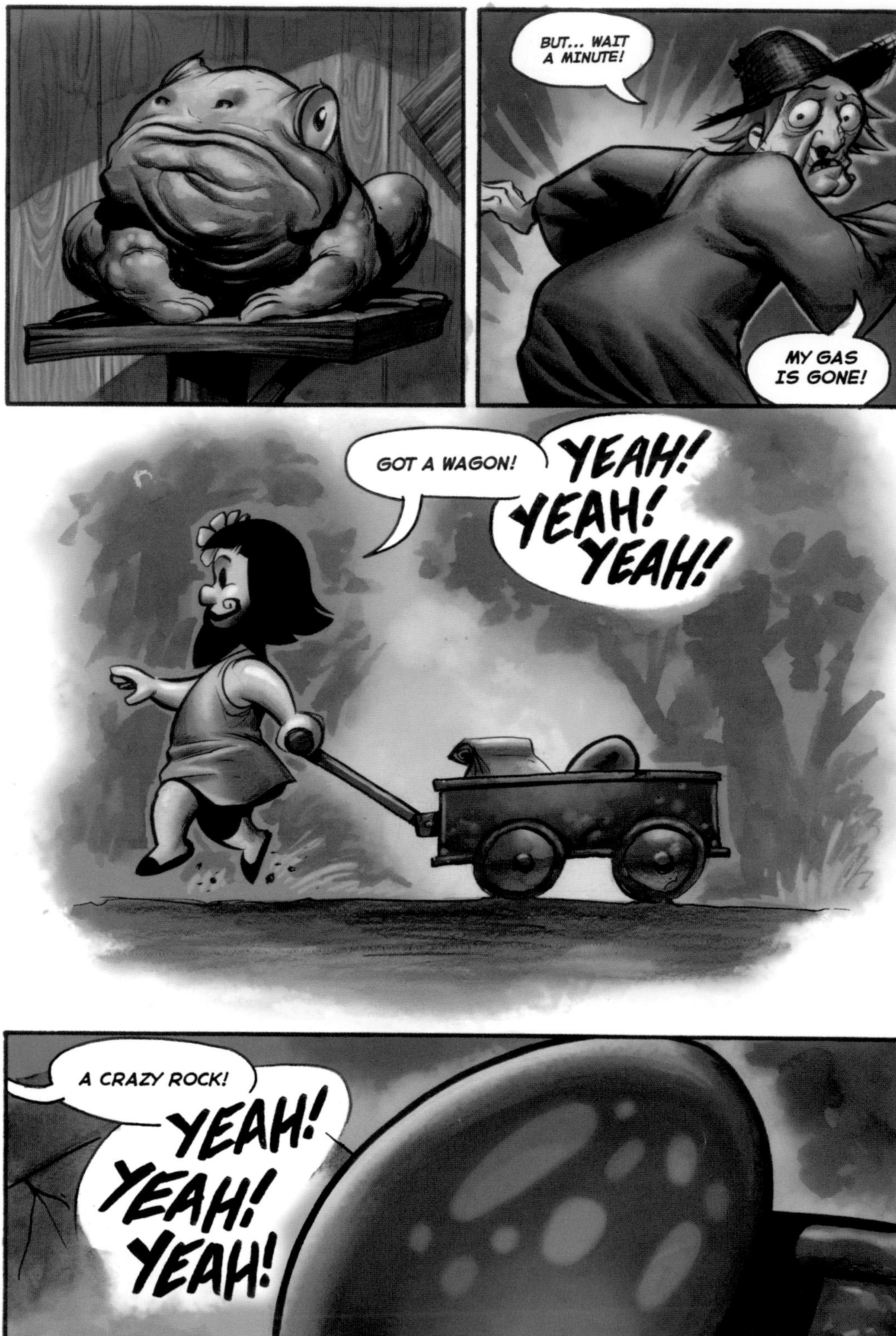
BUT... WAIT A MINUTE!
MY GAS IS GONE!
GOT A WAGON!
YEAH! YEAH! YEAH!
A CRAZY ROCK!
YEAH! YEAH! YEAH!

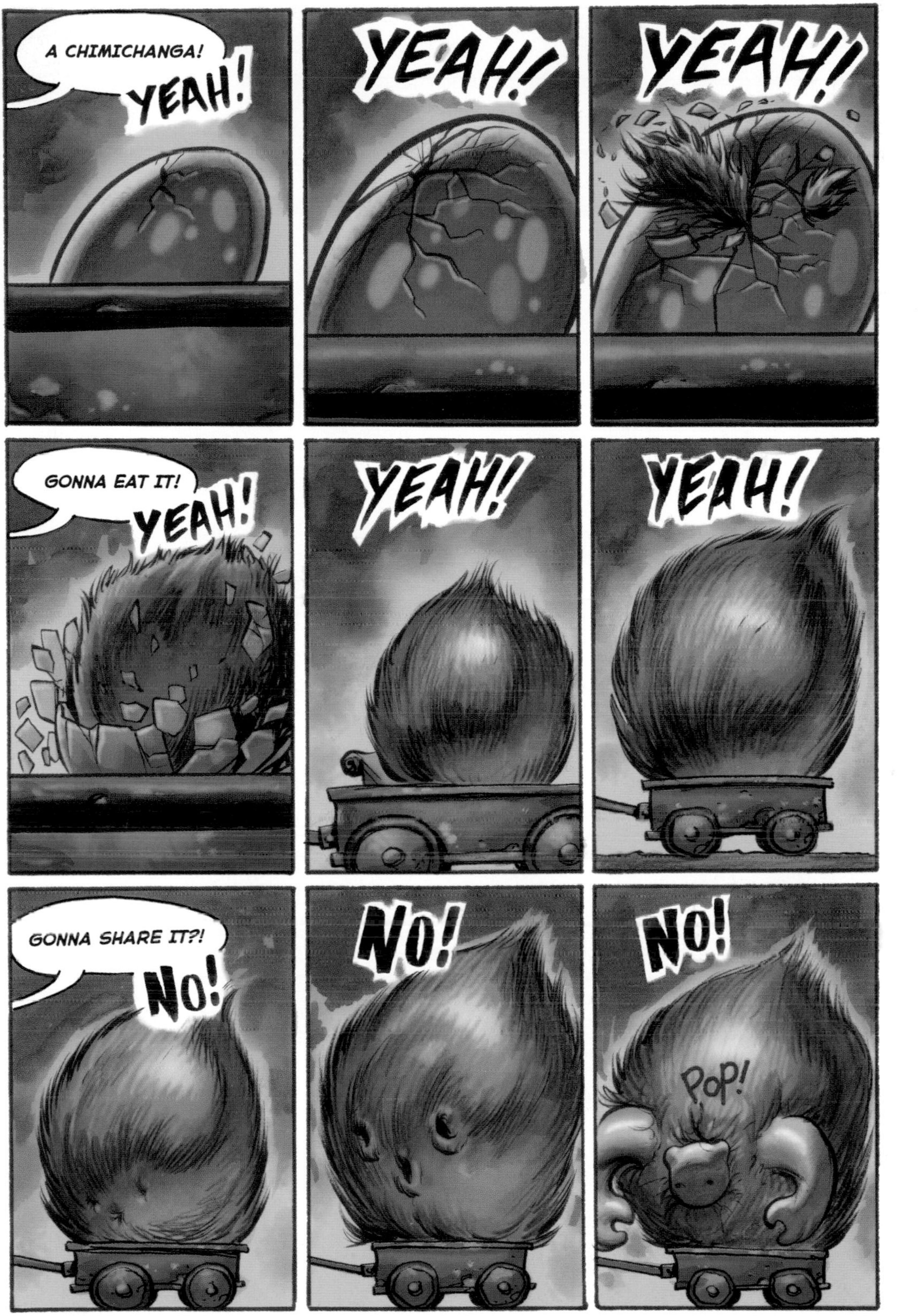

A CHIMICHANGA!
YEAH!
YEAH!
YEAH!
GONNA EAT IT!
YEAH!
YEAH!
YEAH!
GONNA SHARE IT?!
NO!
NO!
NO!
POP!

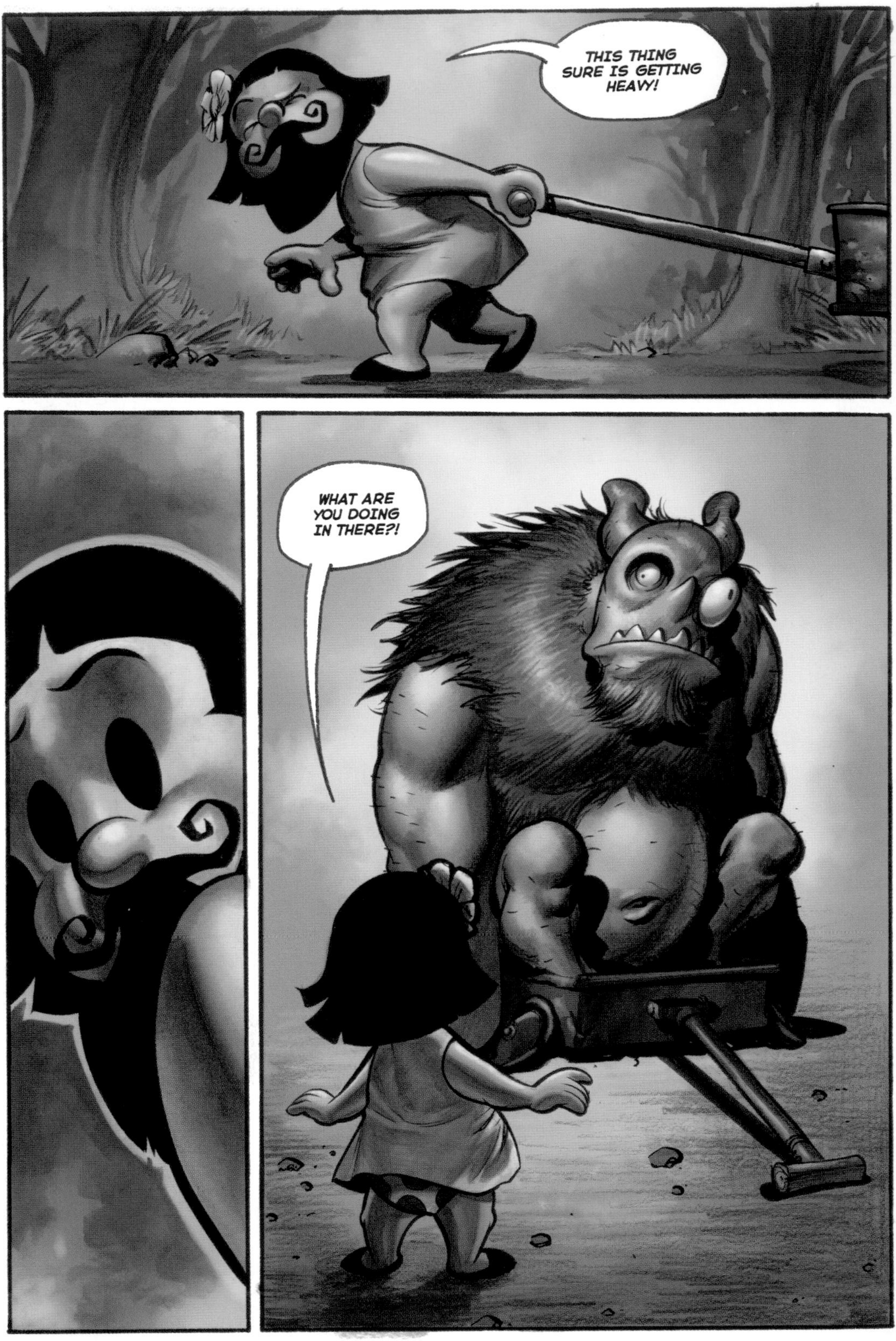
THIS THING SURE IS GETTING HEAVY!
WHAT ARE YOU DOING IN THERE?!

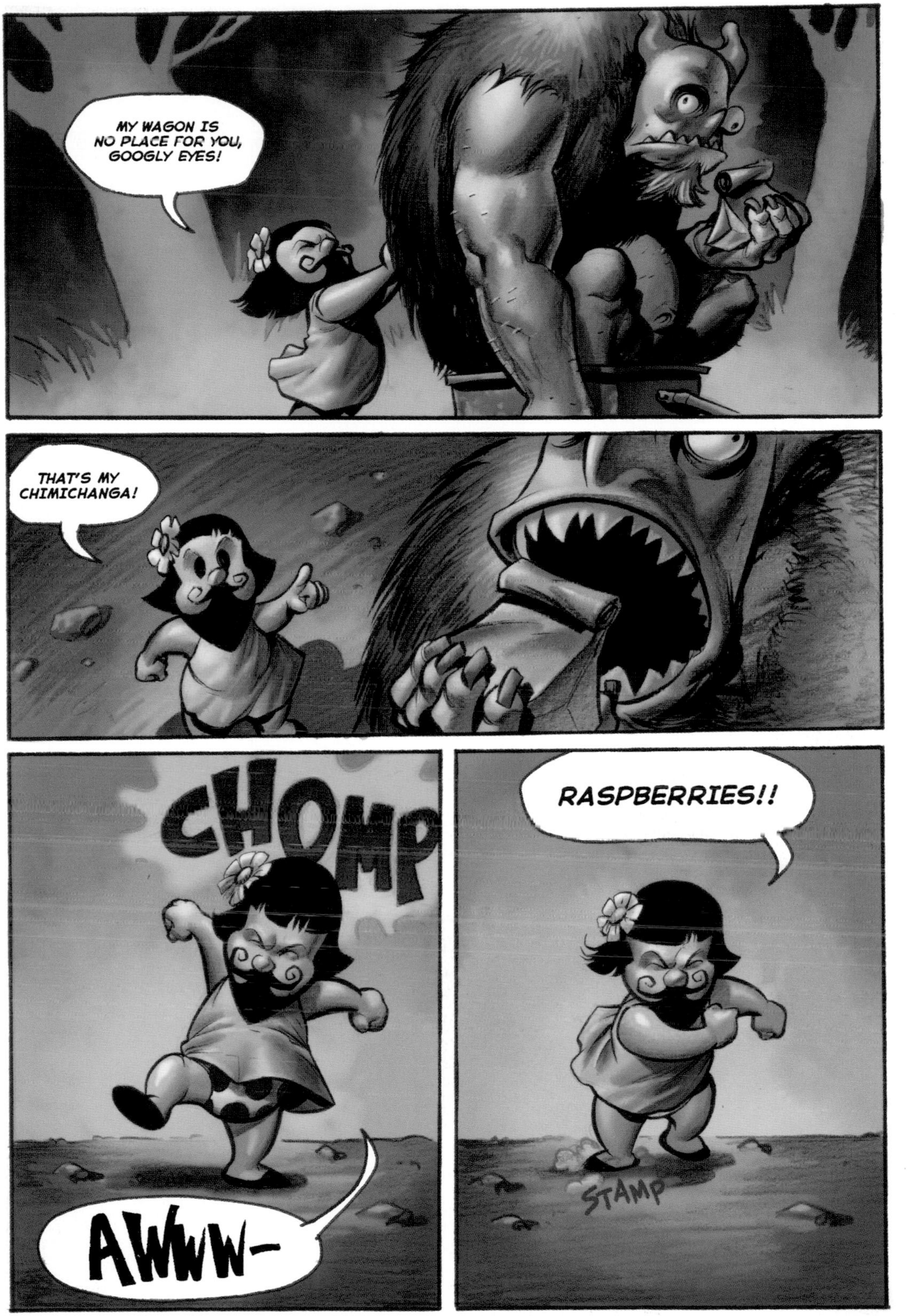
MY WAGON IS NO PLACE FOR YOU, GOOGLY EYES!
THAT'S MY CHIMICHANGA!
CHOMP
AWWW-
RASPBERRIES!!
STAMP

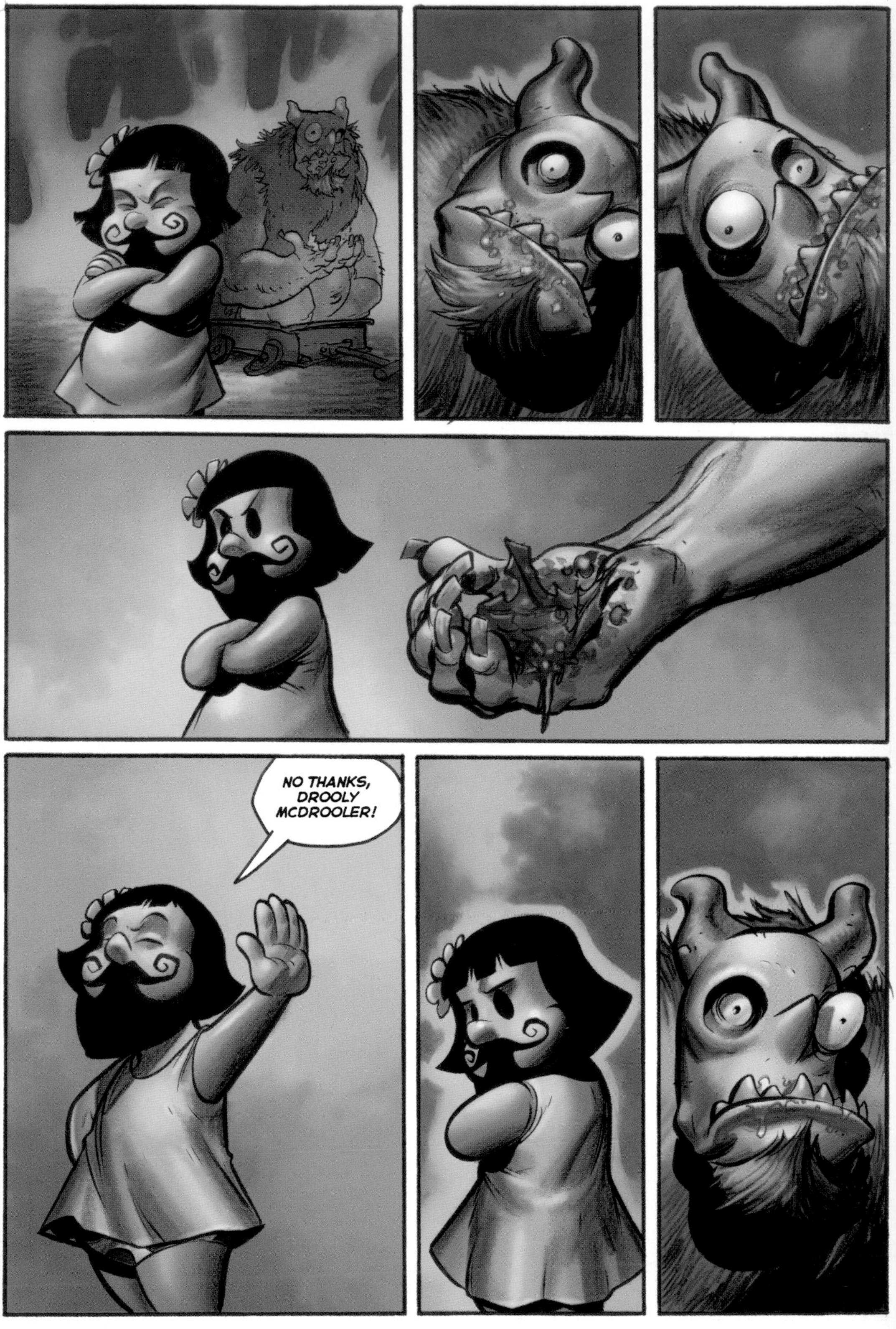
NO THANKS, DROOLY MCDROOLER!

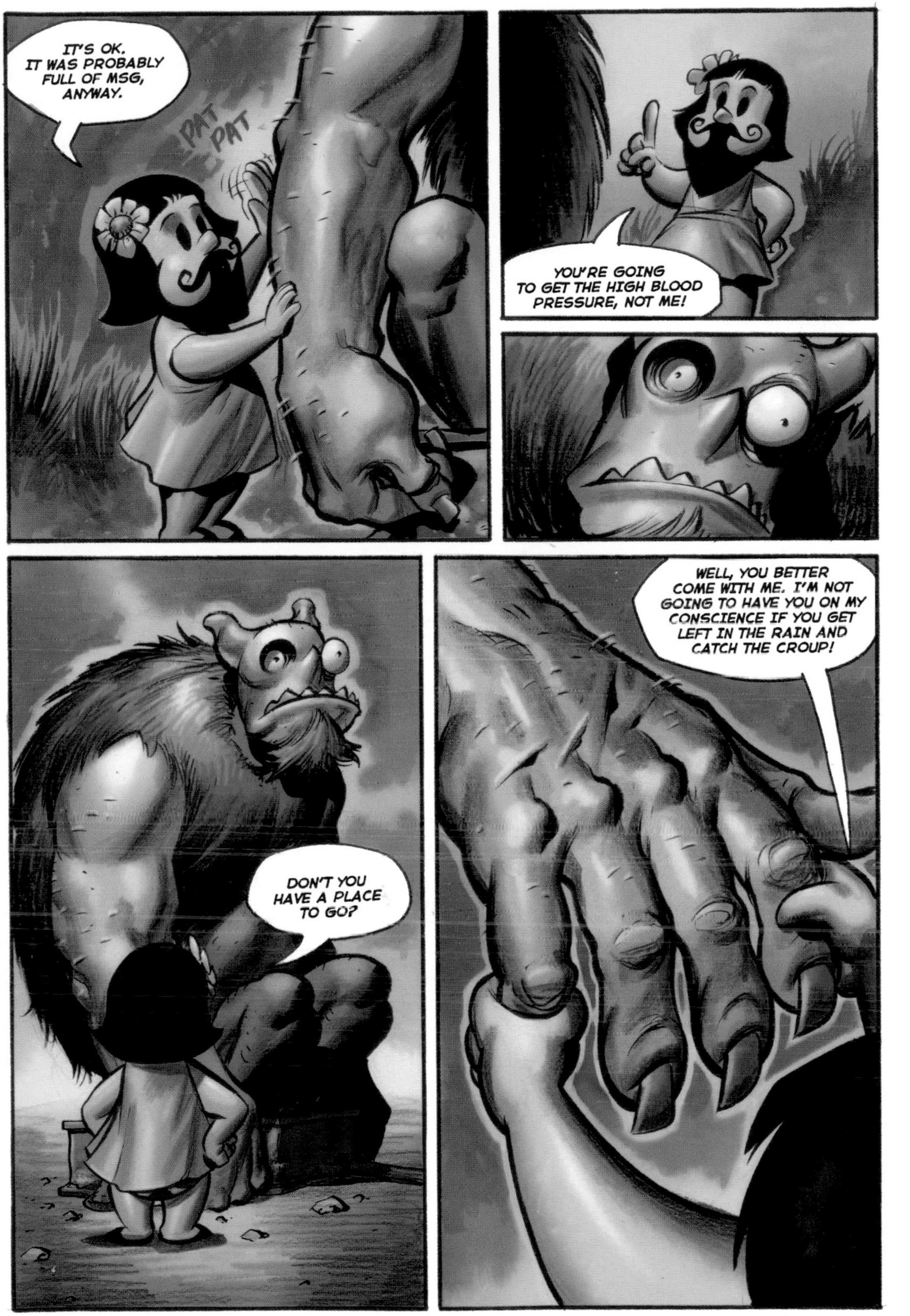
IT'S OK. IT WAS PROBABLY FULL OF MSG, ANYWAY.
PAT PAT
YOU'RE GOING TO GET THE HIGH BLOOD PRESSURE, NOT ME!
DON'T YOU HAVE A PLACE TO GO?
WELL, YOU BETTER COME WITH ME. I'M NOT GOING TO HAVE YOU ON MY CONSCIENCE IF YOU GET LEFT IN THE RAIN AND CATCH THE CROUP!

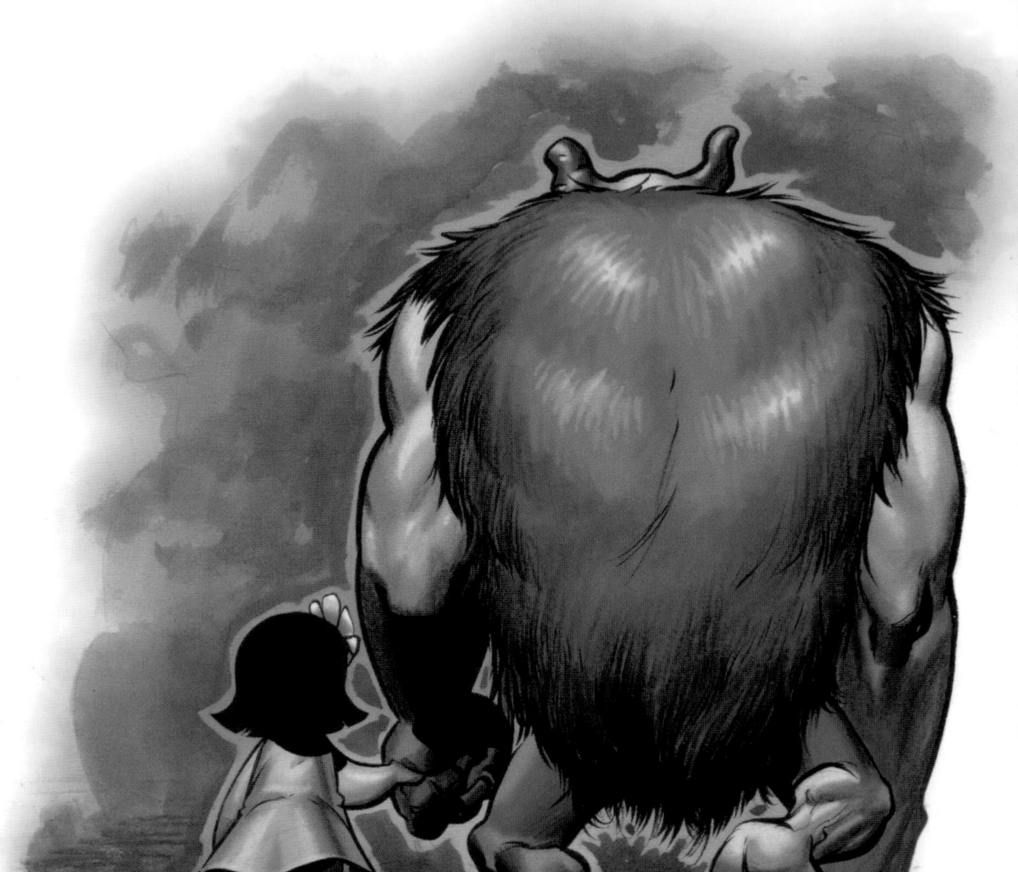

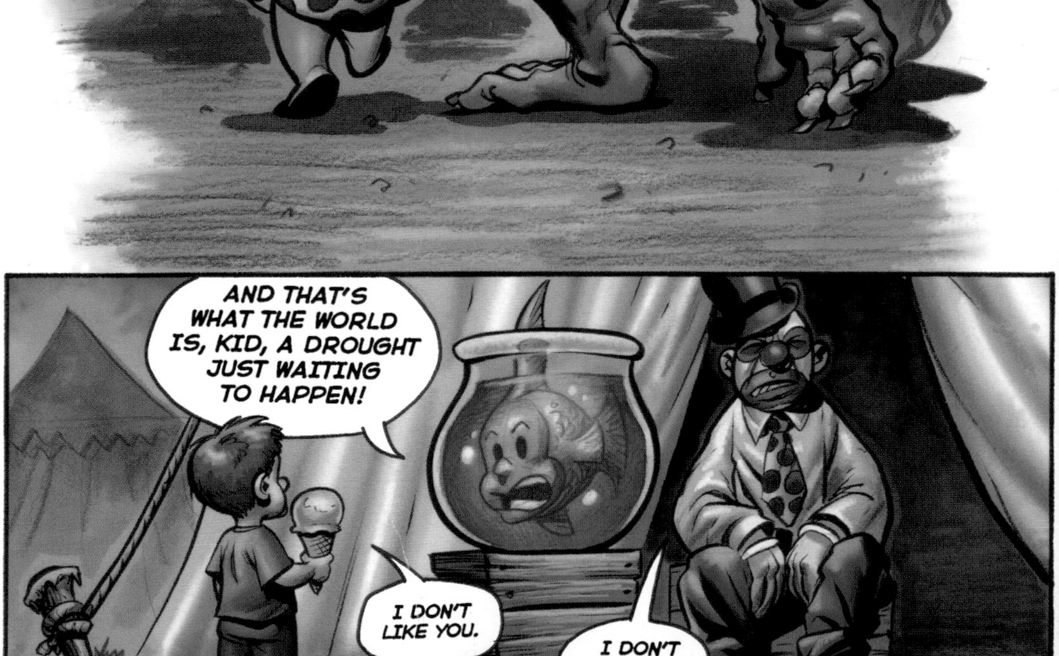
AND THAT'S WHAT THE WORLD IS, KID, A DROUGHT JUST WAITING TO HAPPEN!
I DON'T LIKE YOU.
I DON'T LIKE HIM EITHER.

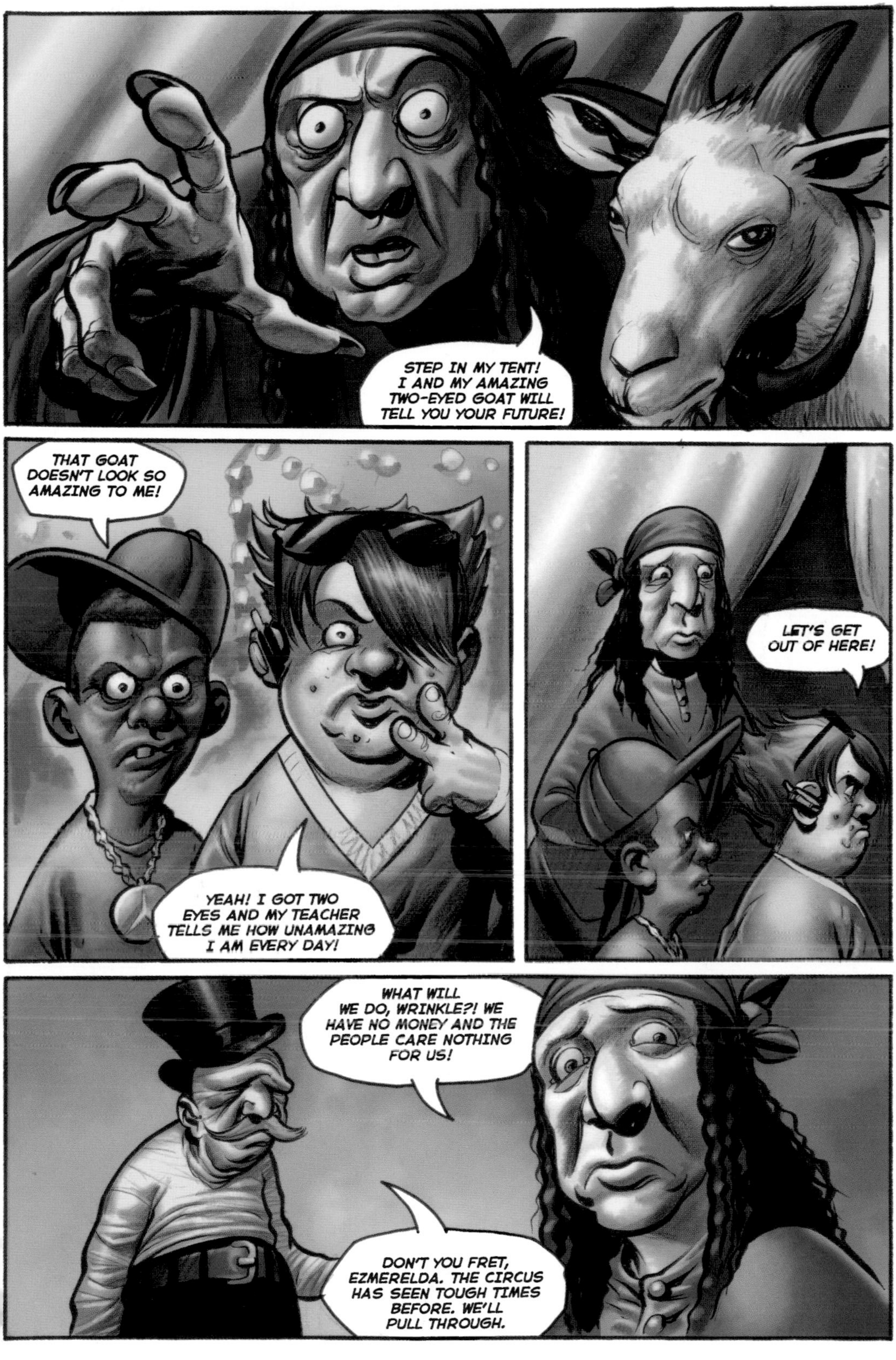
STEP IN MY TENT! I AND MY AMAZING TWO-EYED GOAT WILL TELL YOU YOUR FUTURE!
THAT GOAT DOESN'T LOOK SO AMAZING TO ME!
YEAH! I GOT TWO EYES AND MY TEACHER TELLS ME HOW UNAMAZING I AM EVERY DAY!
LET'S GET OUT OF HERE!
WHAT WILL WE DO, WRINKLE?! WE HAVE NO MONEY AND THE PEOPLE CARE NOTHING FOR US!
DON'T YOU FRET, EZMERELDA. THE CIRCUS HAS SEEN TOUGH TIMES BEFORE. WE'LL PULL THROUGH.

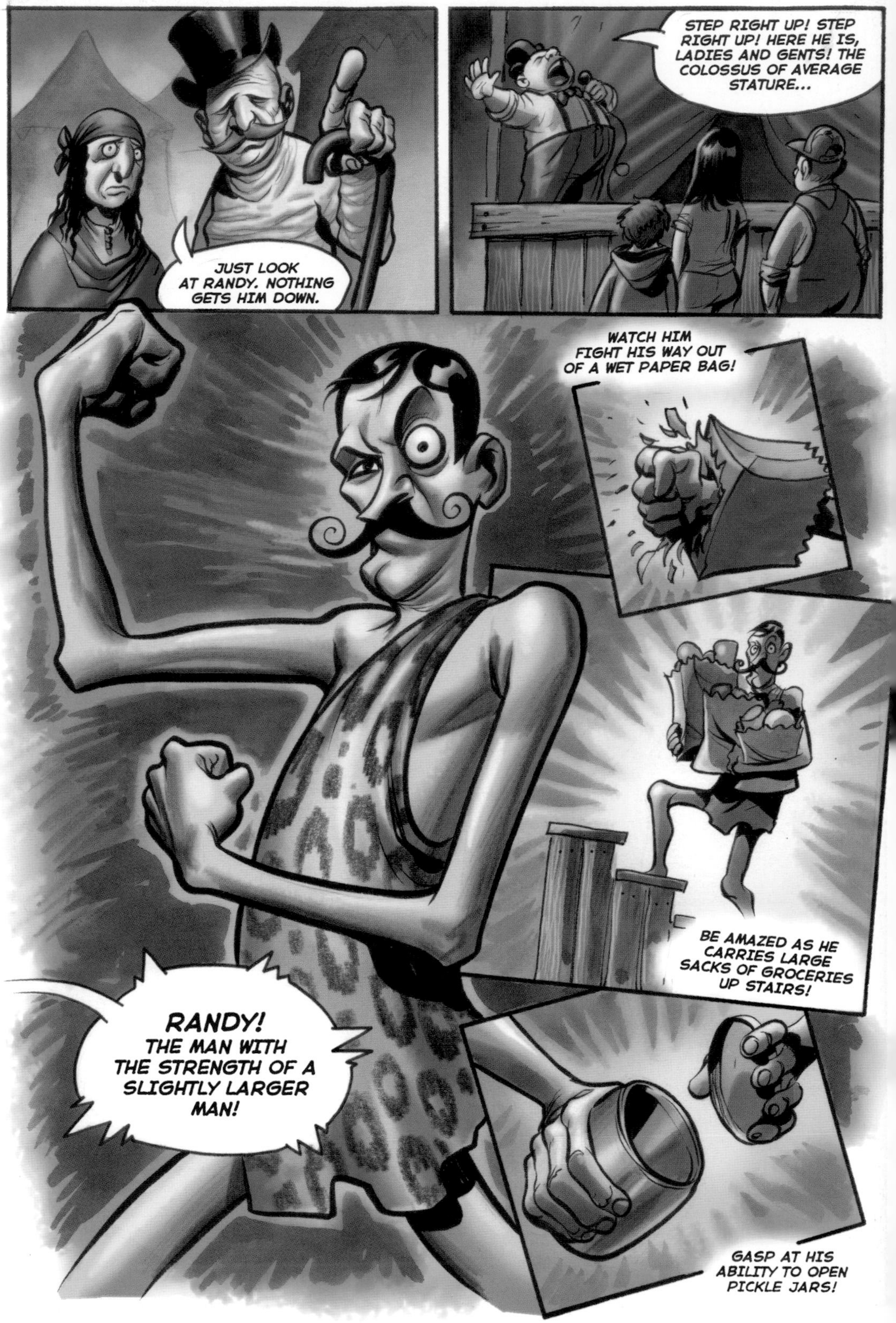
JUST LOOK AT RANDY. NOTHING GETS HIM DOWN.
STEP RIGHT UP! STEP RIGHT UP! HERE HE IS, LADIES AND GENTS! THE COLOSSUS OF AVERAGE STATURE...
RANDY! THE MAN WITH THE STRENGTH OF A SLIGHTLY LARGER MAN!
WATCH HIM FIGHT HIS WAY OUT OF A WET PAPER BAG!
BE AMAZED AS HE CARRIES LARGE SACKS OF GROCERIES UP STAIRS!
GASP AT HIS ABILITY TO OPEN PICKLE JARS!

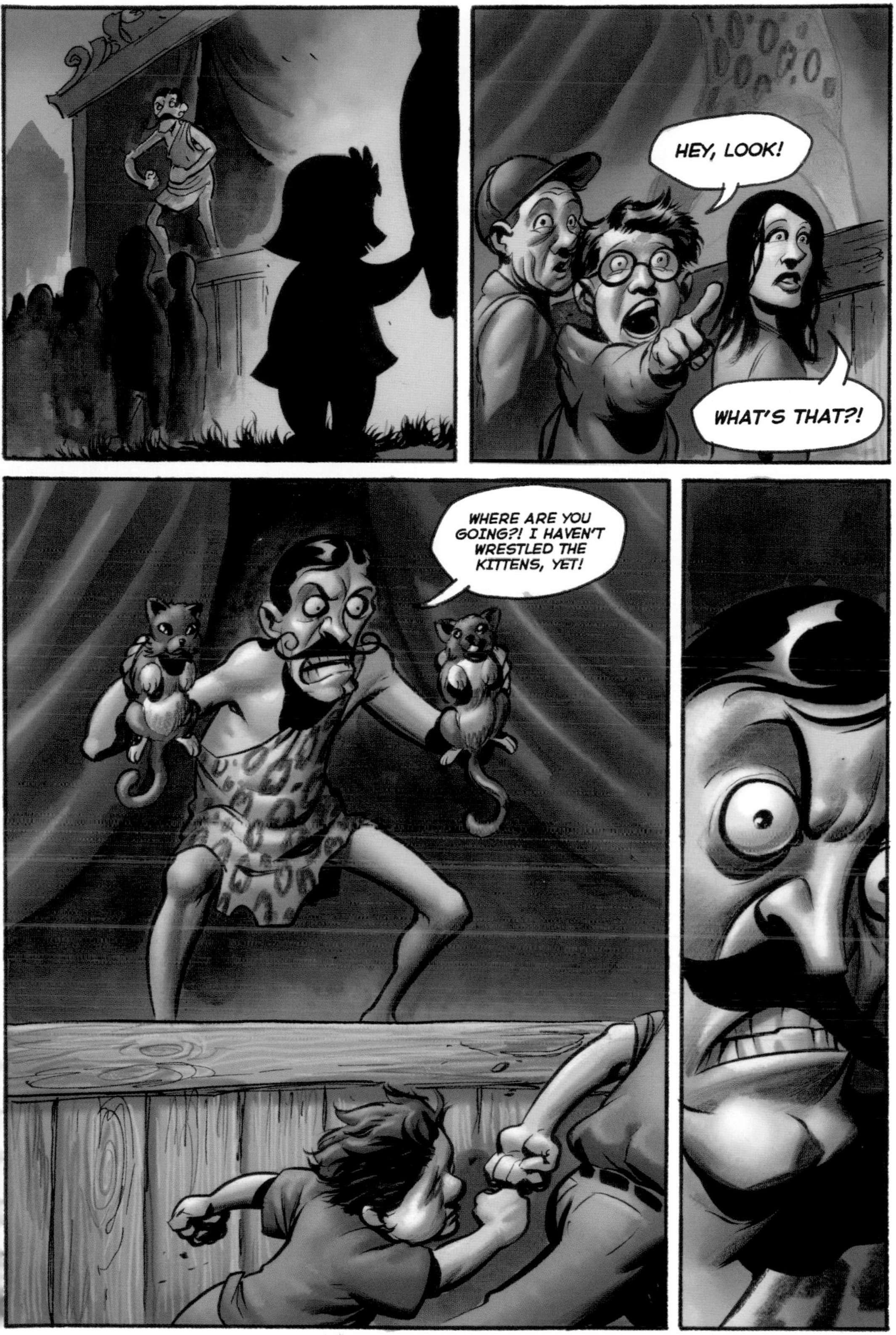
HEY, LOOK!
WHAT'S THAT?!
WHERE ARE YOU GOING?! I HAVEN'T WRESTLED THE KITTENS, YET!

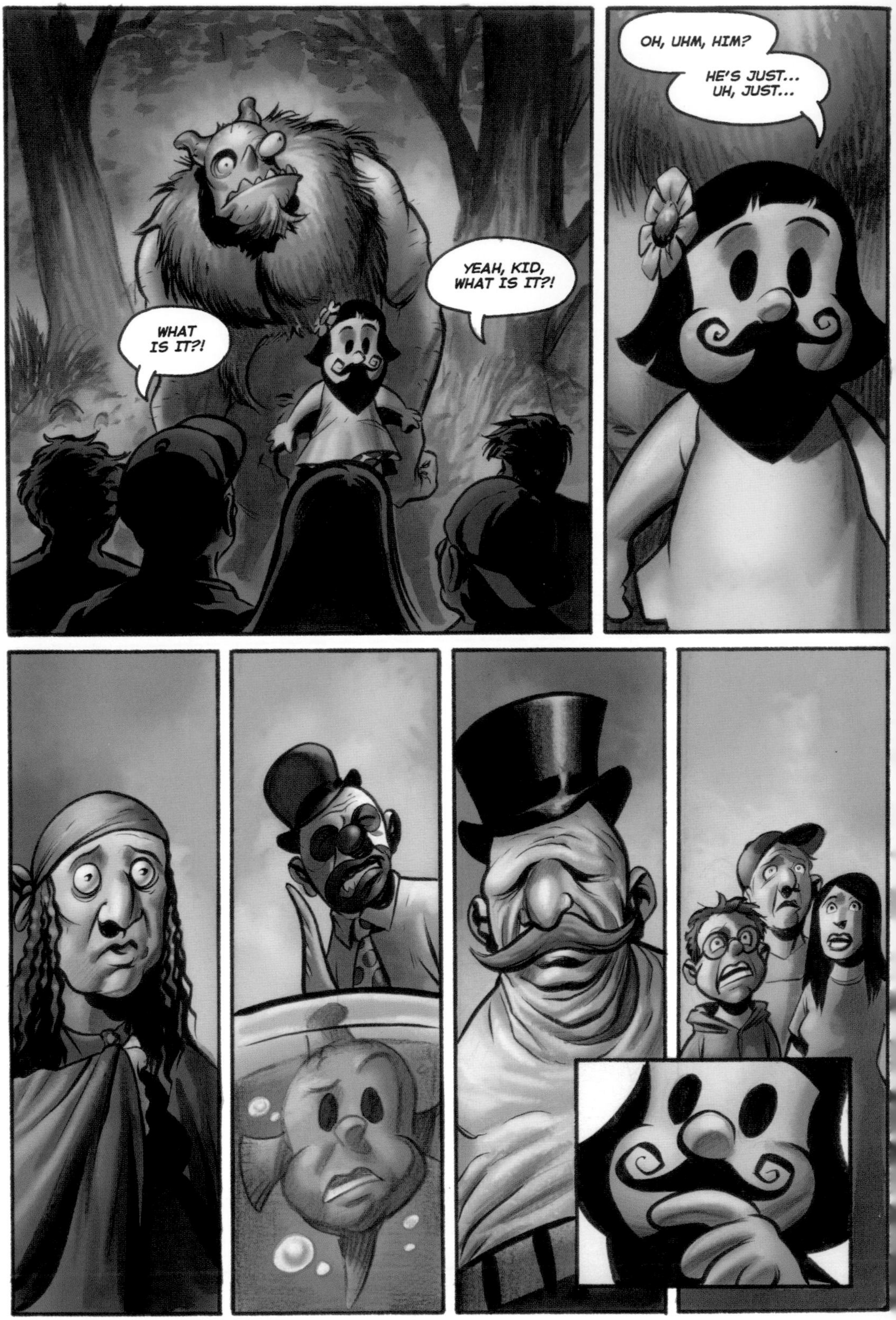
WHAT IS IT?!
YEAH, KID, WHAT IS IT?!
OH, UHM, HIM?
HE'S JUST... UH, JUST...

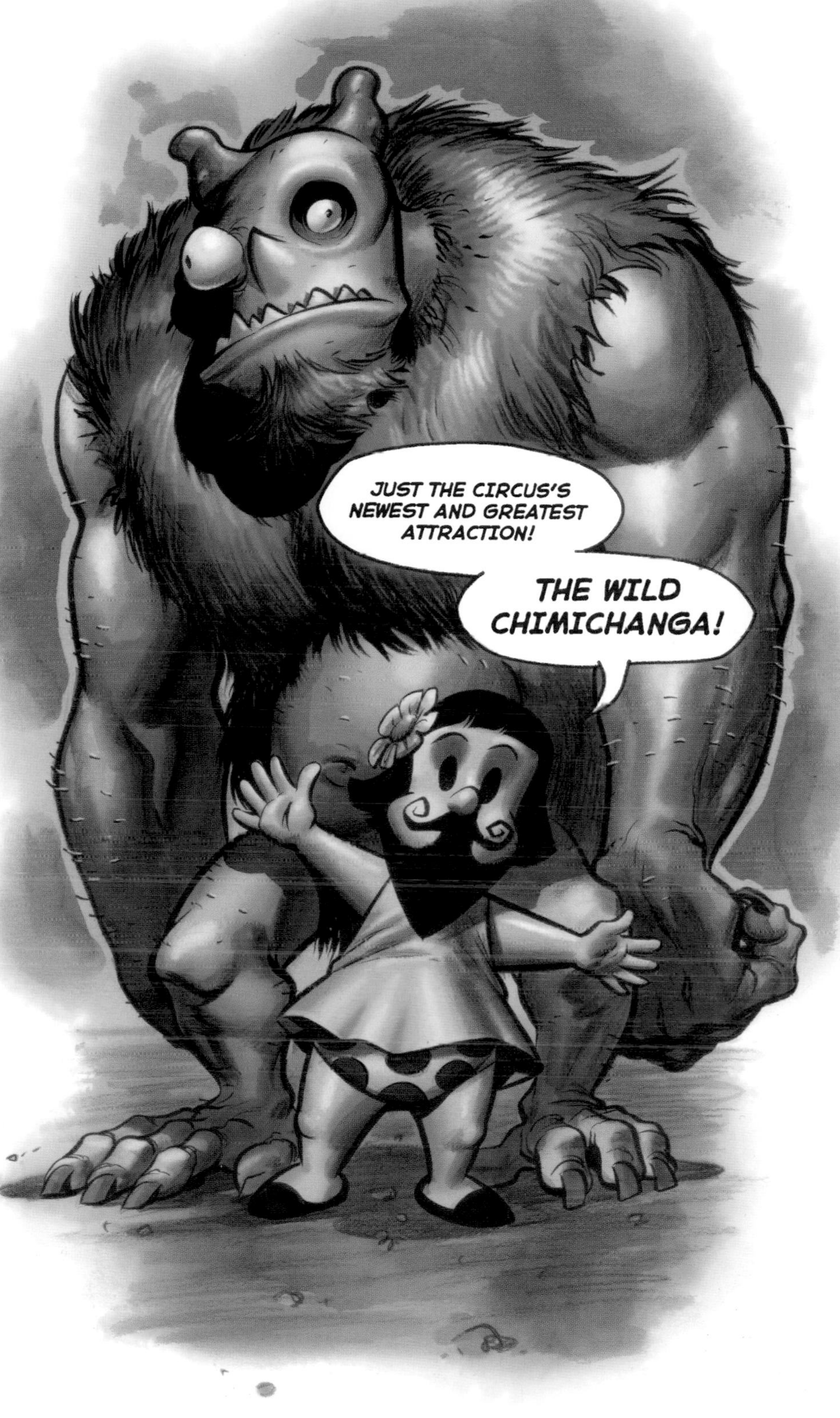
JUST THE CIRCUS'S NEWEST AND GREATEST ATTRACTION!
THE WILD CHIMICHANGA!

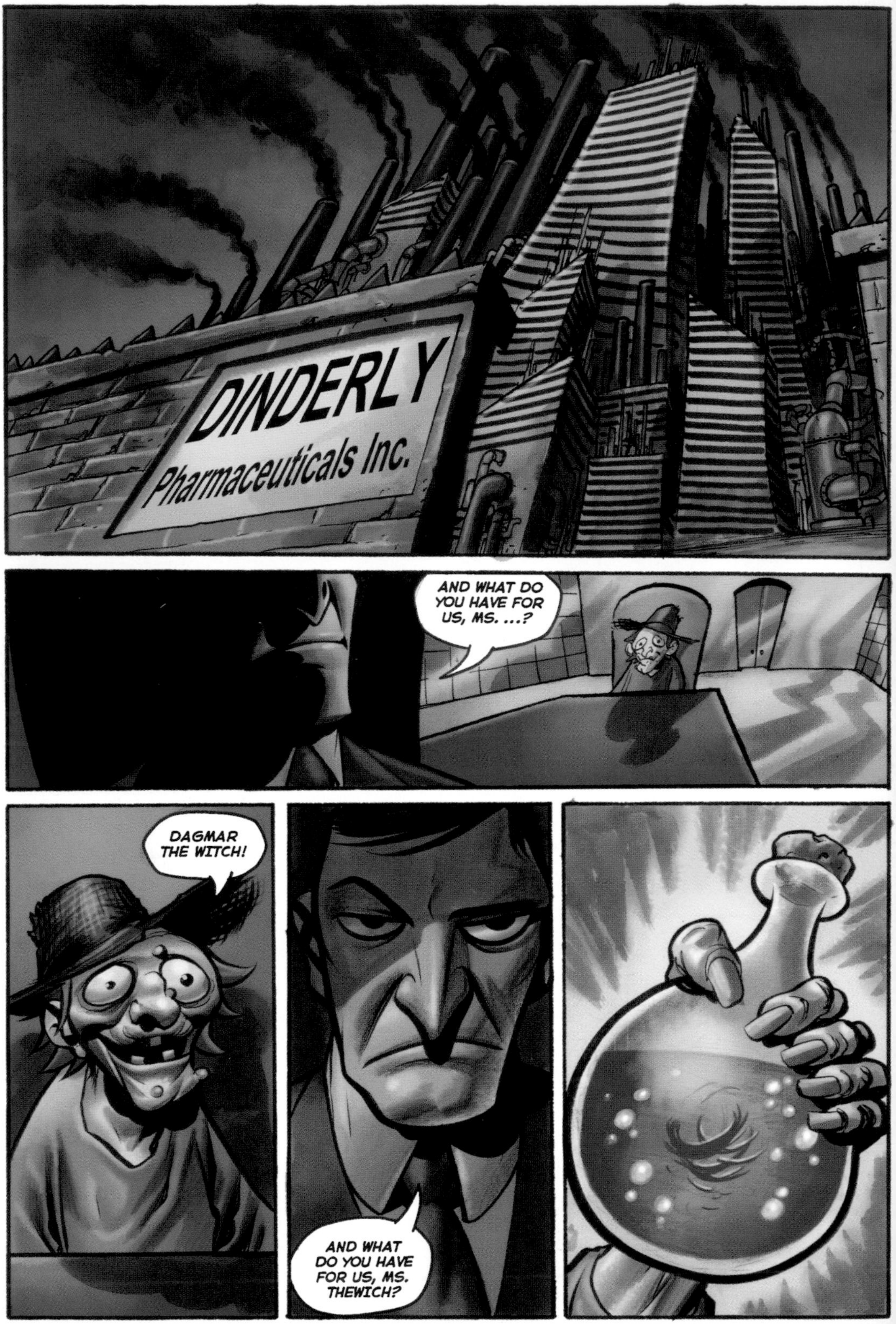
DINDERLY
Pharmaceuticals Inc.
AND WHAT DO YOU HAVE FOR US, MS. ...?
DAGMAR THE WITCH!
AND WHAT DO YOU HAVE FOR US, MS. THEWICH?

Chapter Two

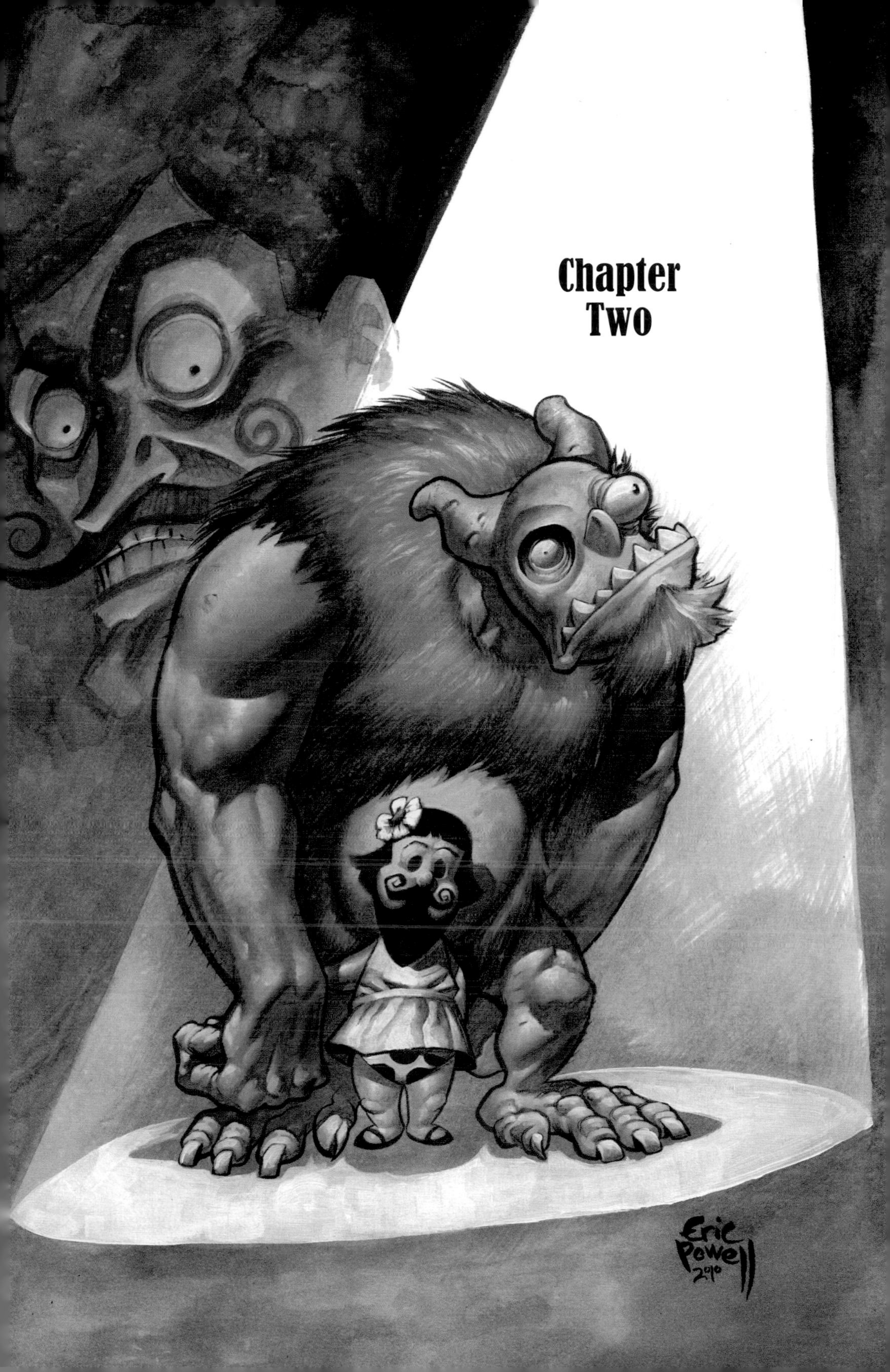
Eric Powell 2010

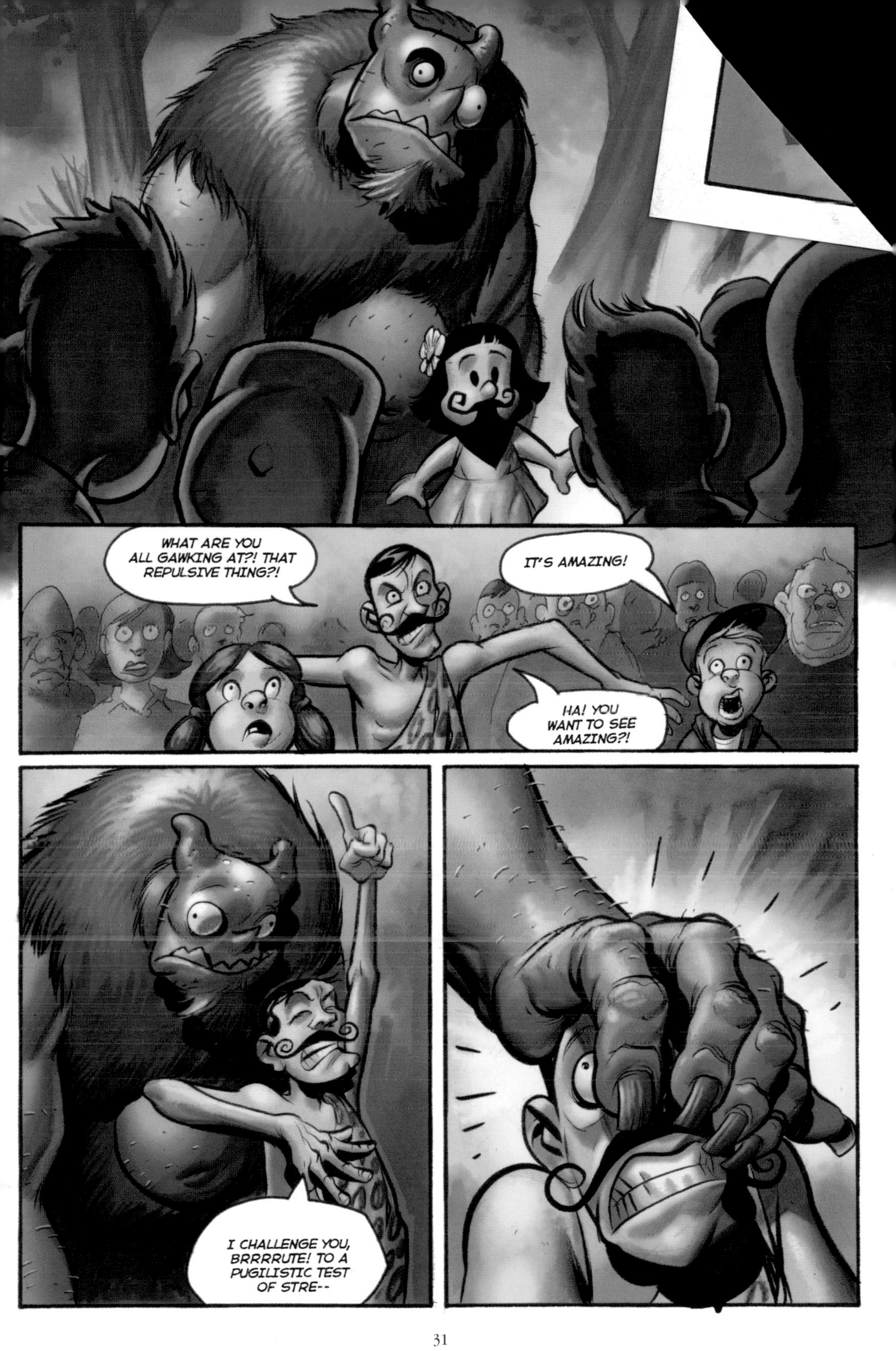

WHAT ARE YOU ALL GAWKING AT?! THAT REPULSIVE THING?!
IT'S AMAZING!
HA! YOU WANT TO SEE AMAZING?!
I CHALLENGE YOU, BRRRRUTE! TO A PUGILISTIC TEST OF STRE--

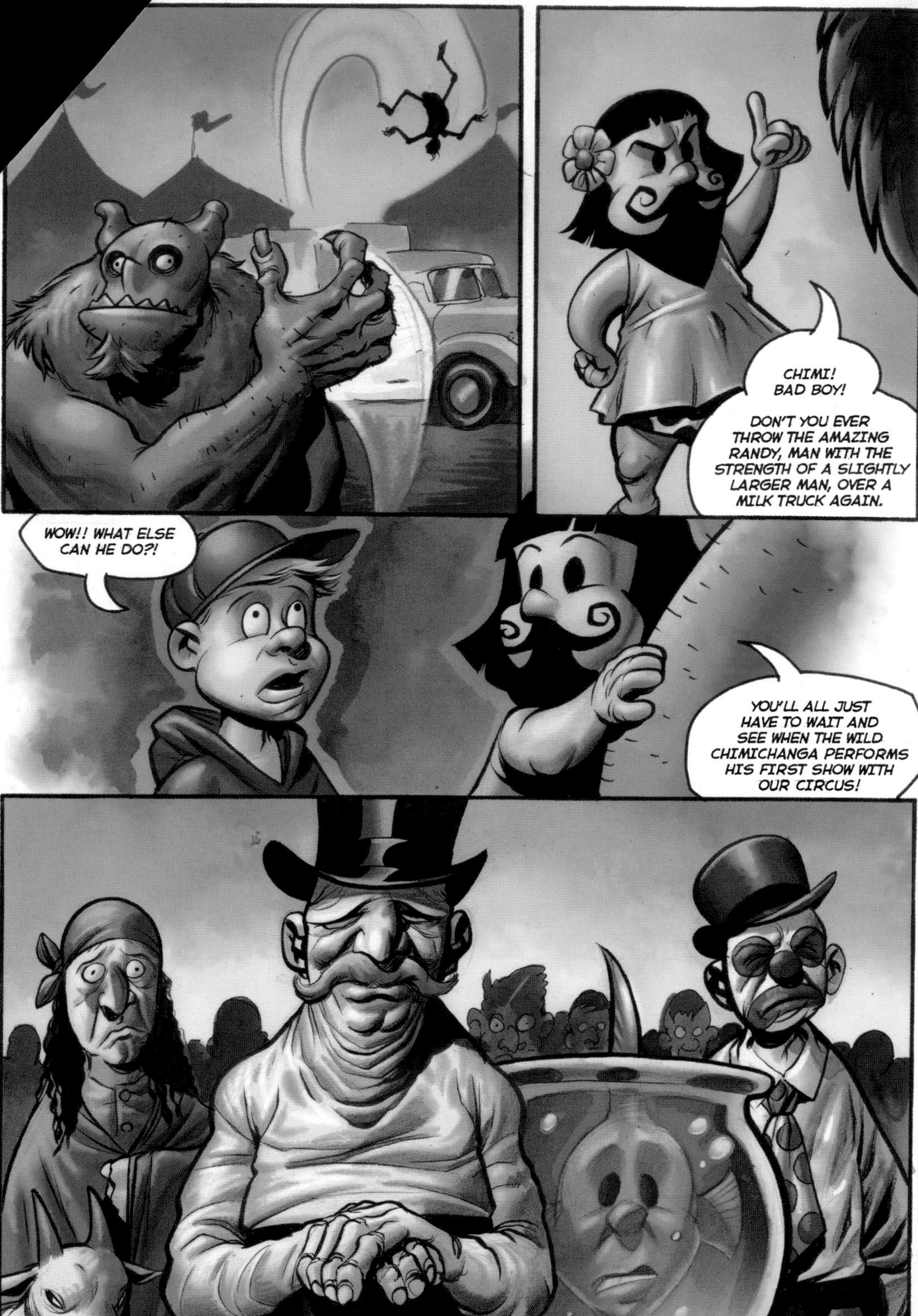
CHIMI! BAD BOY!
DON'T YOU EVER THROW THE AMAZING RANDY, MAN WITH THE STRENGTH OF A SLIGHTLY LARGER MAN, OVER A MILK TRUCK AGAIN.
WOW!! WHAT ELSE CAN HE DO?!
YOU'LL ALL JUST HAVE TO WAIT AND SEE WHEN THE WILD CHIMICHANGA PERFORMS HIS FIRST SHOW WITH OUR CIRCUS!

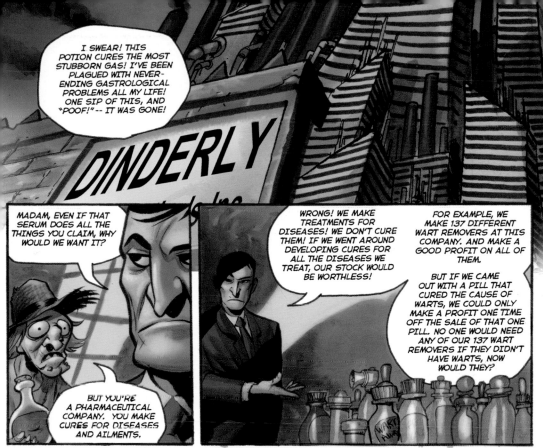

I SWEAR! THIS POTION CURES THE MOST STUBBORN GAS! I'VE BEEN PLAGUED WITH NEVER-ENDING GASTROLOGICAL PROBLEMS ALL MY LIFE! ONE SIP OF THIS, AND "POOF!"-- IT WAS GONE!

DINDERLY

MADAM, EVEN IF THAT SERUM DOES ALL THE THINGS YOU CLAIM, WHY WOULD WE WANT IT?

BUT YOU'RE A PHARMACEUTICAL COMPANY. YOU MAKE CURES FOR DISEASES AND AILMENTS.

WRONG! WE MAKE TREATMENTS FOR DISEASES! WE DON'T CURE THEM! IF WE WENT AROUND DEVELOPING CURES FOR ALL THE DISEASES WE TREAT, OUR STOCK WOULD BE WORTHLESS!

FOR EXAMPLE, WE MAKE 137 DIFFERENT WART REMOVERS AT THIS COMPANY. AND MAKE A GOOD PROFIT ON ALL OF THEM.

BUT IF WE CAME OUT WITH A PILL THAT CURED THE CAUSE OF WARTS, WE COULD ONLY MAKE A PROFIT ONE TIME OFF THE SALE OF THAT ONE PILL. NO ONE WOULD NEED ANY OF OUR 137 WART REMOVERS IF THEY DIDN'T HAVE WARTS, NOW WOULD THEY?

FILTHY LITTLE CHILDREN DESERVE TO GET KNOTTY GROWTHS ON THEIR HANDS THAT HAVE TO BE BURNED OFF WITH ACID, ANYWAY. TEACHES THEM CLEANLINESS.

BUT--

FWARK!

OW!

OH, NO! IT'S BACK! THE GAS!

WORSE THAN EVER!

BWART!

WAIT! ARE YOU TELLING ME THAT THIS SERUM MADE YOUR GAS GO AWAY FOR A LITTLE WHILE AND THEN RETURN WORSE THAN EVER BEFORE?!

PWOOOOT!

WHAT DO YOU THINK?!

BWART!

IT'S A DREAM COME TRUE! BUILT-IN REPEAT CONSUMERS! ONE SIP AND THEY'LL HAVE TO COME BACK FOR MORE!

MS. THEWICH, I BELIEVE WE CAN DO BUSINESS!

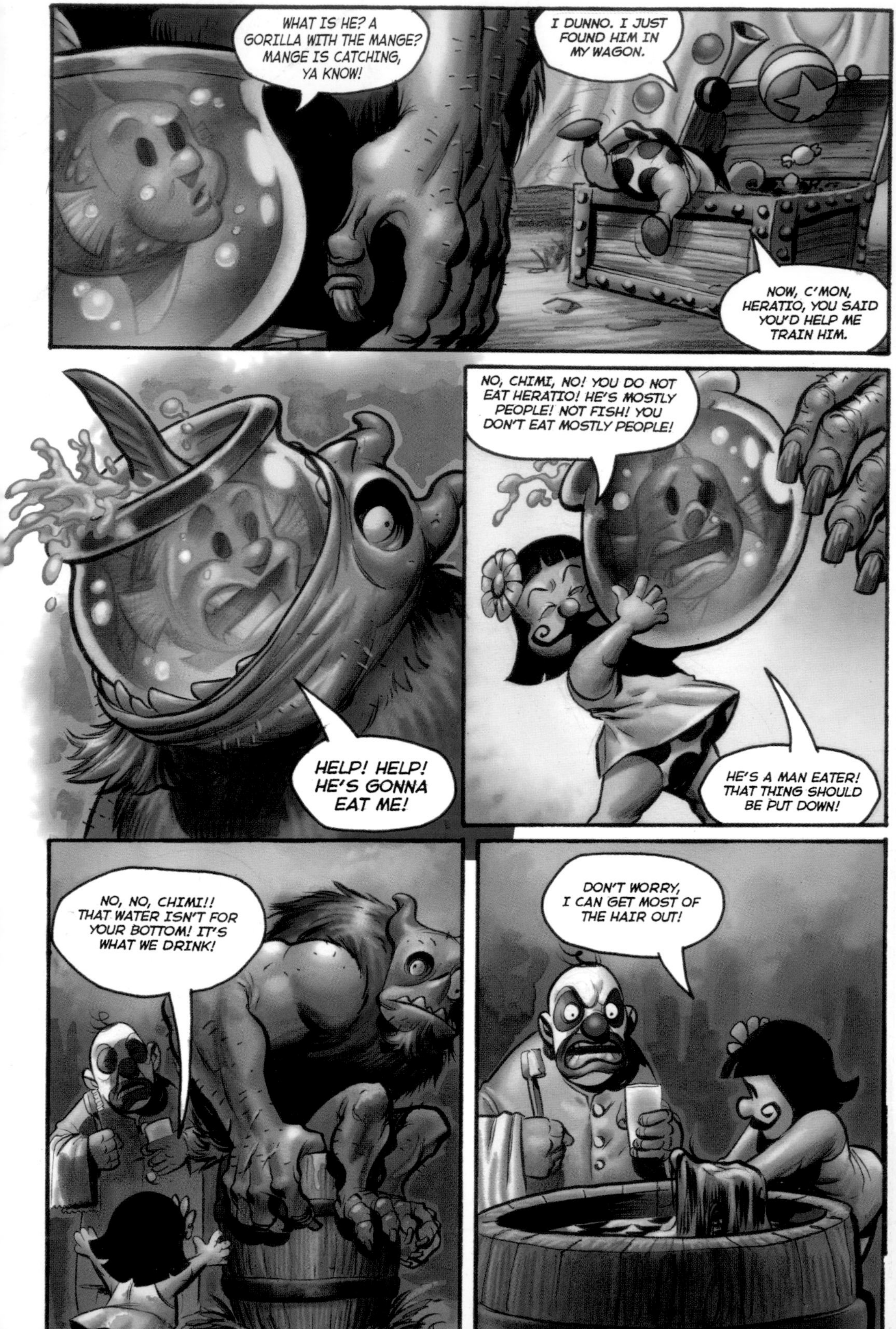
WHAT IS HE? A GORILLA WITH THE MANGE? MANGE IS CATCHING, YA KNOW!
I DUNNO. I JUST FOUND HIM IN MY WAGON.
NOW, C'MON, HERATIO, YOU SAID YOU'D HELP ME TRAIN HIM.
HELP! HELP! HE'S GONNA EAT ME!
NO, CHIMI, NO! YOU DO NOT EAT HERATIO! HE'S MOSTLY PEOPLE! NOT FISH! YOU DON'T EAT MOSTLY PEOPLE!
HE'S A MAN EATER! THAT THING SHOULD BE PUT DOWN!
NO, NO, CHIMI!! THAT WATER ISN'T FOR YOUR BOTTOM! IT'S WHAT WE DRINK!
DON'T WORRY, I CAN GET MOST OF THE HAIR OUT!

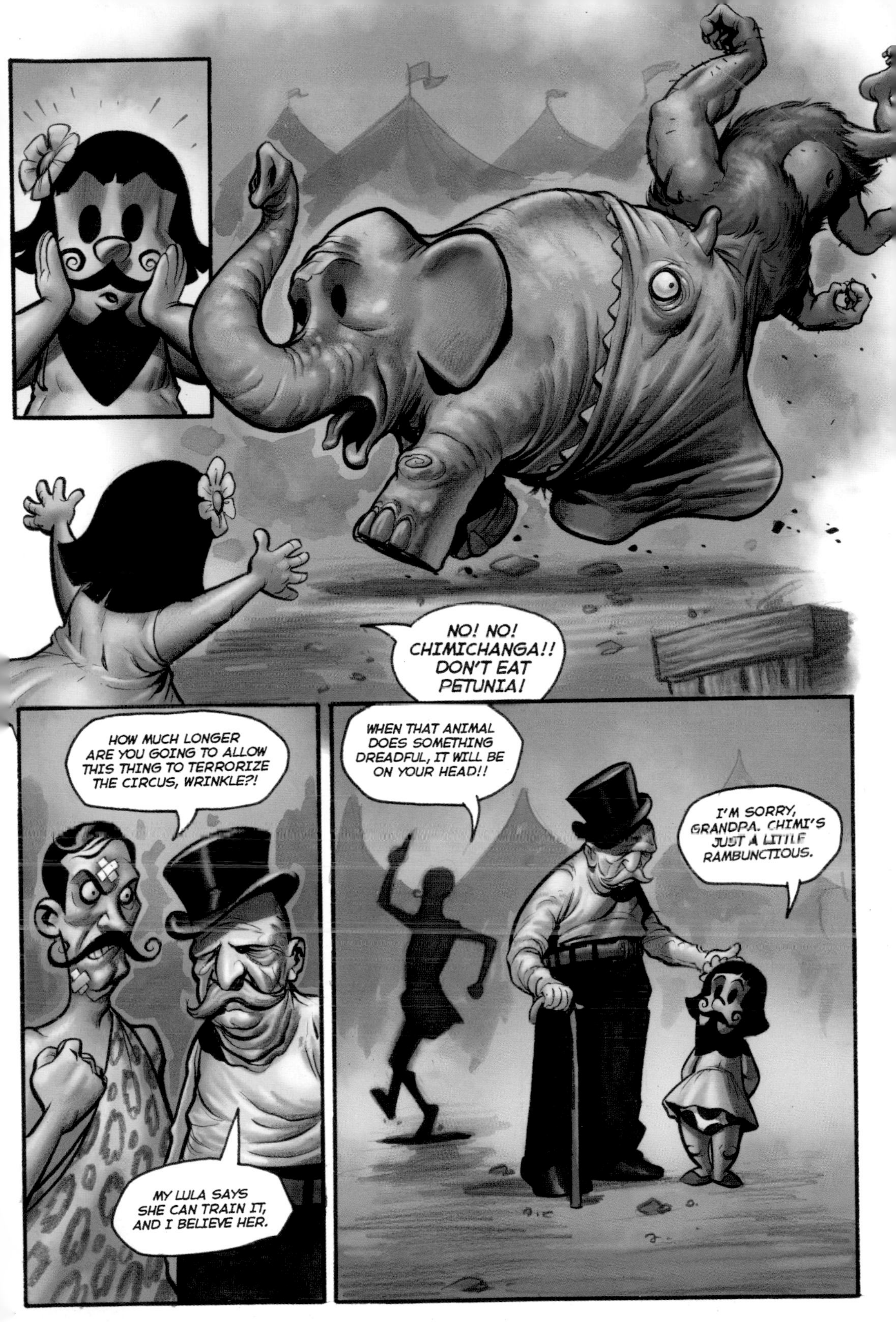
NO! NO! CHIMICHANGA!! DON'T EAT PETUNIA!
HOW MUCH LONGER ARE YOU GOING TO ALLOW THIS THING TO TERRORIZE THE CIRCUS, WRINKLE?!
MY LULA SAYS SHE CAN TRAIN IT, AND I BELIEVE HER.
WHEN THAT ANIMAL DOES SOMETHING DREADFUL, IT WILL BE ON YOUR HEAD!!
I'M SORRY, GRANDPA. CHIMI'S JUST A LITTLE RAMBUNCTIOUS.

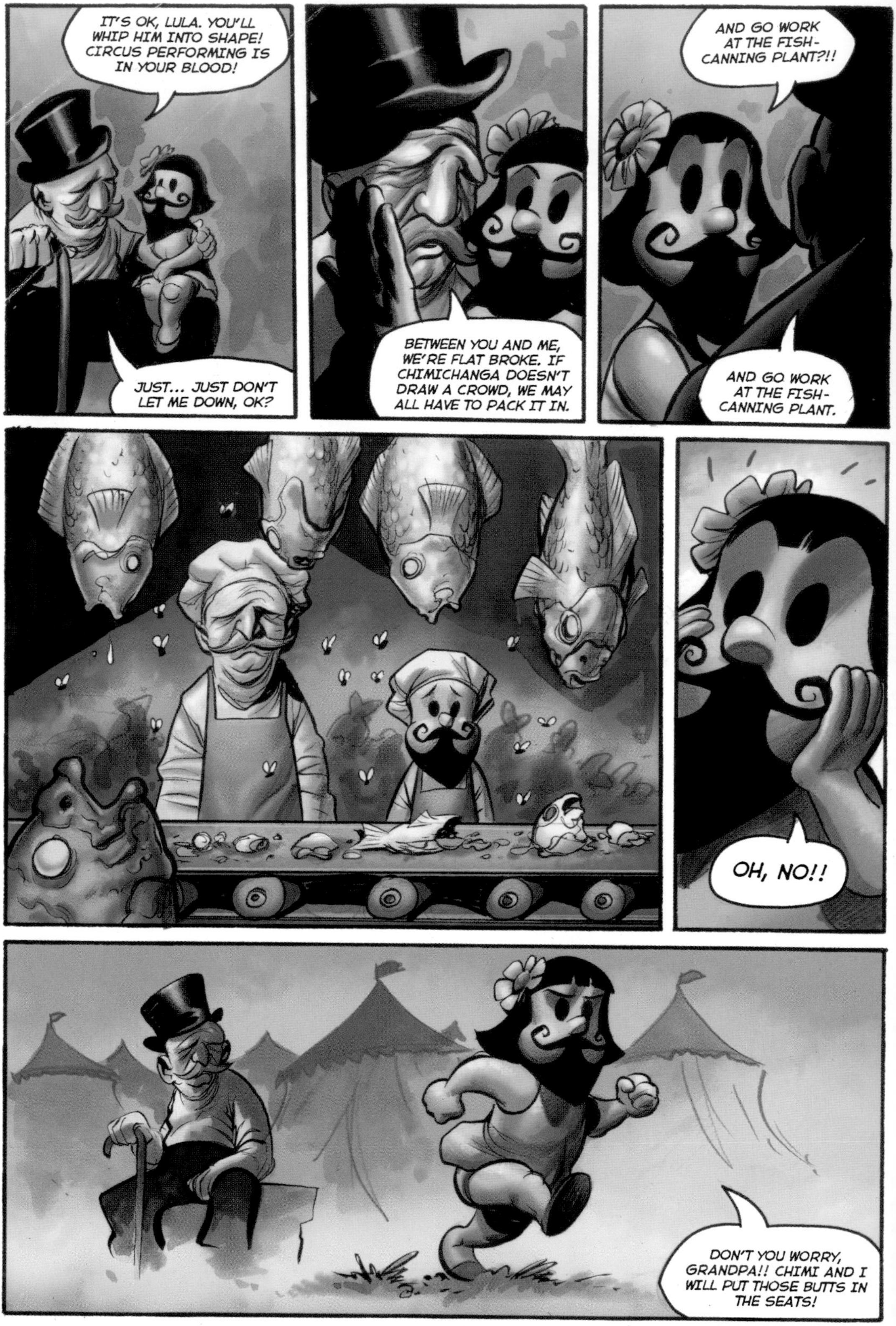
IT'S OK, LULA. YOU'LL WHIP HIM INTO SHAPE! CIRCUS PERFORMING IS IN YOUR BLOOD!
JUST... JUST DON'T LET ME DOWN, OK?
BETWEEN YOU AND ME, WE'RE FLAT BROKE. IF CHIMICHANGA DOESN'T DRAW A CROWD, WE MAY ALL HAVE TO PACK IT IN.
AND GO WORK AT THE FISH-CANNING PLANT?!!
AND GO WORK AT THE FISH-CANNING PLANT.
OH, NO!!
DON'T YOU WORRY, GRANDPA!! CHIMI AND I WILL PUT THOSE BUTTS IN THE SEATS!

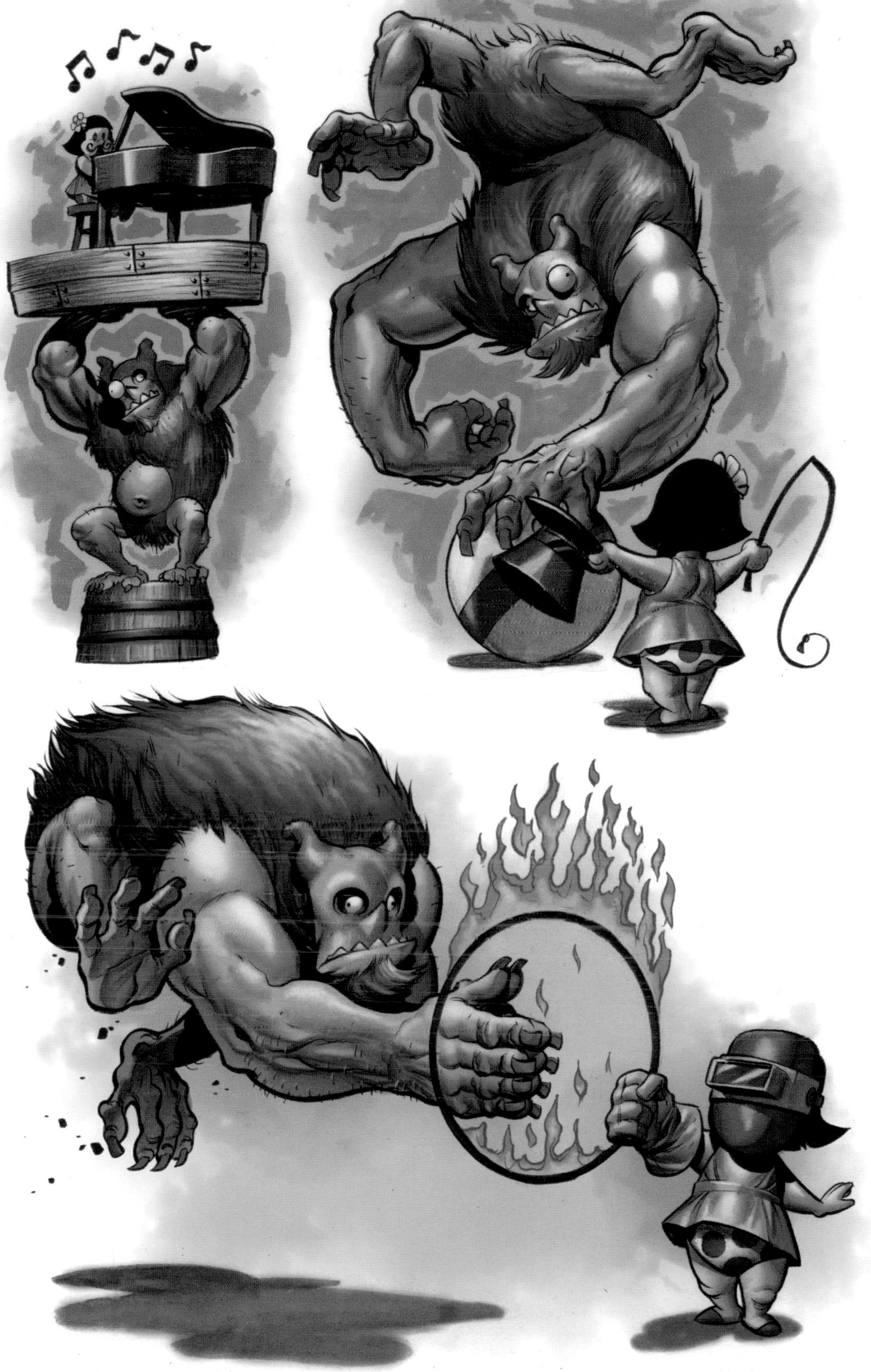

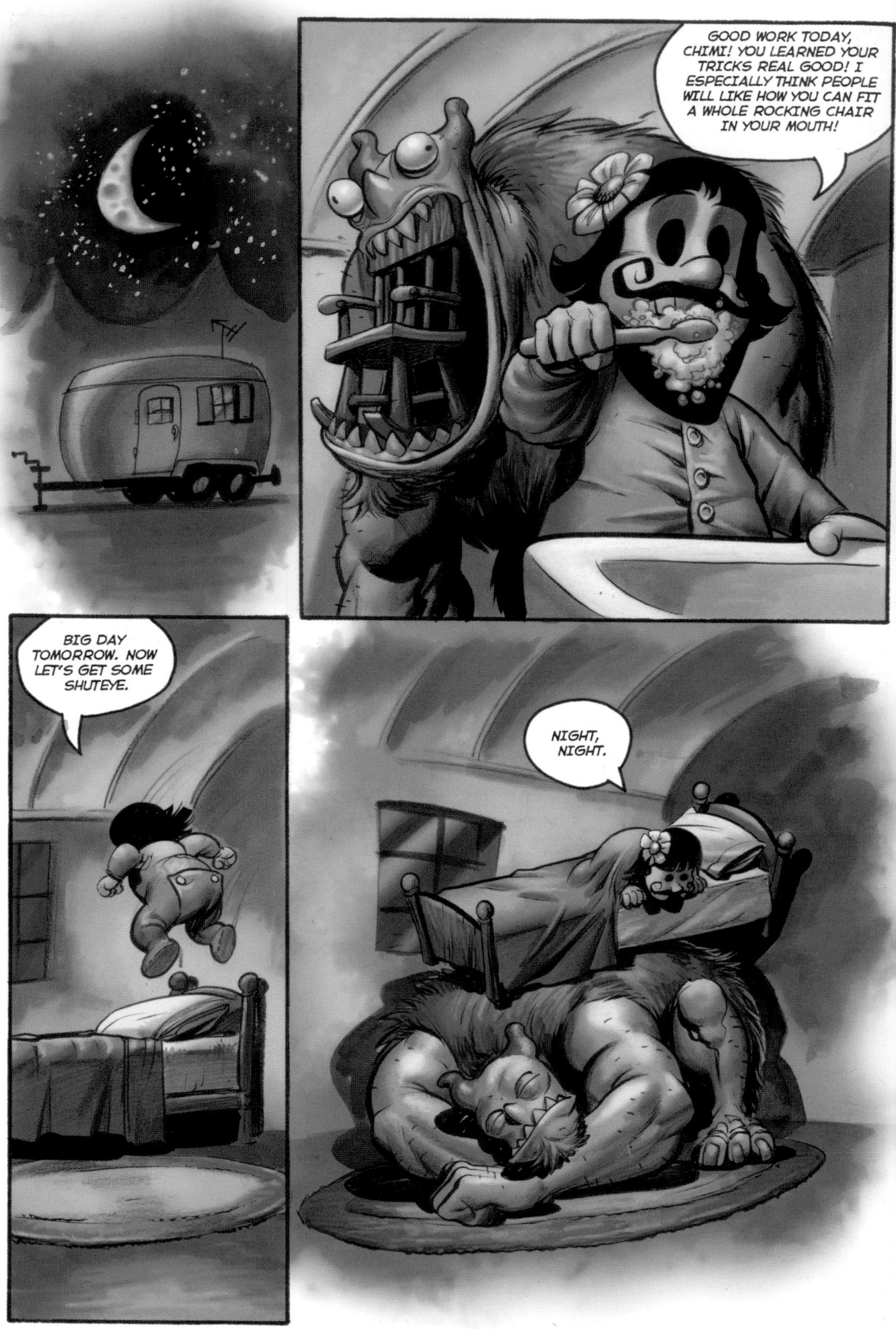
GOOD WORK TODAY, CHIMI! YOU LEARNED YOUR TRICKS REAL GOOD! I ESPECIALLY THINK PEOPLE WILL LIKE HOW YOU CAN FIT A WHOLE ROCKING CHAIR IN YOUR MOUTH!
BIG DAY TOMORROW. NOW LET'S GET SOME SHUTEYE.
NIGHT, NIGHT.

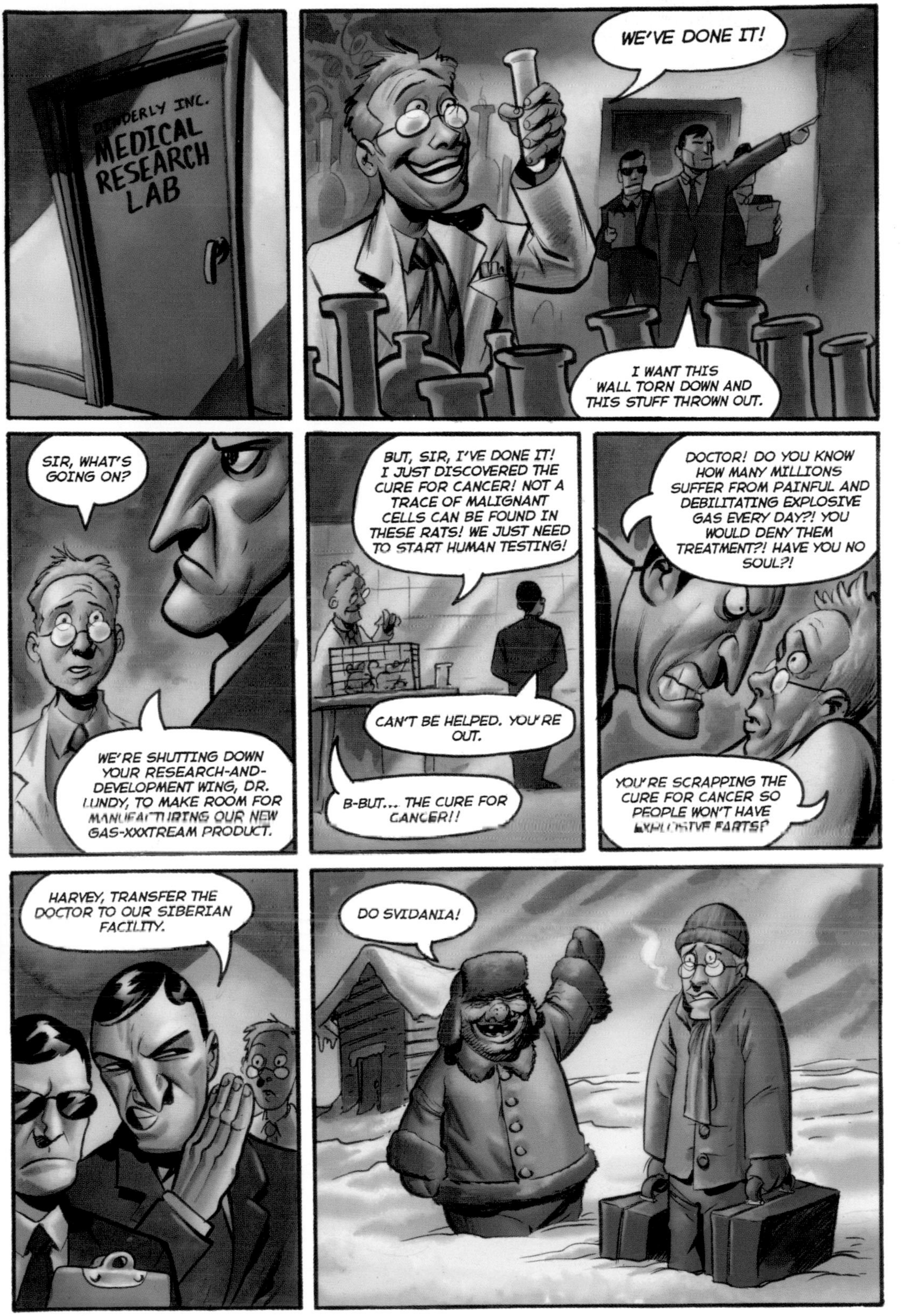
MEDICAL RESEARCH LAB
WE'VE DONE IT!
I WANT THIS WALL TORN DOWN AND THIS STUFF THROWN OUT.
SIR, WHAT'S GOING ON?
WE'RE SHUTTING DOWN YOUR RESEARCH-AND-DEVELOPMENT WING, DR. LUNDY, TO MAKE ROOM FOR MANUFACTURING OUR NEW GAS-XXXTREAM PRODUCT.
BUT, SIR, I'VE DONE IT! I JUST DISCOVERED THE CURE FOR CANCER! NOT A TRACE OF MALIGNANT CELLS CAN BE FOUND IN THESE RATS! WE JUST NEED TO START HUMAN TESTING!
CAN'T BE HELPED. YOU'RE OUT.
B-BUT... THE CURE FOR CANCER!!
DOCTOR! DO YOU KNOW HOW MANY MILLIONS SUFFER FROM PAINFUL AND DEBILITATING EXPLOSIVE GAS EVERY DAY?! YOU WOULD DENY THEM TREATMENT?! HAVE YOU NO SOUL?!
YOU'RE SCRAPPING THE CURE FOR CANCER SO PEOPLE WON'T HAVE EXPLOSIVE FARTS?
HARVEY, TRANSFER THE DOCTOR TO OUR SIBERIAN FACILITY.
DO SVIDANIA!

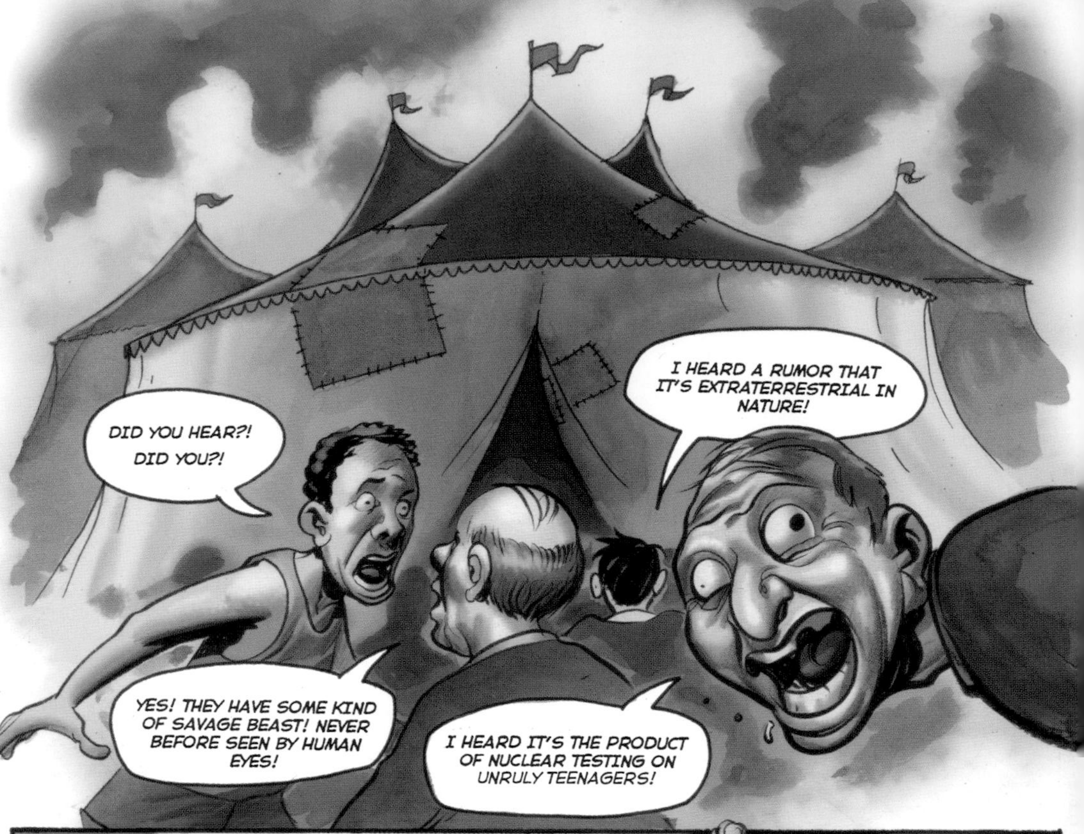
DID YOU HEAR?! DID YOU?!
I HEARD A RUMOR THAT IT'S EXTRATERRESTRIAL IN NATURE!
YES! THEY HAVE SOME KIND OF SAVAGE BEAST! NEVER BEFORE SEEN BY HUMAN EYES!
I HEARD IT'S THE PRODUCT OF NUCLEAR TESTING ON UNRULY TEENAGERS!

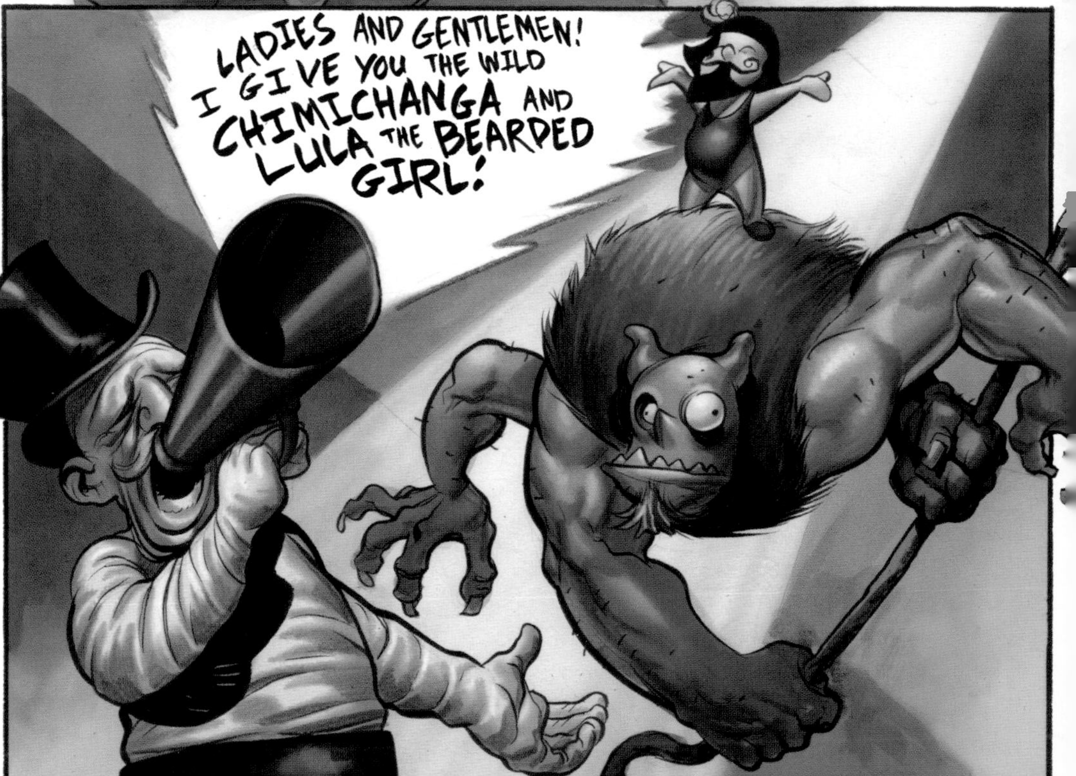
LADIES AND GENTLEMEN! I GIVE YOU THE WILD CHIMICHANGA AND LULA THE BEARDED GIRL!

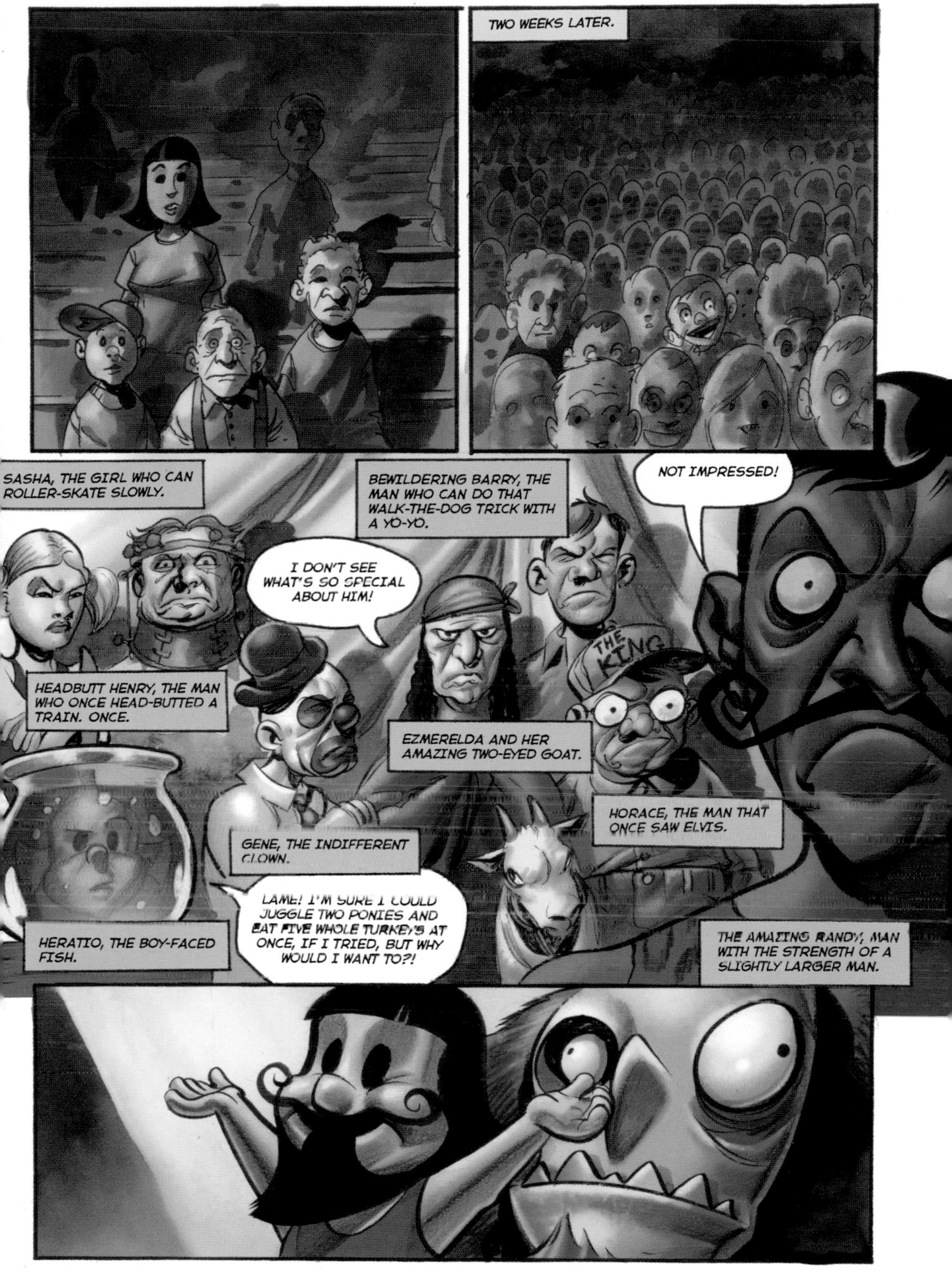
TWO WEEKS LATER.
SASHA, THE GIRL WHO CAN ROLLER-SKATE SLOWLY.
BEWILDERING BARRY, THE MAN WHO CAN DO THAT WALK-THE-DOG TRICK WITH A YO-YO.
NOT IMPRESSED!
I DON'T SEE WHAT'S SO SPECIAL ABOUT HIM!
HEADBUTT HENRY, THE MAN WHO ONCE HEAD-BUTTED A TRAIN. ONCE.
EZMERELDA AND HER AMAZING TWO-EYED GOAT.
HORACE, THE MAN THAT ONCE SAW ELVIS.
GENE, THE INDIFFERENT CLOWN.
LAME! I'M SURE I COULD JUGGLE TWO PONIES AND EAT FIVE WHOLE TURKEYS AT ONCE, IF I TRIED, BUT WHY WOULD I WANT TO?!
HERATIO, THE BOY-FACED FISH.
THE AMAZING RANDY, MAN WITH THE STRENGTH OF A SLIGHTLY LARGER MAN.
THE KING

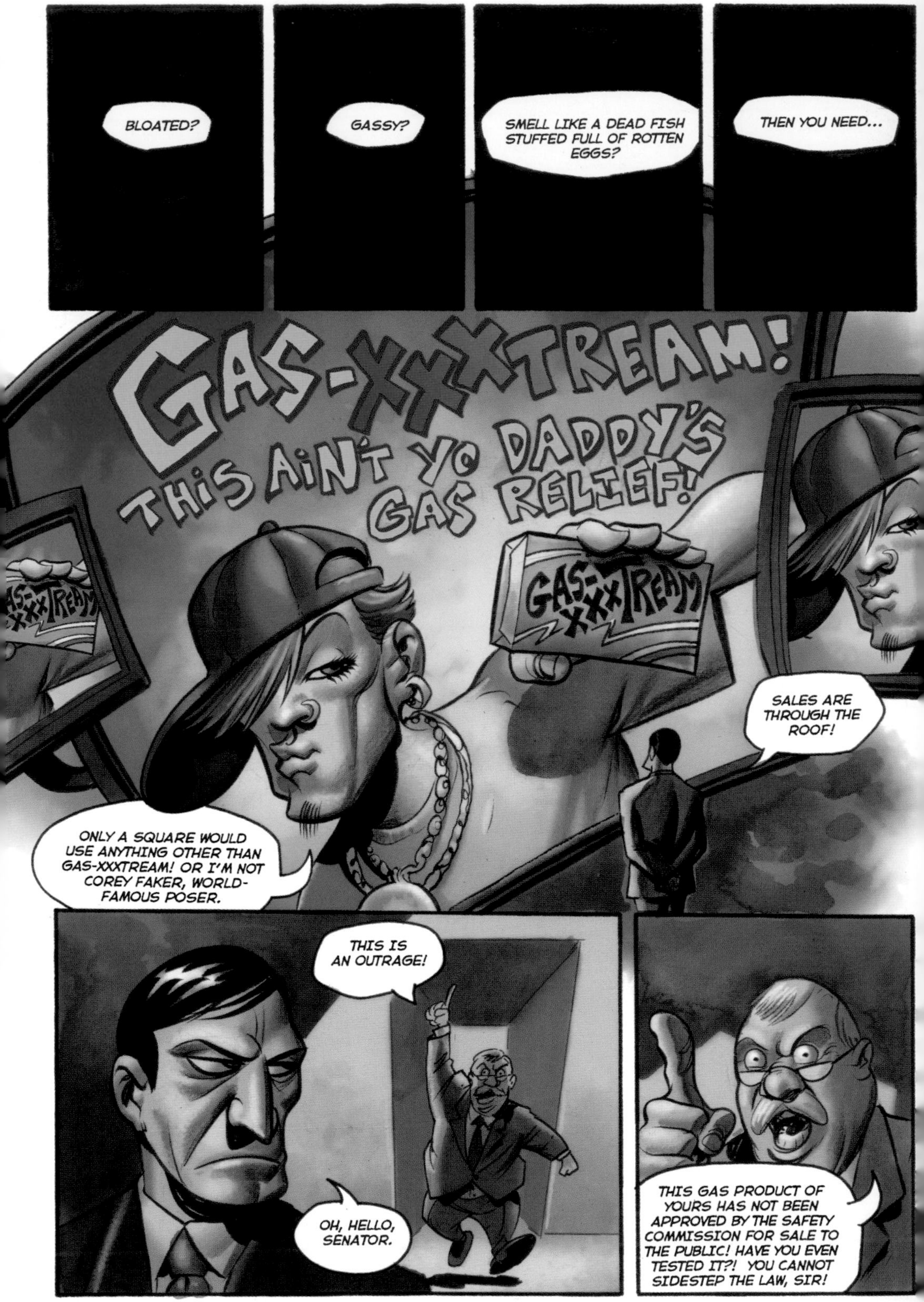
BLOATED?
GASSY?
SMELL LIKE A DEAD FISH STUFFED FULL OF ROTTEN EGGS?
THEN YOU NEED...
GAS-XXXTREAM!
THIS AIN'T YO DADDY'S GAS RELIEF!
GAS-XXXTREAM
SALES ARE THROUGH THE ROOF!
ONLY A SQUARE WOULD USE ANYTHING OTHER THAN GAS-XXXTREAM! OR I'M NOT COREY FAKER, WORLD-FAMOUS POSER.
THIS IS AN OUTRAGE!
OH, HELLO, SENATOR.
THIS GAS PRODUCT OF YOURS HAS NOT BEEN APPROVED BY THE SAFETY COMMISSION FOR SALE TO THE PUBLIC! HAVE YOU EVEN TESTED IT?! YOU CANNOT SIDESTEP THE LAW, SIR!

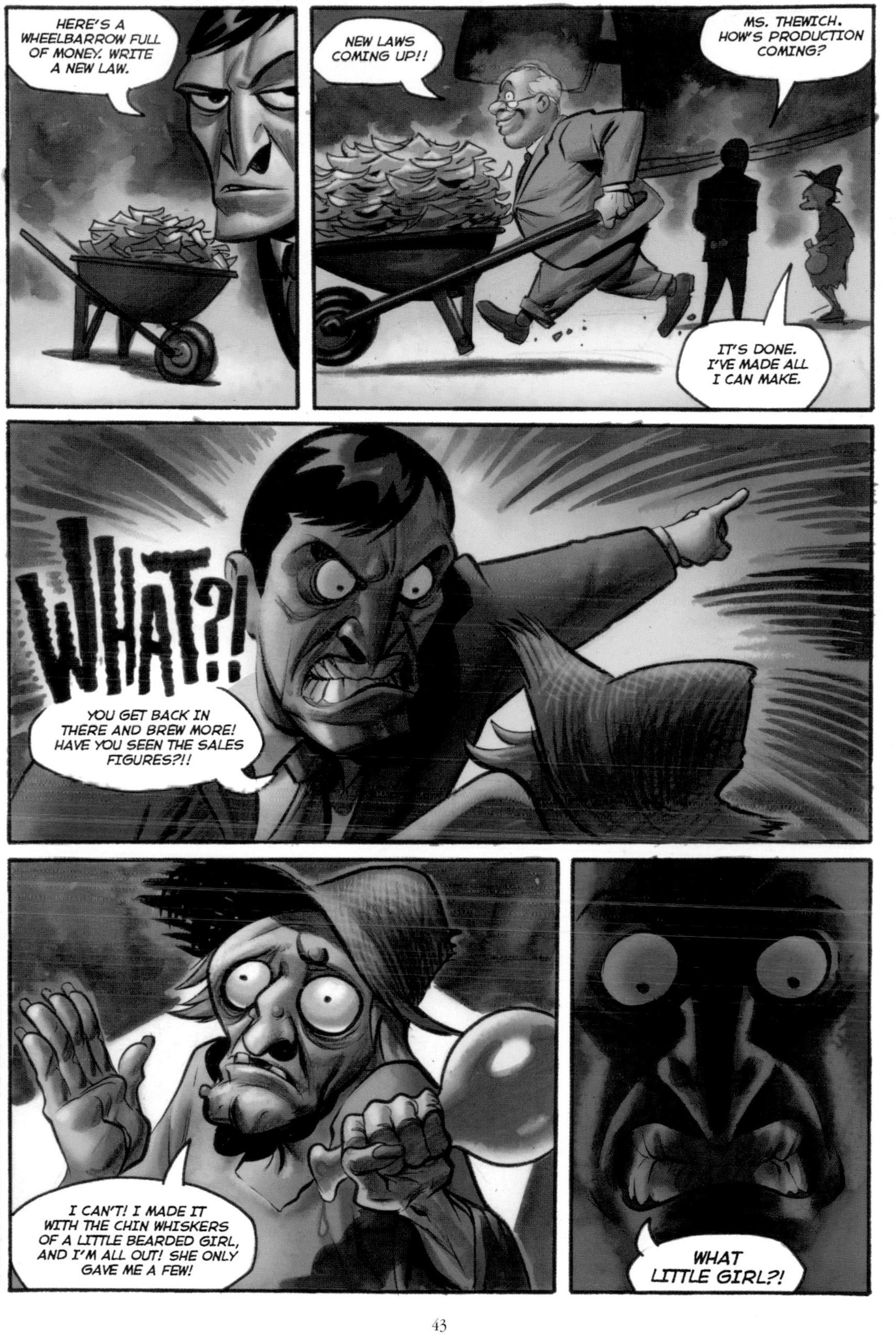
HERE'S A WHEELBARROW FULL OF MONEY. WRITE A NEW LAW.
NEW LAWS COMING UP!!
MS. THEWICH. HOW'S PRODUCTION COMING?
IT'S DONE. I'VE MADE ALL I CAN MAKE.
WHAT?!
YOU GET BACK IN THERE AND BREW MORE! HAVE YOU SEEN THE SALES FIGURES?!!
I CAN'T! I MADE IT WITH THE CHIN WHISKERS OF A LITTLE BEARDED GIRL, AND I'M ALL OUT! SHE ONLY GAVE ME A FEW!
WHAT LITTLE GIRL?!

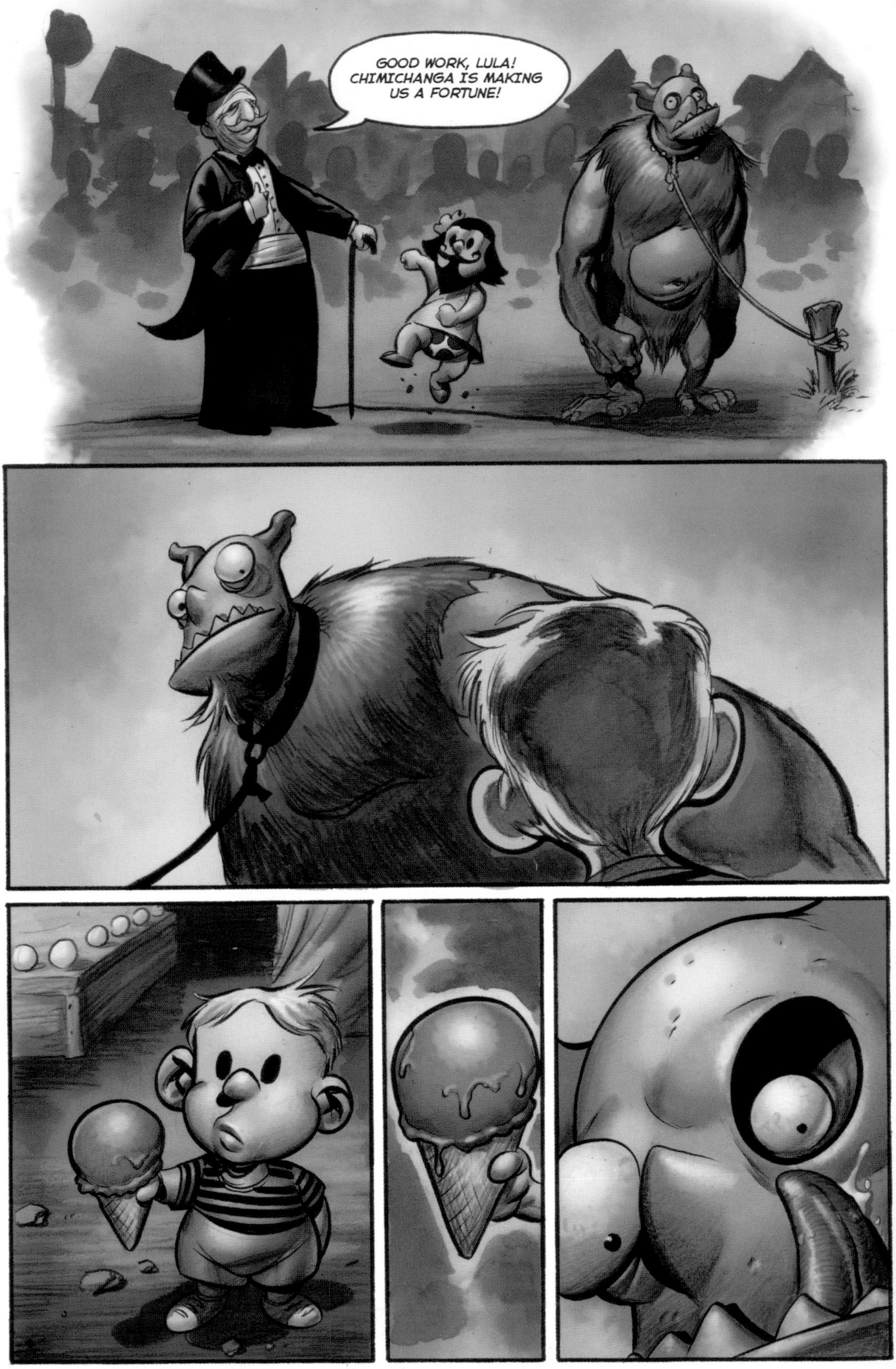
GOOD WORK, LULA! CHIMICHANGA IS MAKING US A FORTUNE!

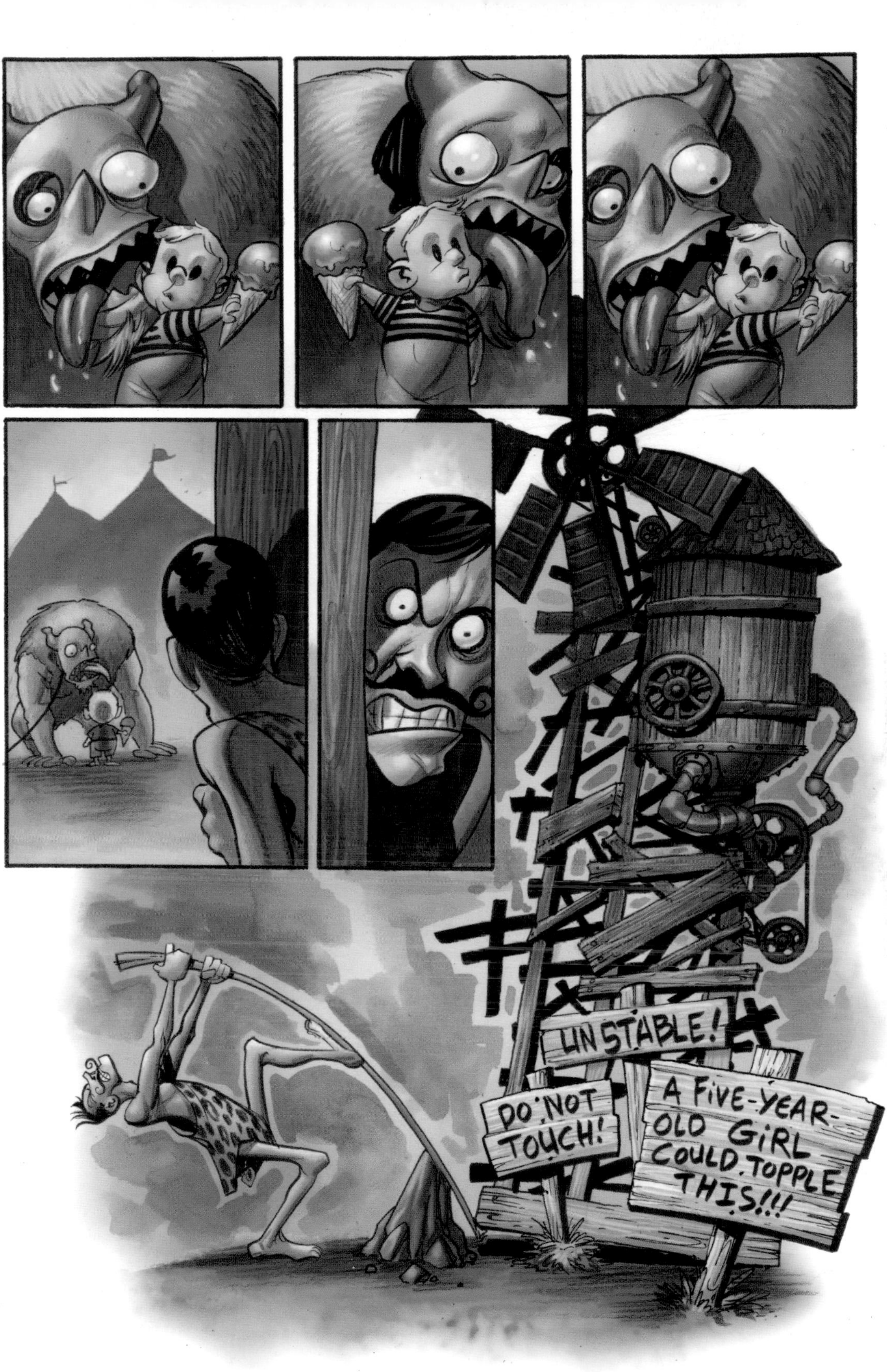
UNSTABLE!
DO NOT TOUCH!
A FIVE-YEAR-OLD GIRL COULD TOPPLE THIS!!!

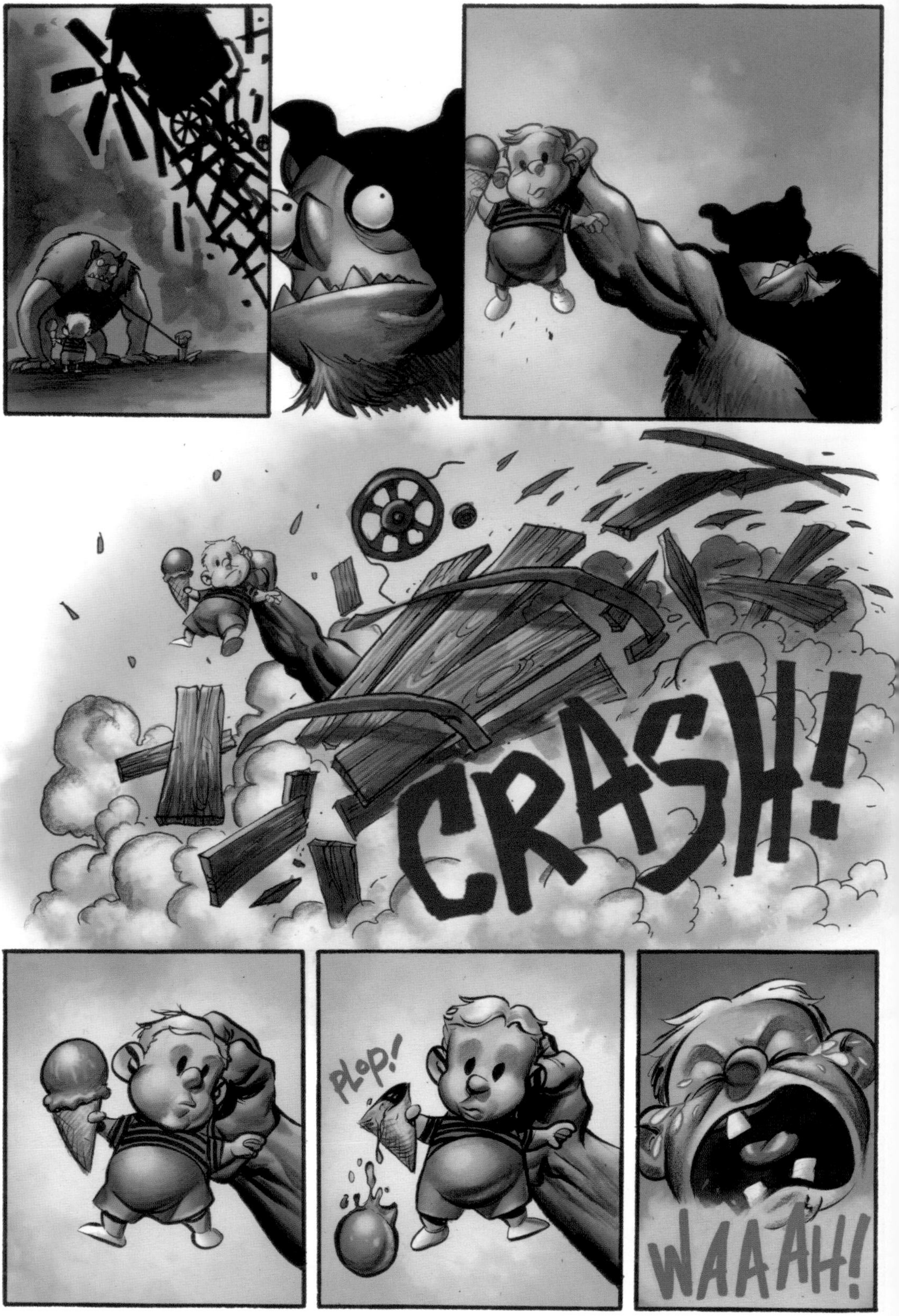
CRASH!
PLOP!
WAAAH!

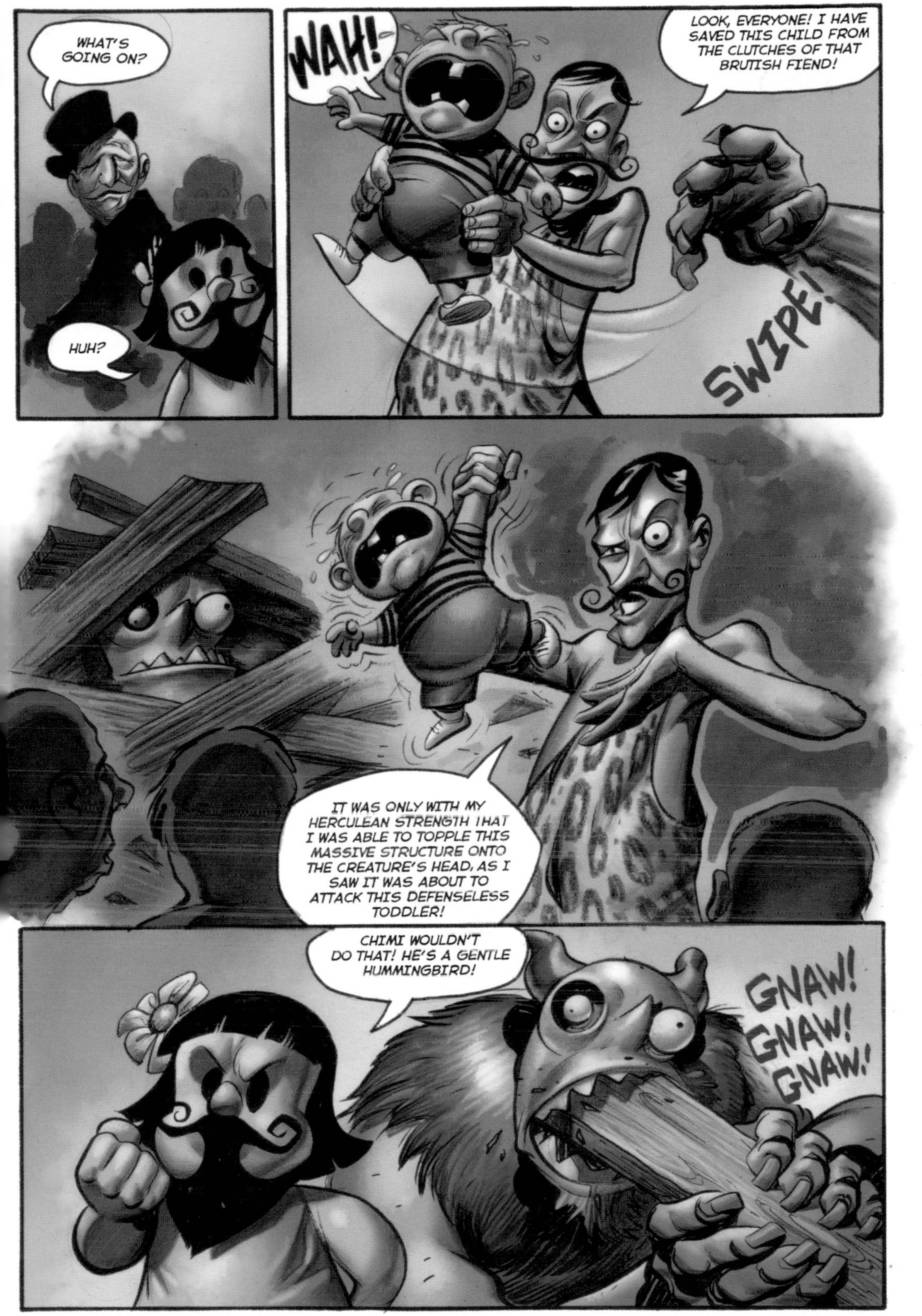
WHAT'S GOING ON?
HUH?
WAH!
LOOK, EVERYONE! I HAVE SAVED THIS CHILD FROM THE CLUTCHES OF THAT BRUTISH FIEND!
SWIPE!
IT WAS ONLY WITH MY HERCULEAN STRENGTH THAT I WAS ABLE TO TOPPLE THIS MASSIVE STRUCTURE ONTO THE CREATURE'S HEAD, AS I SAW IT WAS ABOUT TO ATTACK THIS DEFENSELESS TODDLER!
CHIMI WOULDN'T DO THAT! HE'S A GENTLE HUMMINGBIRD!
GNAW! GNAW! GNAW!

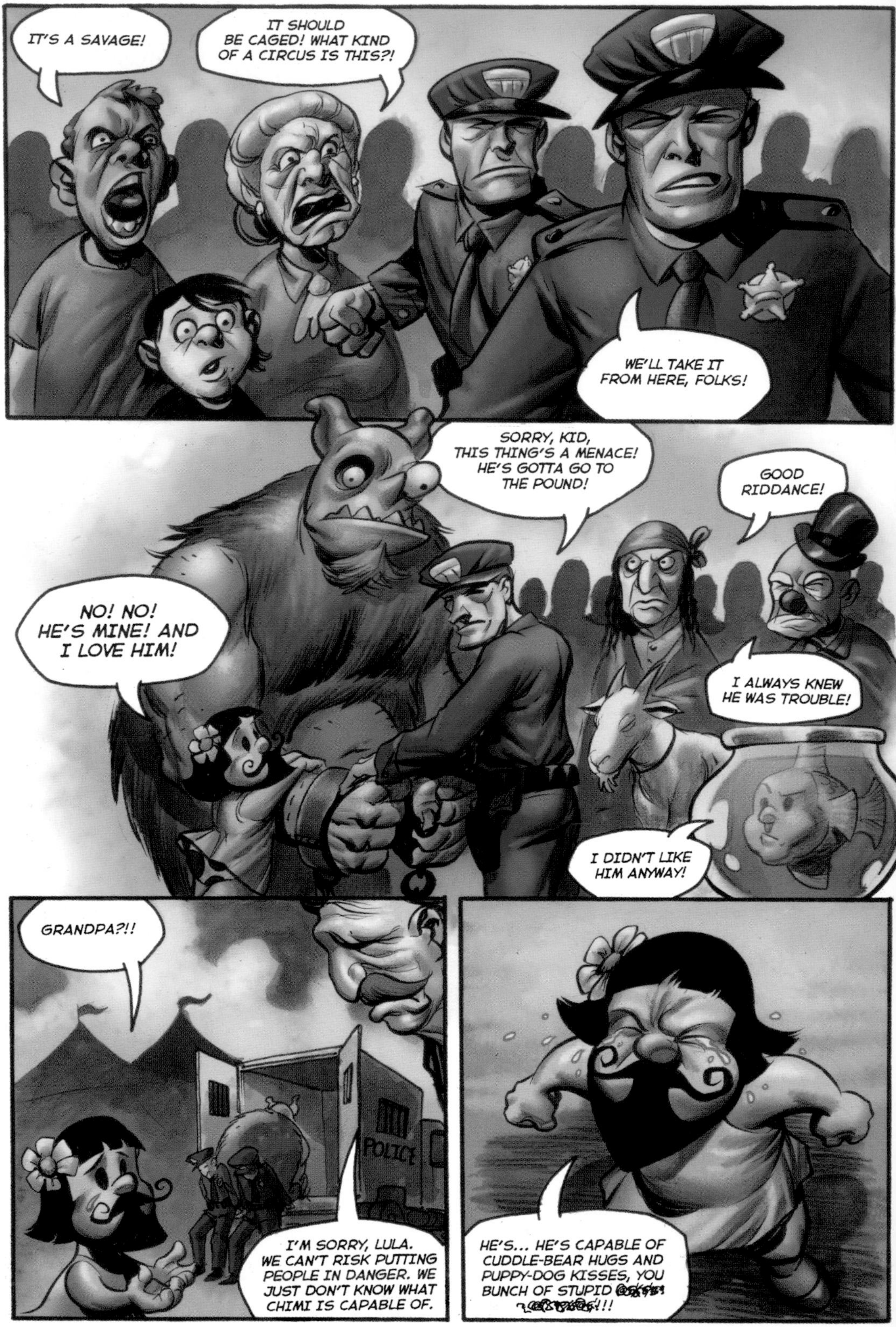
IT'S A SAVAGE!
IT SHOULD BE CAGED! WHAT KIND OF A CIRCUS IS THIS?!
WE'LL TAKE IT FROM HERE, FOLKS!
SORRY, KID, THIS THING'S A MENACE! HE'S GOTTA GO TO THE POUND!
GOOD RIDDANCE!
NO! NO! HE'S MINE! AND I LOVE HIM!
I ALWAYS KNEW HE WAS TROUBLE!
I DIDN'T LIKE HIM ANYWAY!
GRANDPA?!!
POLICE
I'M SORRY, LULA. WE CAN'T RISK PUTTING PEOPLE IN DANGER. WE JUST DON'T KNOW WHAT CHIMI IS CAPABLE OF.
HE'S... HE'S CAPABLE OF CUDDLE-BEAR HUGS AND PUPPY-DOG KISSES, YOU BUNCH OF STUPID

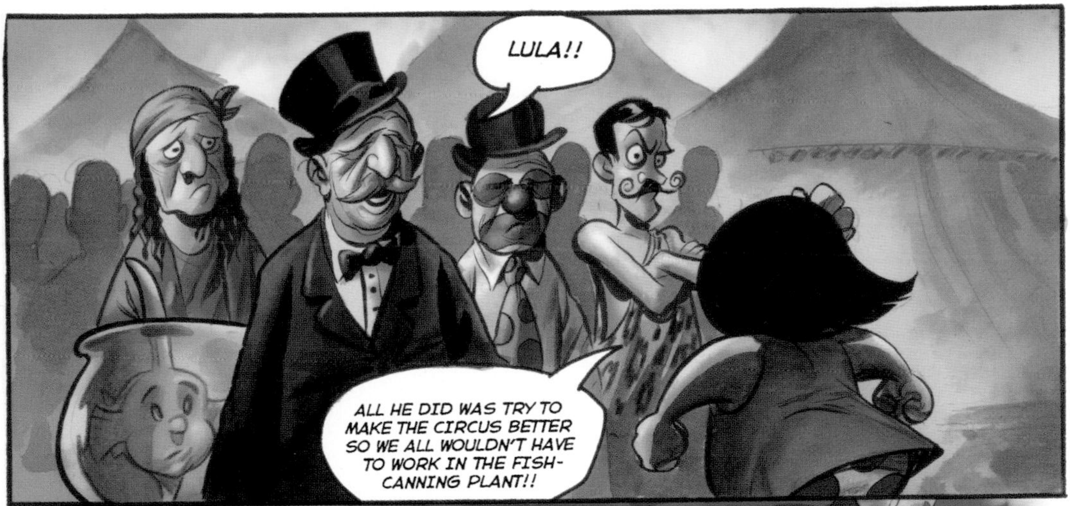
LULA!!
ALL HE DID WAS TRY TO MAKE THE CIRCUS BETTER SO WE ALL WOULDN'T HAVE TO WORK IN THE FISH-CANNING PLANT!!

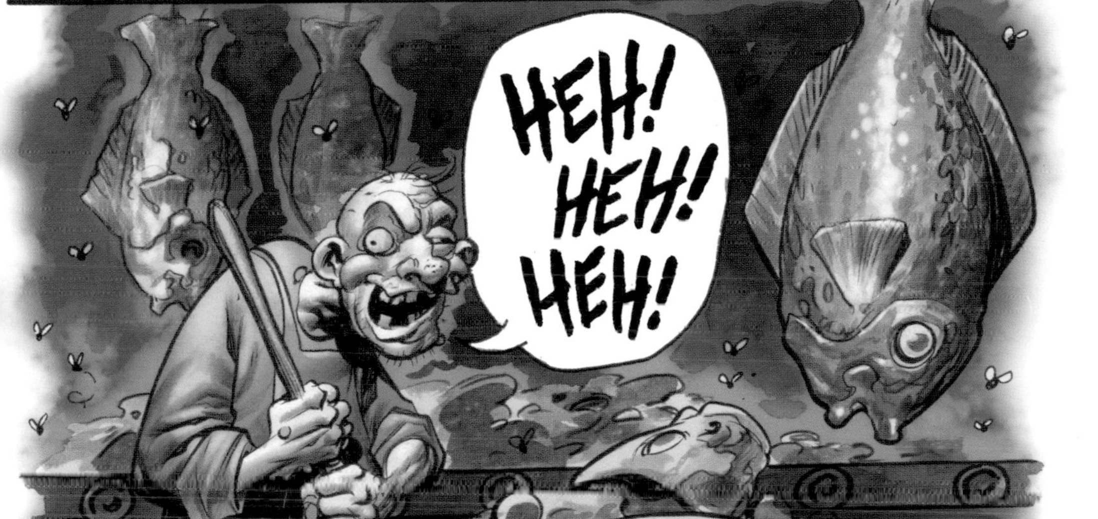
HEH! HEH! HEH!

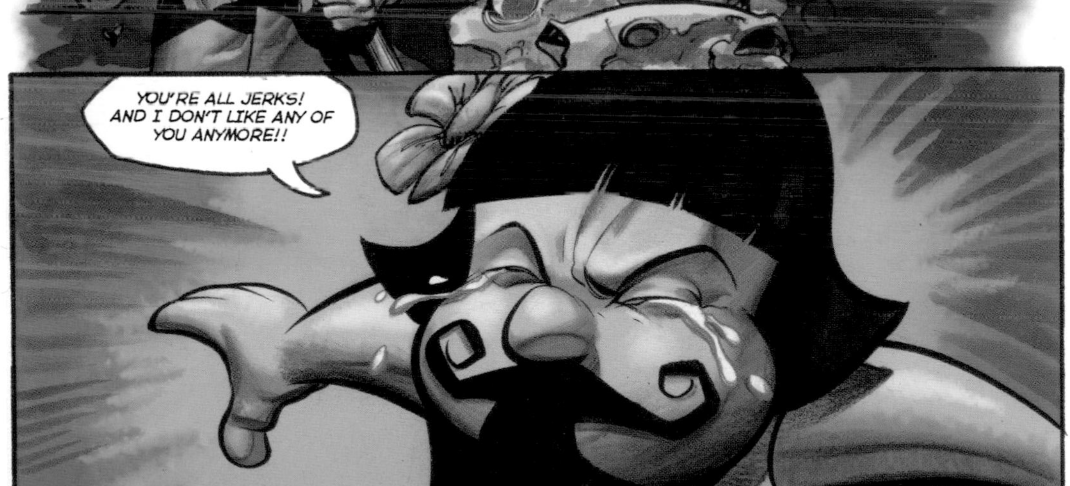
YOU'RE ALL JERKS! AND I DON'T LIKE ANY OF YOU ANYMORE!!

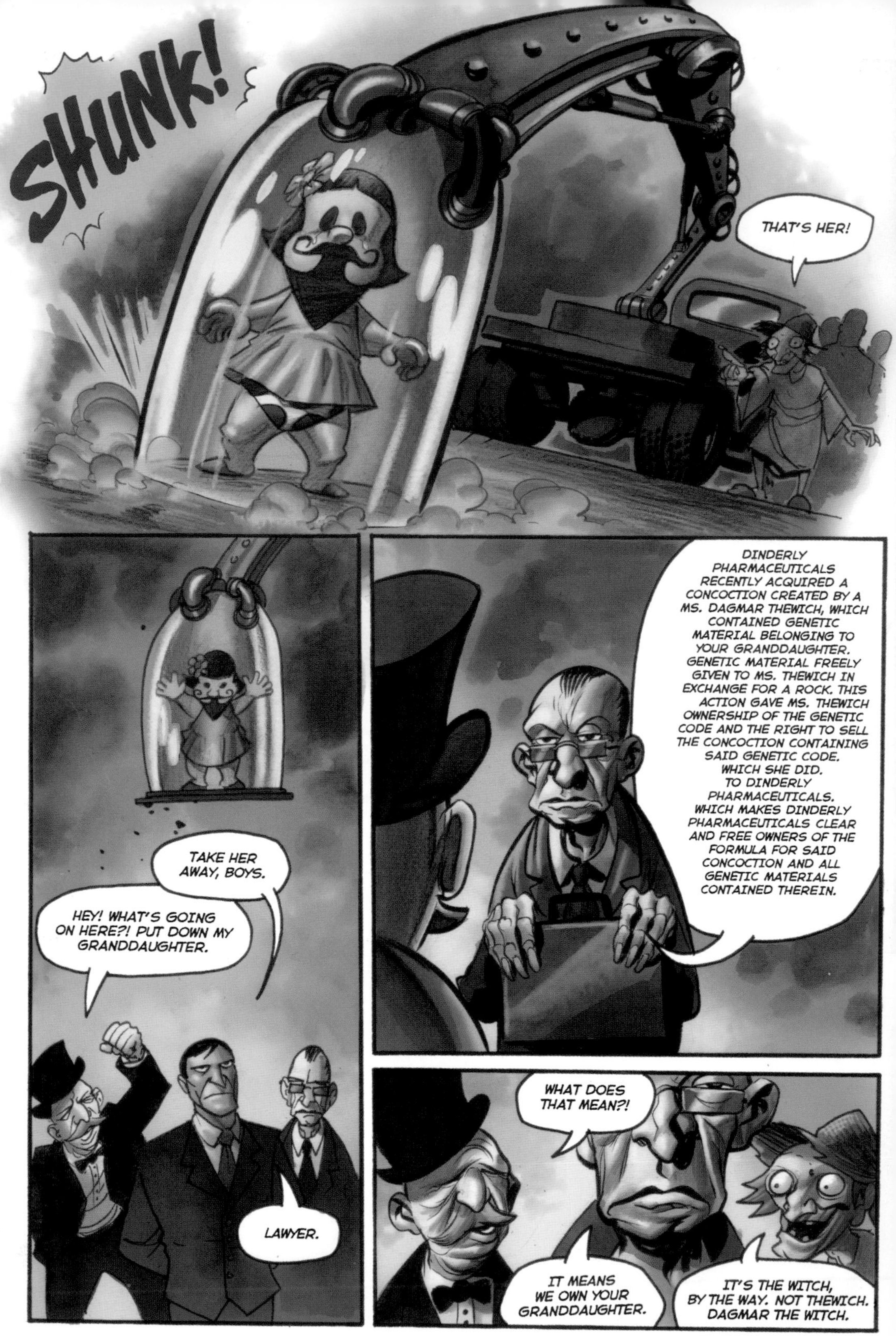
SHUNK!
THAT'S HER!
TAKE HER AWAY, BOYS.
HEY! WHAT'S GOING ON HERE?! PUT DOWN MY GRANDDAUGHTER.
LAWYER.
DINDERLY PHARMACEUTICALS RECENTLY ACQUIRED A CONCOCTION CREATED BY A MS. DAGMAR THEWICH, WHICH CONTAINED GENETIC MATERIAL BELONGING TO YOUR GRANDDAUGHTER. GENETIC MATERIAL FREELY GIVEN TO MS. THEWICH IN EXCHANGE FOR A ROCK. THIS ACTION GAVE MS. THEWICH OWNERSHIP OF THE GENETIC CODE AND THE RIGHT TO SELL THE CONCOCTION CONTAINING SAID GENETIC CODE. WHICH SHE DID. TO DINDERLY PHARMACEUTICALS. WHICH MAKES DINDERLY PHARMACEUTICALS CLEAR AND FREE OWNERS OF THE FORMULA FOR SAID CONCOCTION AND ALL GENETIC MATERIALS CONTAINED THEREIN.
WHAT DOES THAT MEAN?!
IT MEANS WE OWN YOUR GRANDDAUGHTER.
IT'S THE WITCH, BY THE WAY. NOT THEWICH. DAGMAR THE WITCH.

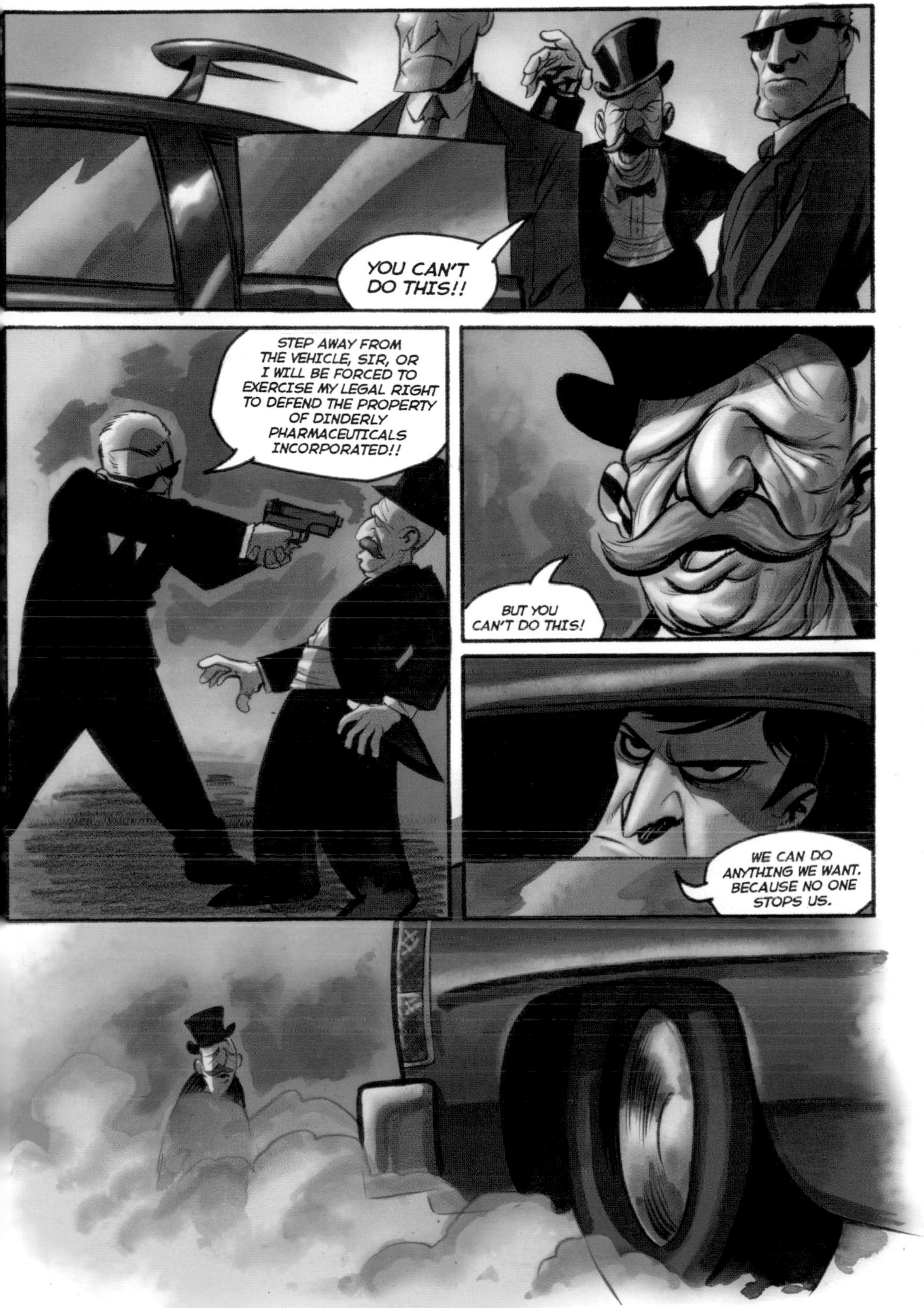
YOU CAN'T DO THIS!!
STEP AWAY FROM THE VEHICLE, SIR, OR I WILL BE FORCED TO EXERCISE MY LEGAL RIGHT TO DEFEND THE PROPERTY OF DINDERLY PHARMACEUTICALS INCORPORATED!!
BUT YOU CAN'T DO THIS!
WE CAN DO ANYTHING WE WANT. BECAUSE NO ONE STOPS US.

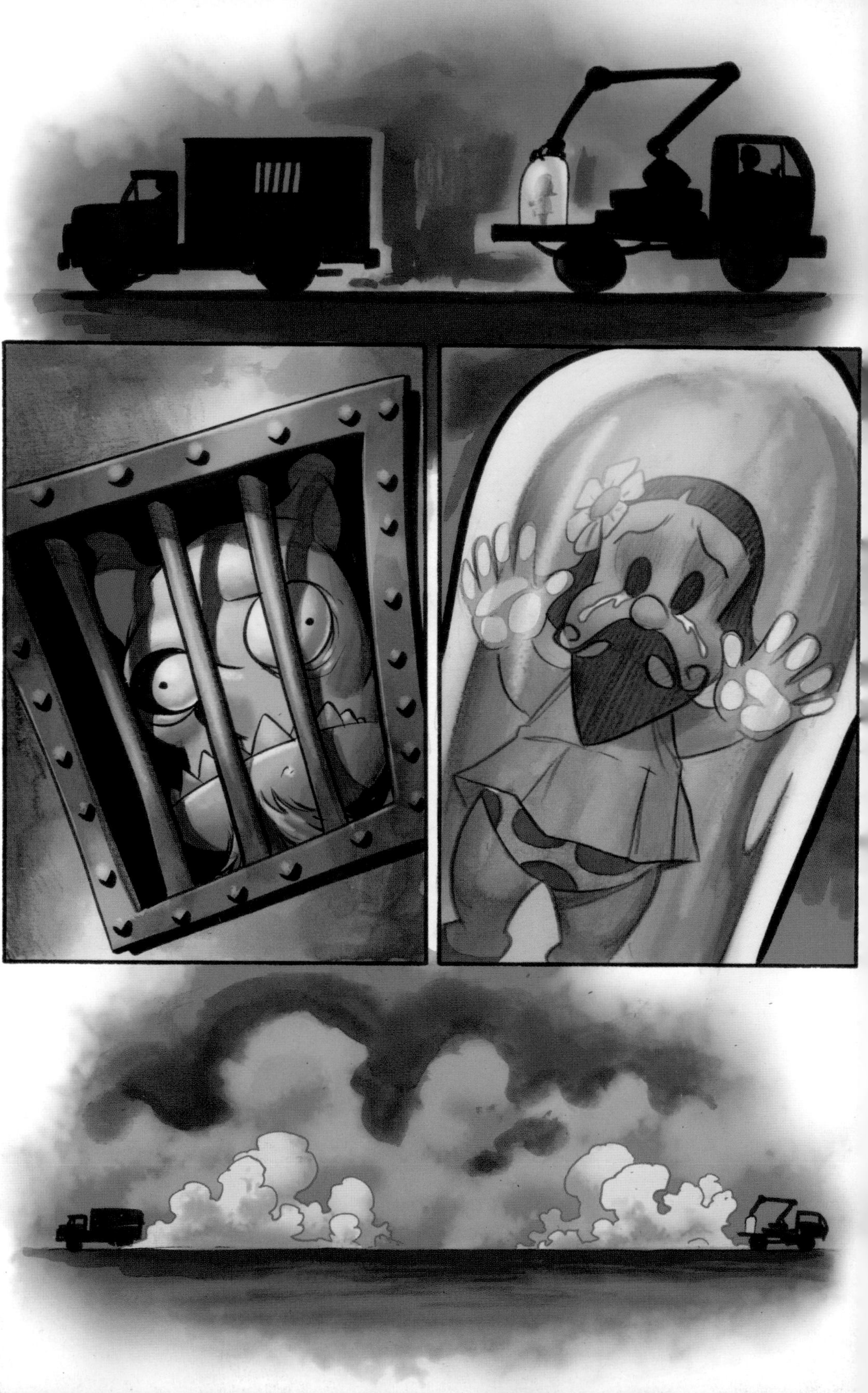

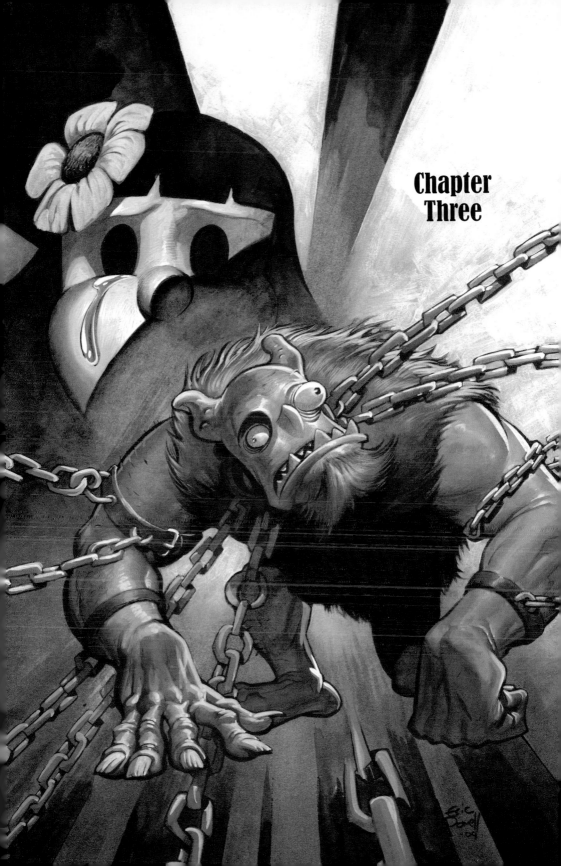

Chapter
Three

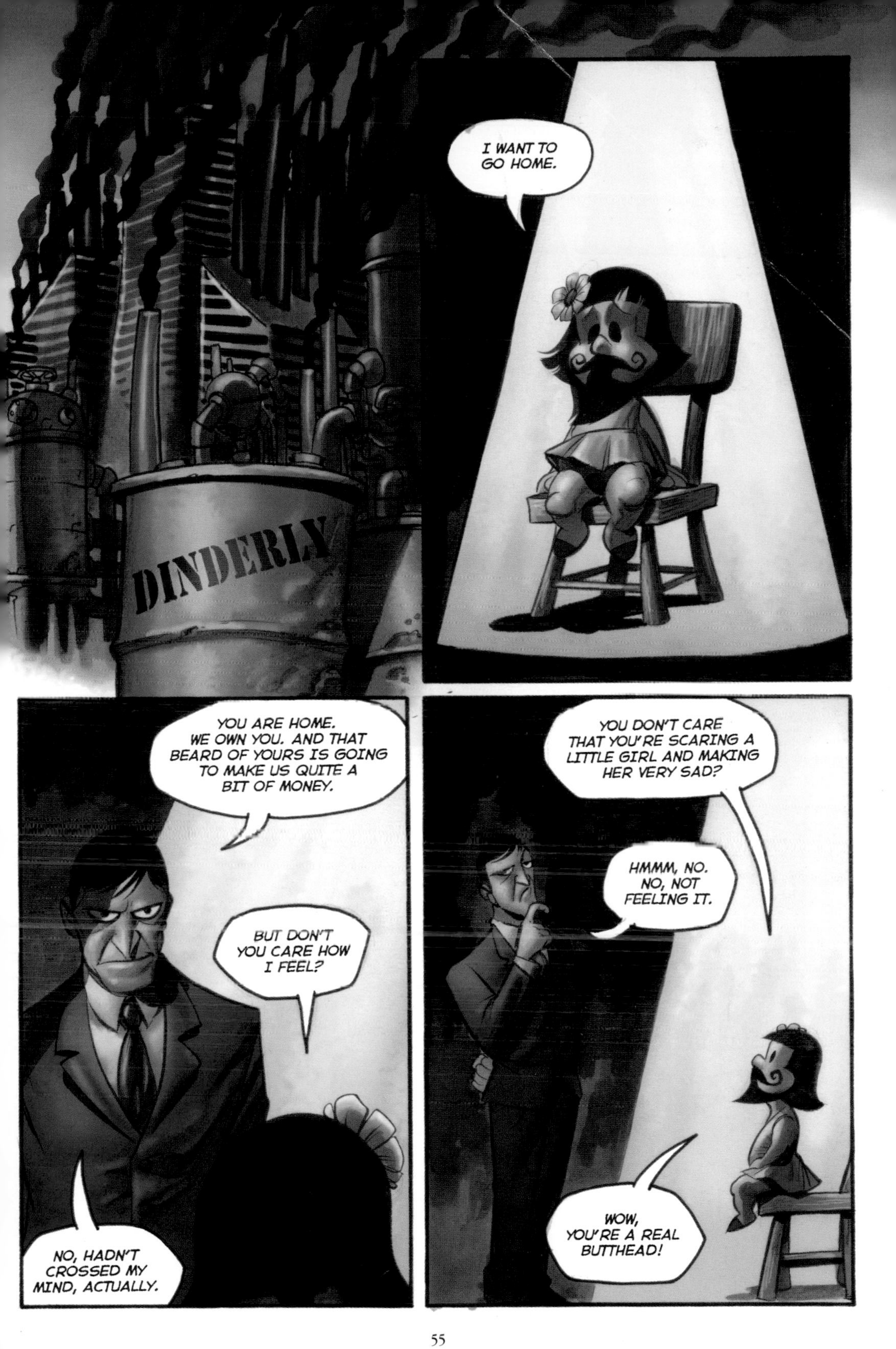
DINDERLY
I WANT TO GO HOME.
YOU ARE HOME. WE OWN YOU. AND THAT BEARD OF YOURS IS GOING TO MAKE US QUITE A BIT OF MONEY.
BUT DON'T YOU CARE HOW I FEEL?
NO, HADN'T CROSSED MY MIND, ACTUALLY.
YOU DON'T CARE THAT YOU'RE SCARING A LITTLE GIRL AND MAKING HER VERY SAD?
HMMM, NO. NO, NOT FEELING IT.
WOW, YOU'RE A REAL BUTTHEAD!

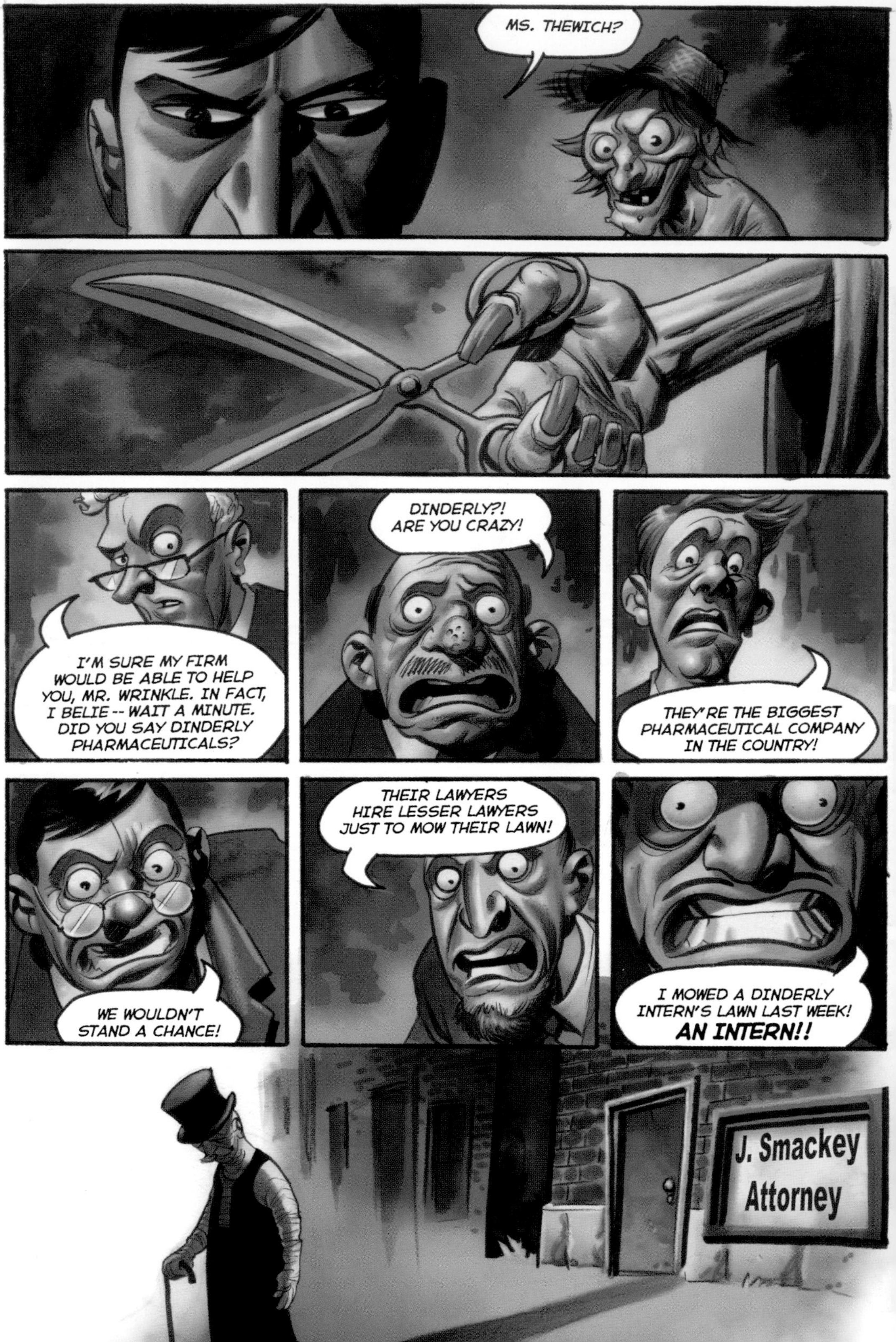
MS. THEWICH?
I'M SURE MY FIRM WOULD BE ABLE TO HELP YOU, MR. WRINKLE. IN FACT, I BELIE -- WAIT A MINUTE. DID YOU SAY DINDERLY PHARMACEUTICALS?
DINDERLY?! ARE YOU CRAZY!
THEY'RE THE BIGGEST PHARMACEUTICAL COMPANY IN THE COUNTRY!
WE WOULDN'T STAND A CHANCE!
THEIR LAWYERS HIRE LESSER LAWYERS JUST TO MOW THEIR LAWN!
I MOWED A DINDERLY INTERN'S LAWN LAST WEEK! **AN INTERN!!**
J. Smackey Attorney

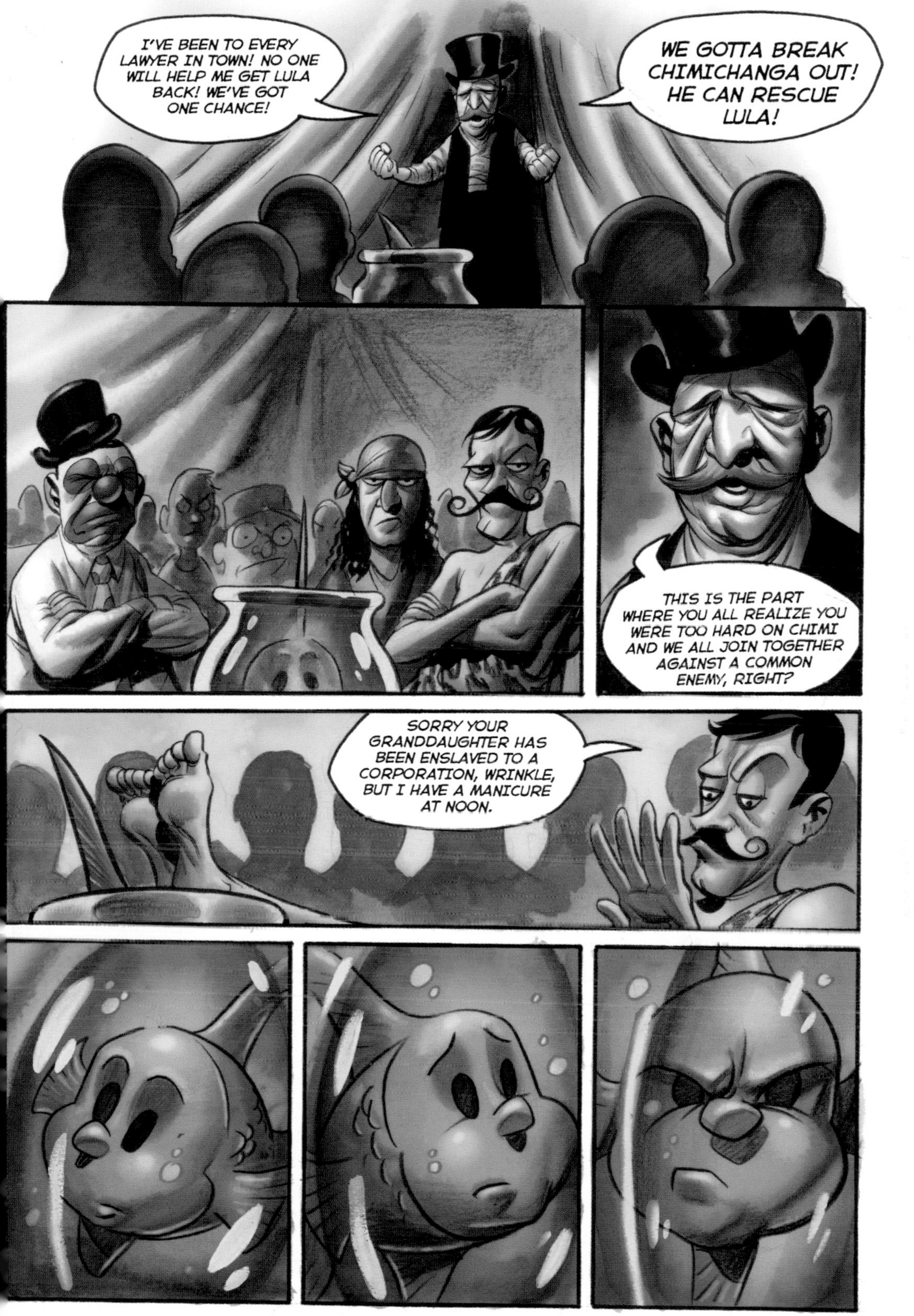
I'VE BEEN TO EVERY LAWYER IN TOWN! NO ONE WILL HELP ME GET LULA BACK! WE'VE GOT ONE CHANCE!
WE GOTTA BREAK CHIMICHANGA OUT! HE CAN RESCUE LULA!
THIS IS THE PART WHERE YOU ALL REALIZE YOU WERE TOO HARD ON CHIMI AND WE ALL JOIN TOGETHER AGAINST A COMMON ENEMY, RIGHT?
SORRY YOUR GRANDDAUGHTER HAS BEEN ENSLAVED TO A CORPORATION, WRINKLE, BUT I HAVE A MANICURE AT NOON.

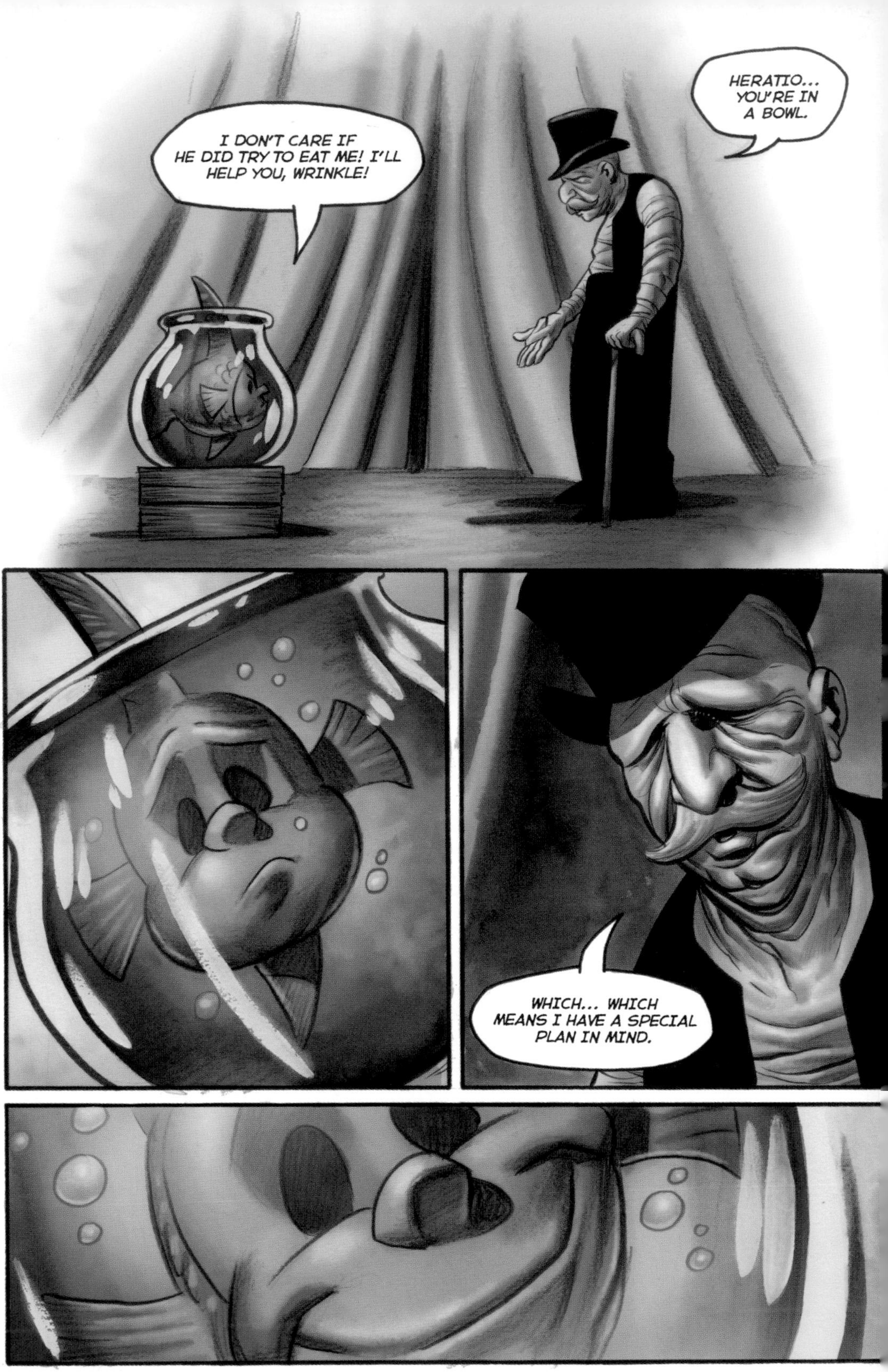
I DON'T CARE IF HE DID TRY TO EAT ME! I'LL HELP YOU, WRINKLE!
HERATIO... YOU'RE IN A BOWL.
WHICH... WHICH MEANS I HAVE A SPECIAL PLAN IN MIND.

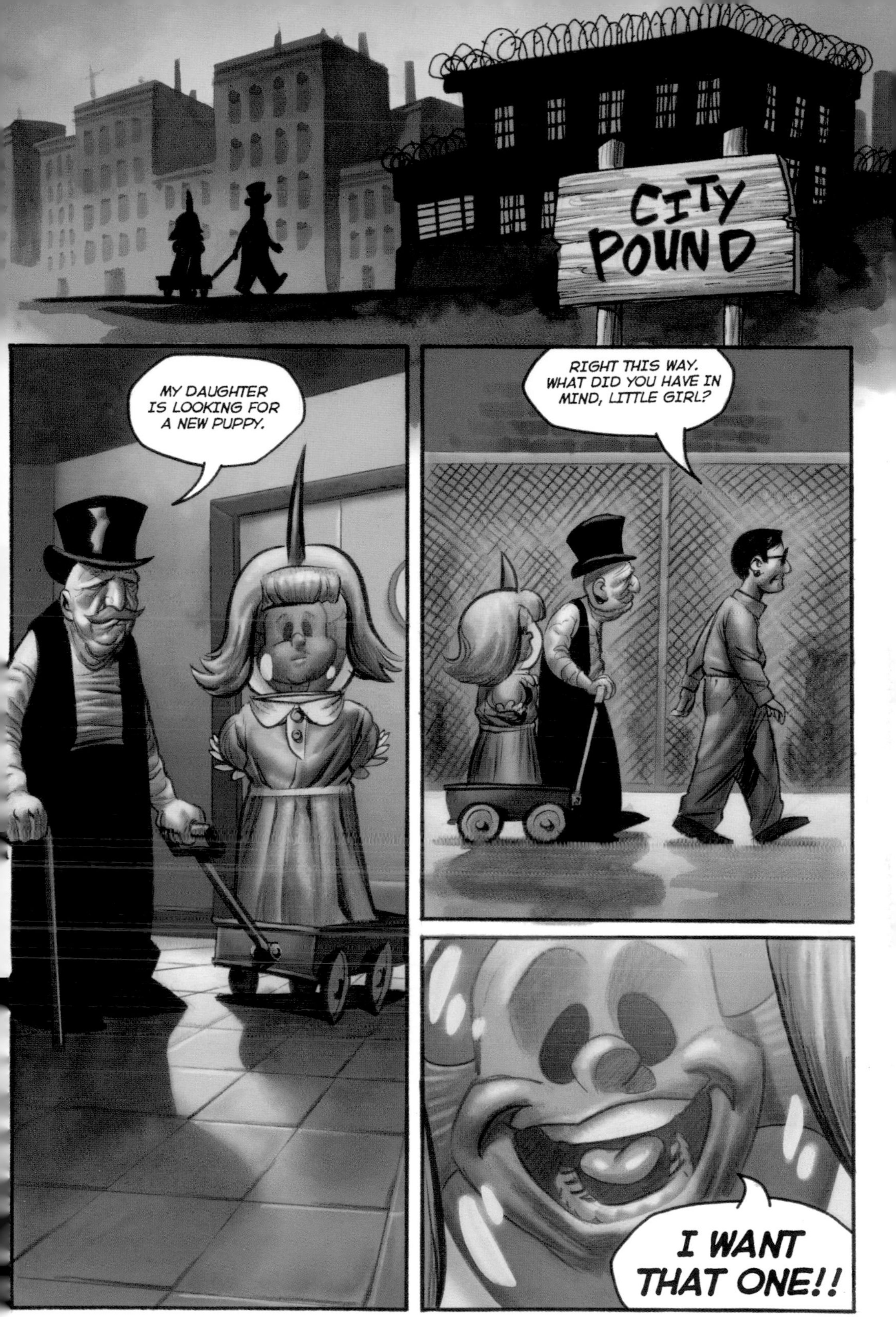
CITY POUND
MY DAUGHTER IS LOOKING FOR A NEW PUPPY.
RIGHT THIS WAY. WHAT DID YOU HAVE IN MIND, LITTLE GIRL?
I WANT THAT ONE!!

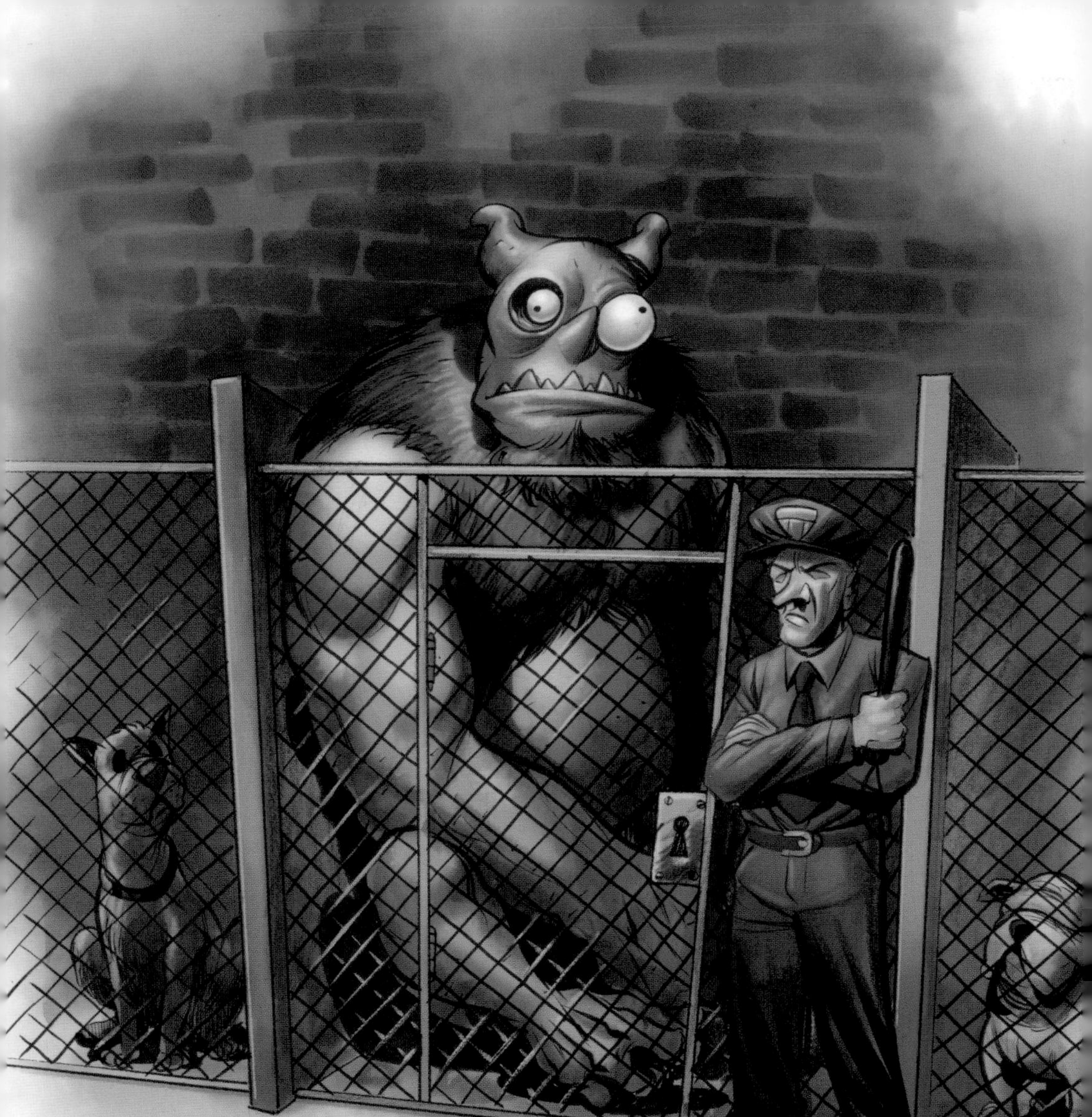

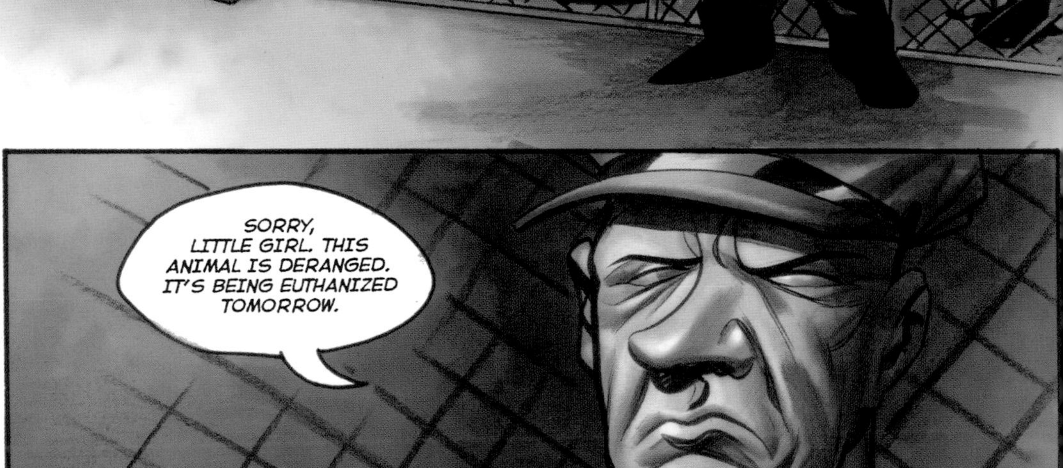
SORRY, LITTLE GIRL. THIS ANIMAL IS DERANGED. IT'S BEING EUTHANIZED TOMORROW.

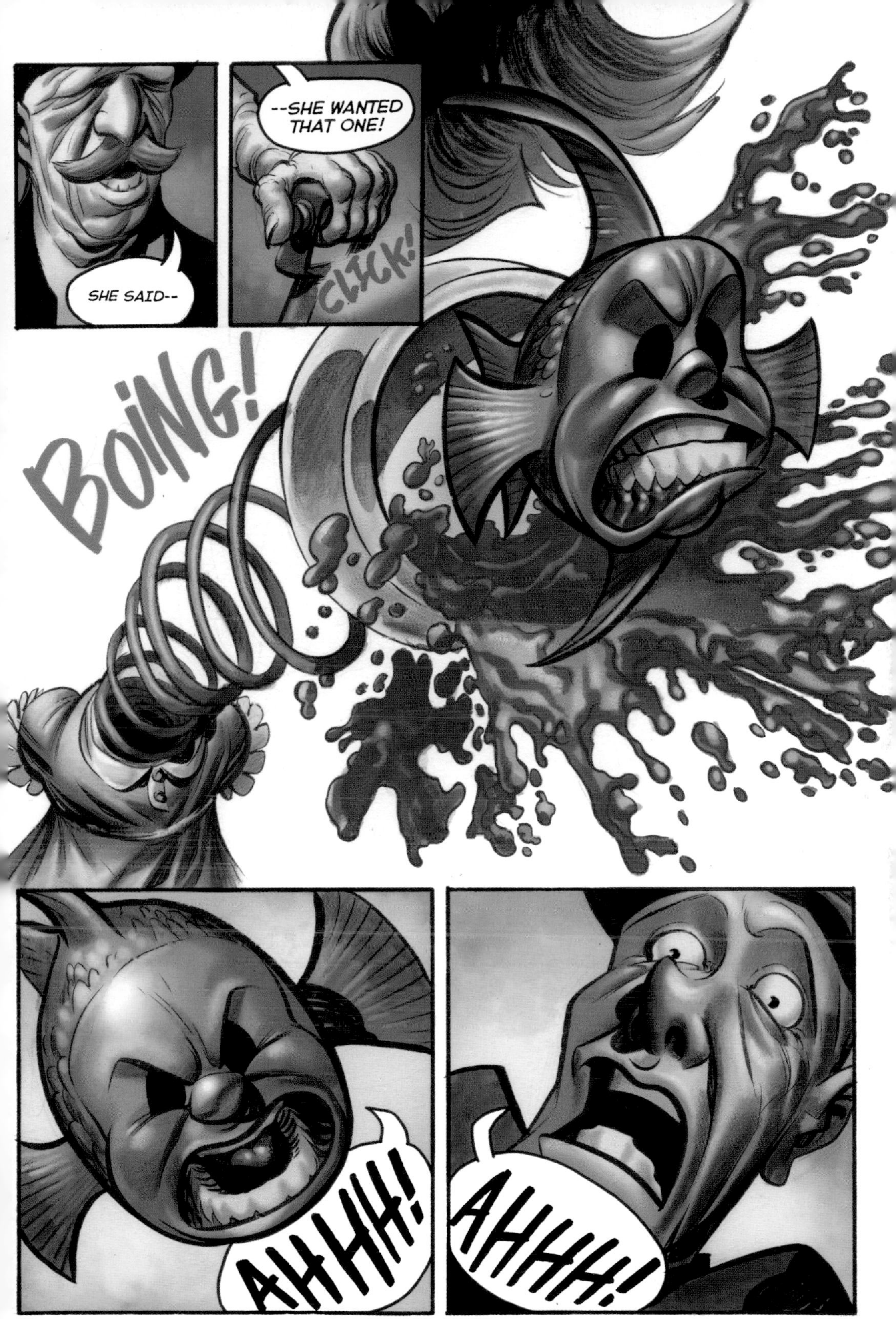
SHE SAID--
--SHE WANTED THAT ONE!
CLICK!
BOING!
AHHH!
AHHH!

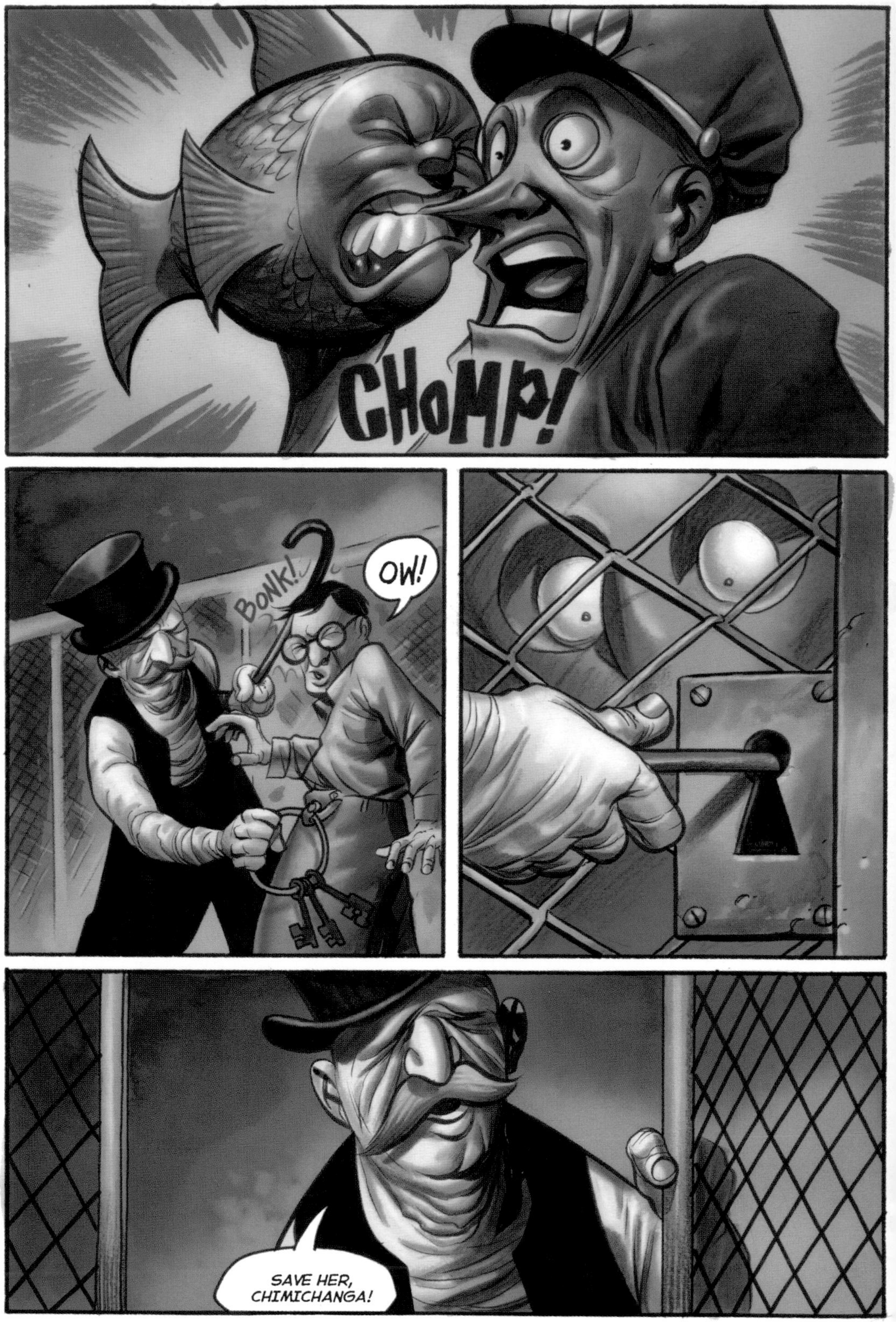
CHOMP!
BONK!
OW!
SAVE HER, CHIMICHANGA!

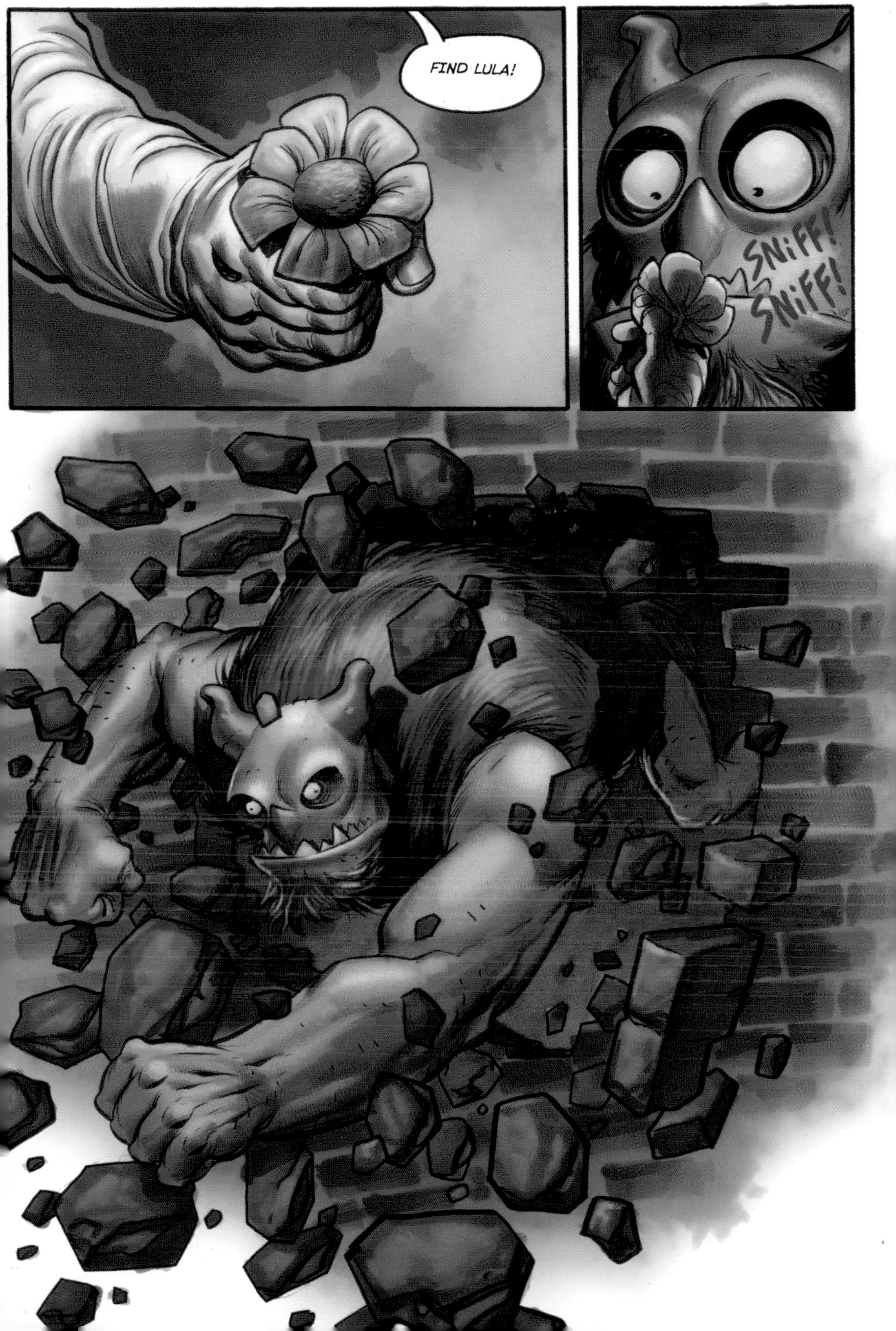
FIND LULA!
SNIFF! SNIFF!

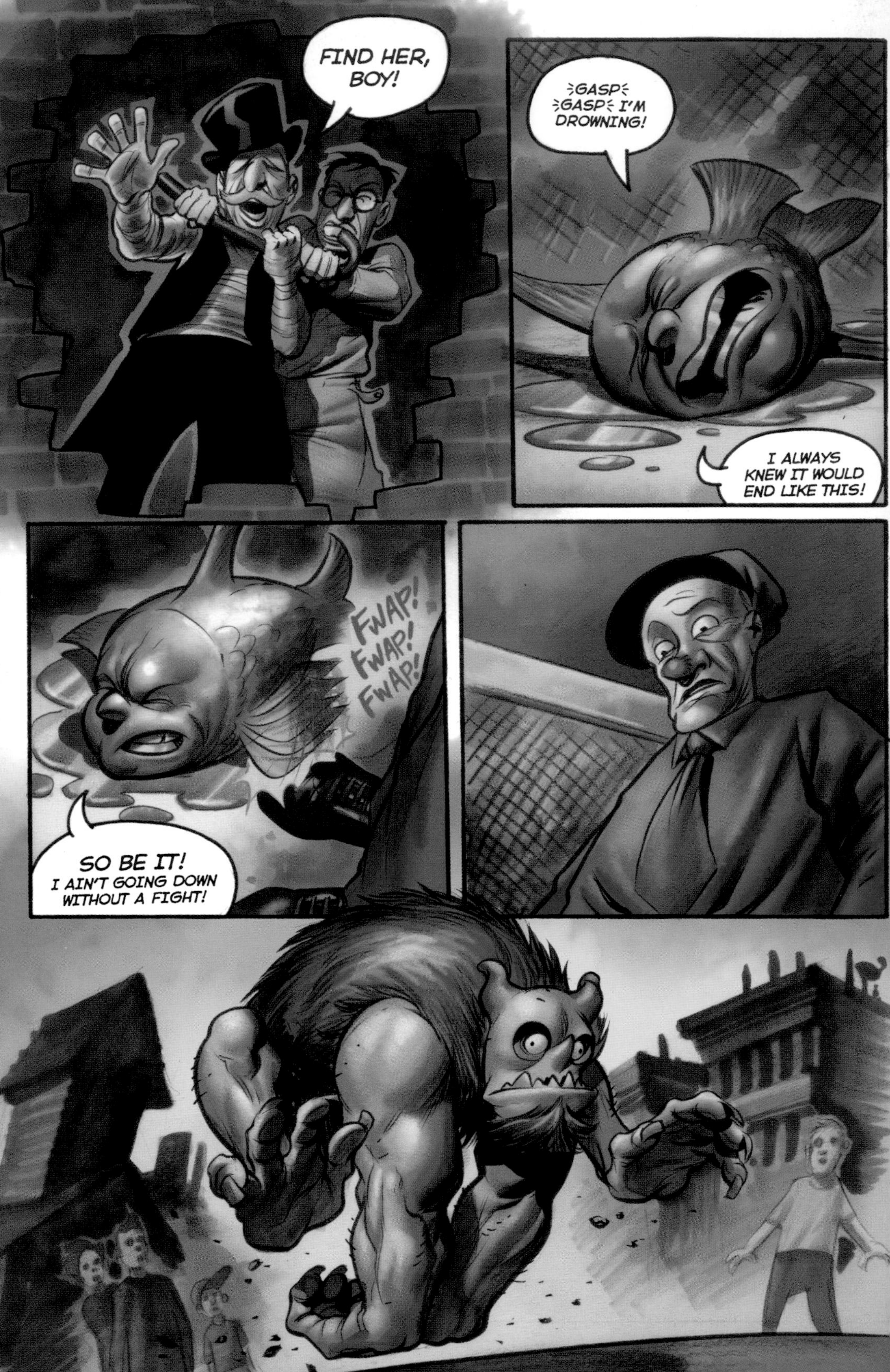
FIND HER, BOY!
GASP GASP I'M DROWNING!
I ALWAYS KNEW IT WOULD END LIKE THIS!
FWAP! FWAP! FWAP!
SO BE IT! I AIN'T GOING DOWN WITHOUT A FIGHT!

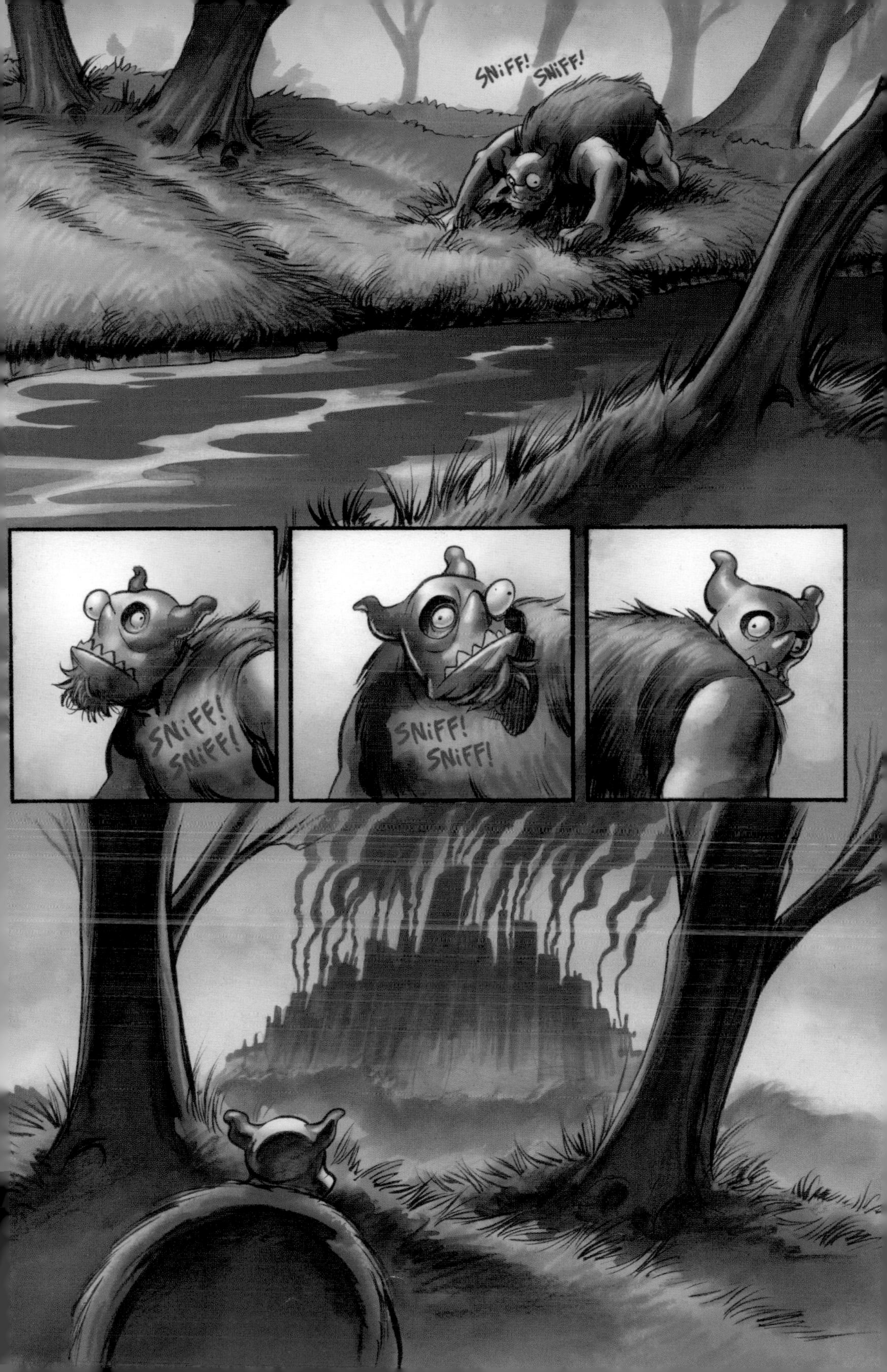
SNiFF! SNiFF!
SNiFF! SNiFF!
SNiFF! SNiFF!

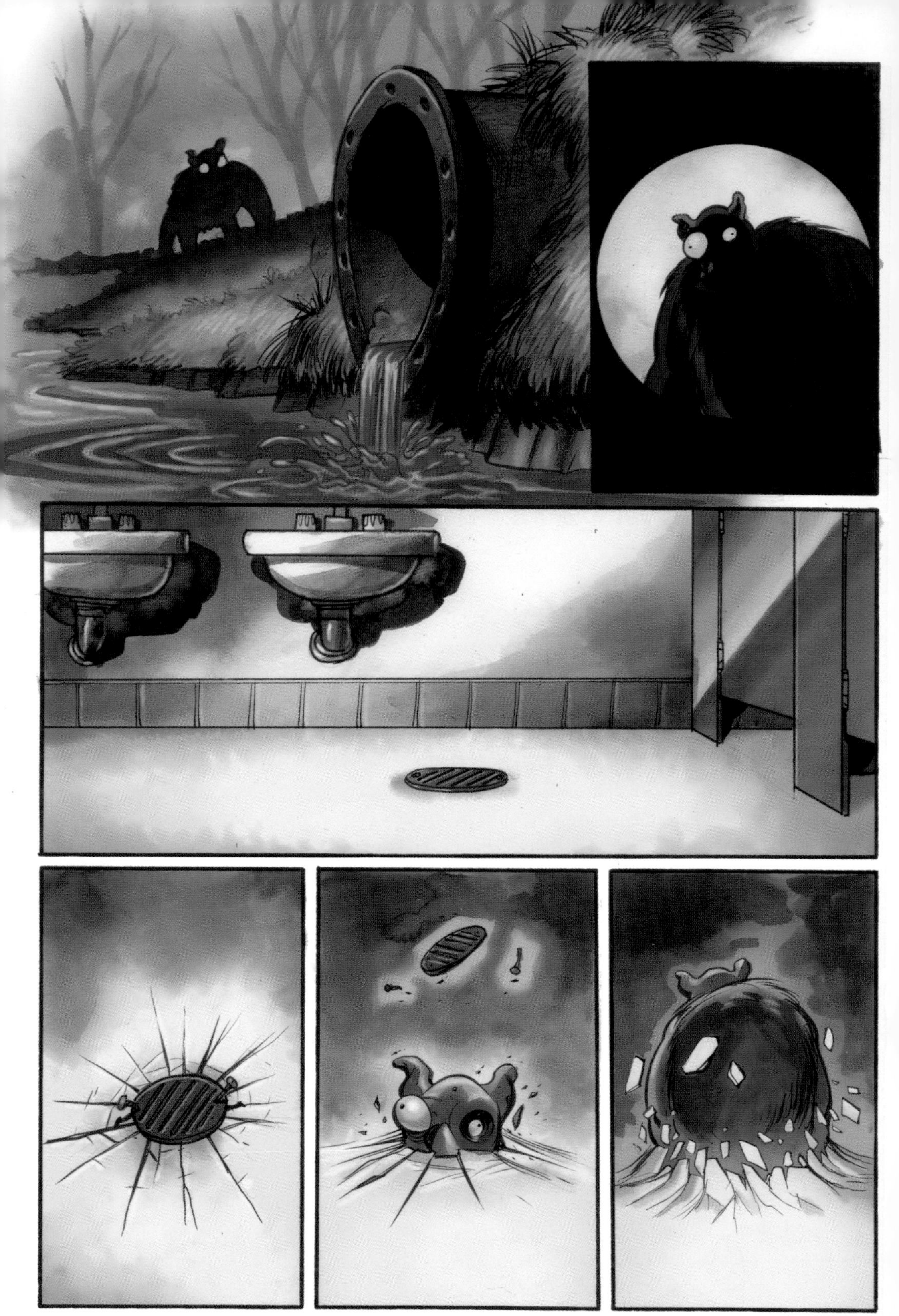

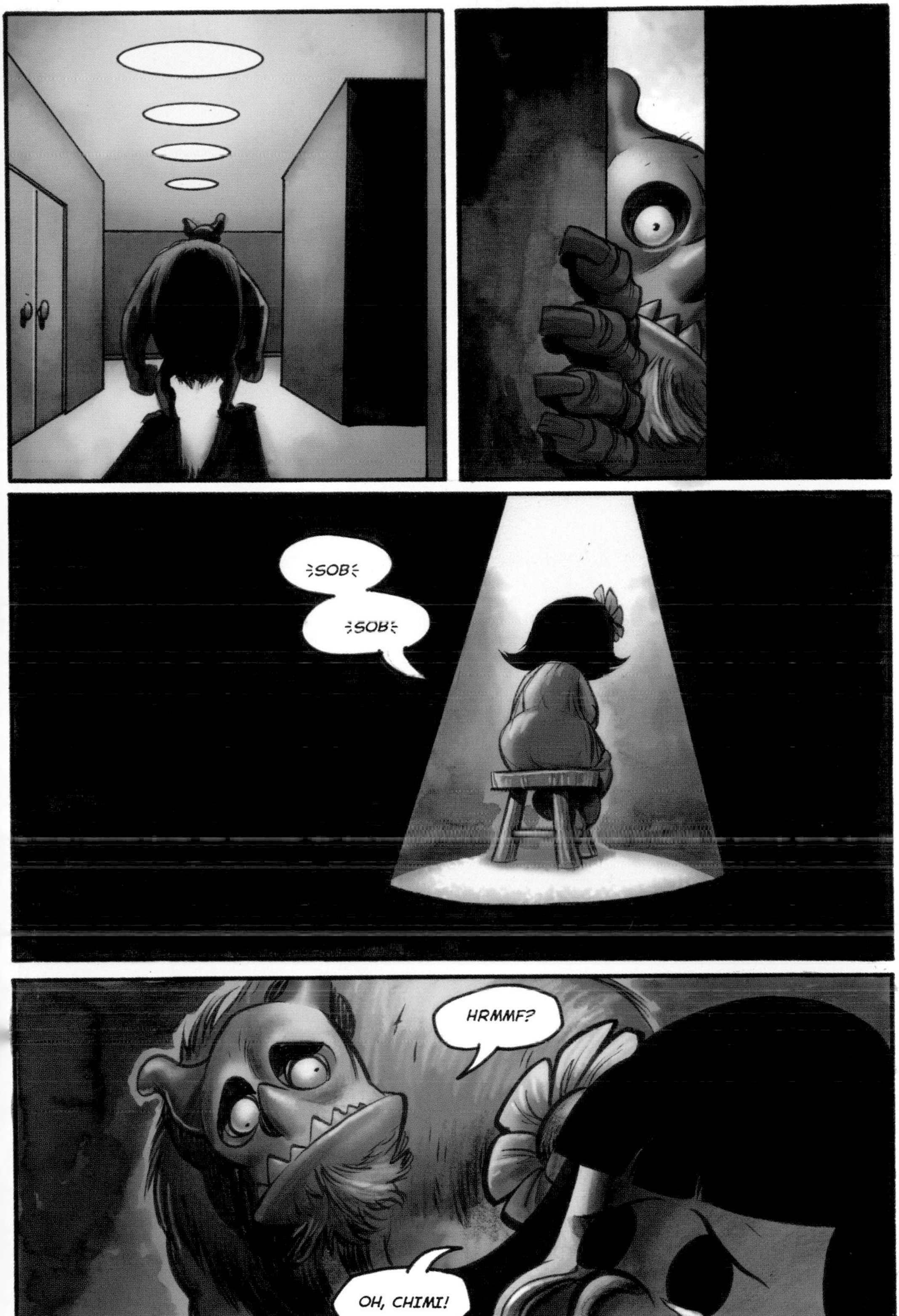
SOB
SOB
HRMMF?
OH, CHIMI!

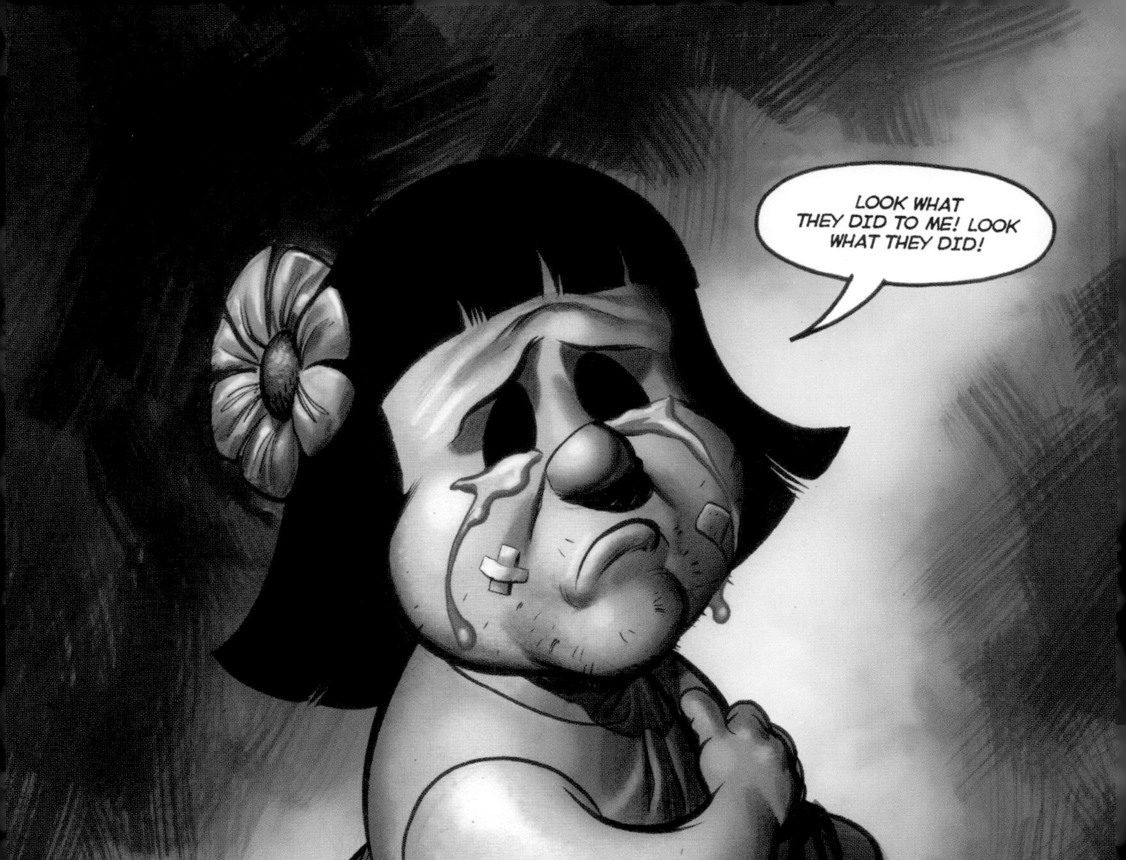
LOOK WHAT THEY DID TO ME! LOOK WHAT THEY DID!

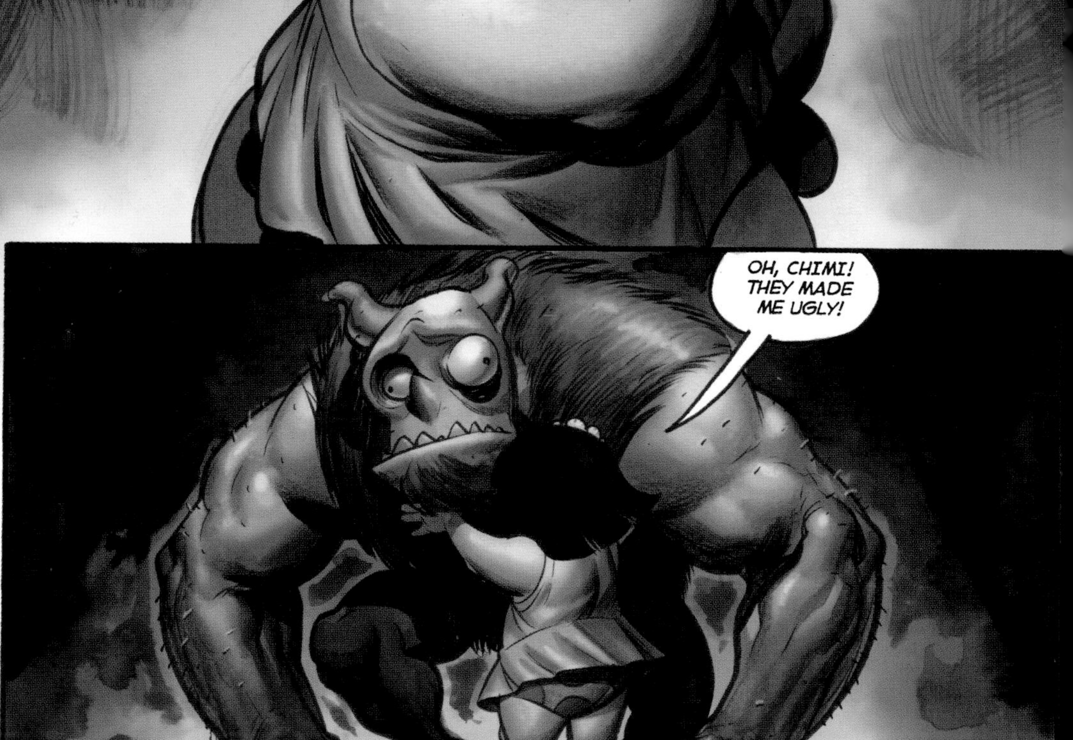
OH, CHIMI! THEY MADE ME UGLY!

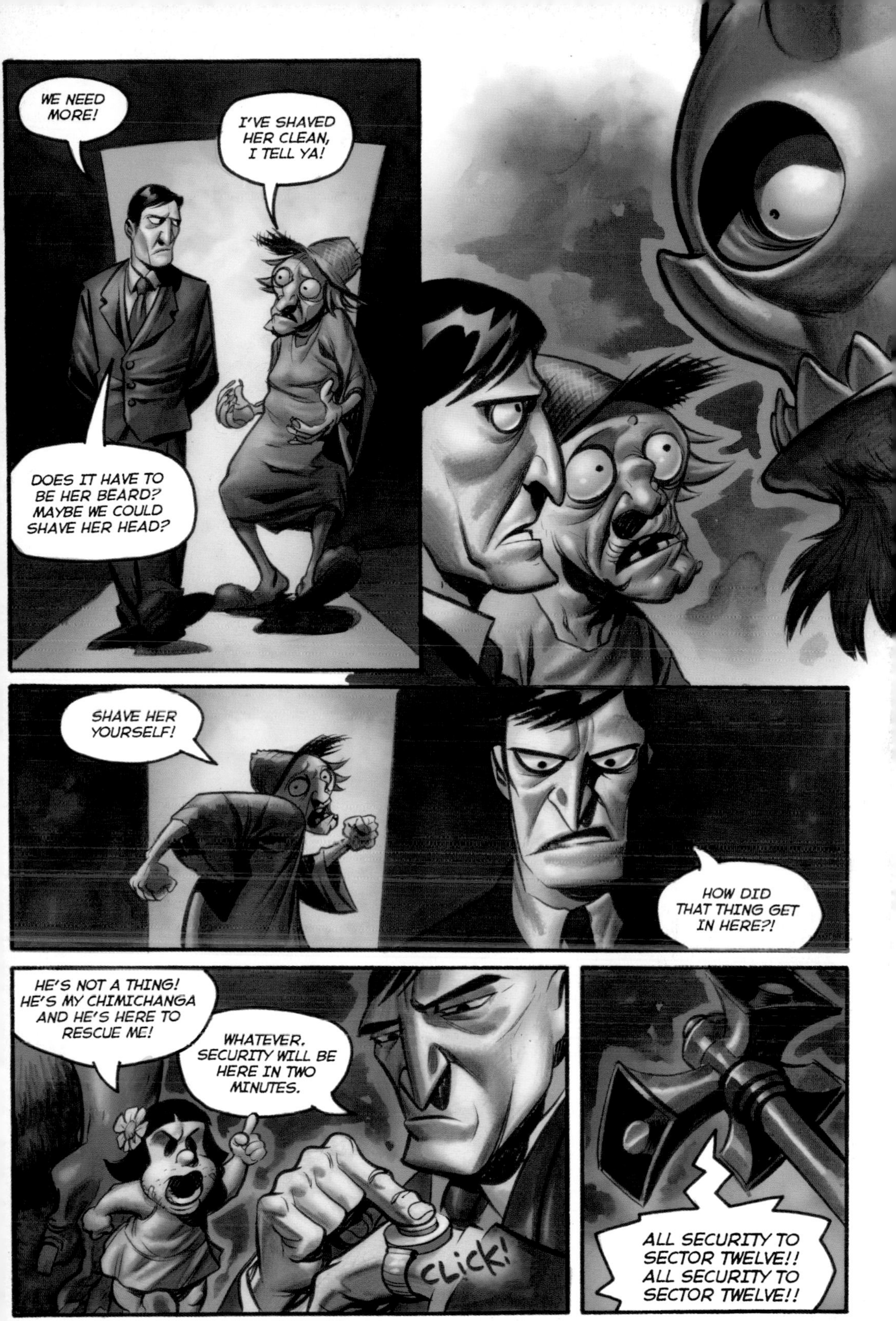
WE NEED MORE!
I'VE SHAVED HER CLEAN, I TELL YA!
DOES IT HAVE TO BE HER BEARD? MAYBE WE COULD SHAVE HER HEAD?
SHAVE HER YOURSELF!
HOW DID THAT THING GET IN HERE?!
HE'S NOT A THING! HE'S MY CHIMICHANGA AND HE'S HERE TO RESCUE ME!
WHATEVER. SECURITY WILL BE HERE IN TWO MINUTES.
CLICK!
ALL SECURITY TO SECTOR TWELVE!! ALL SECURITY TO SECTOR TWELVE!!

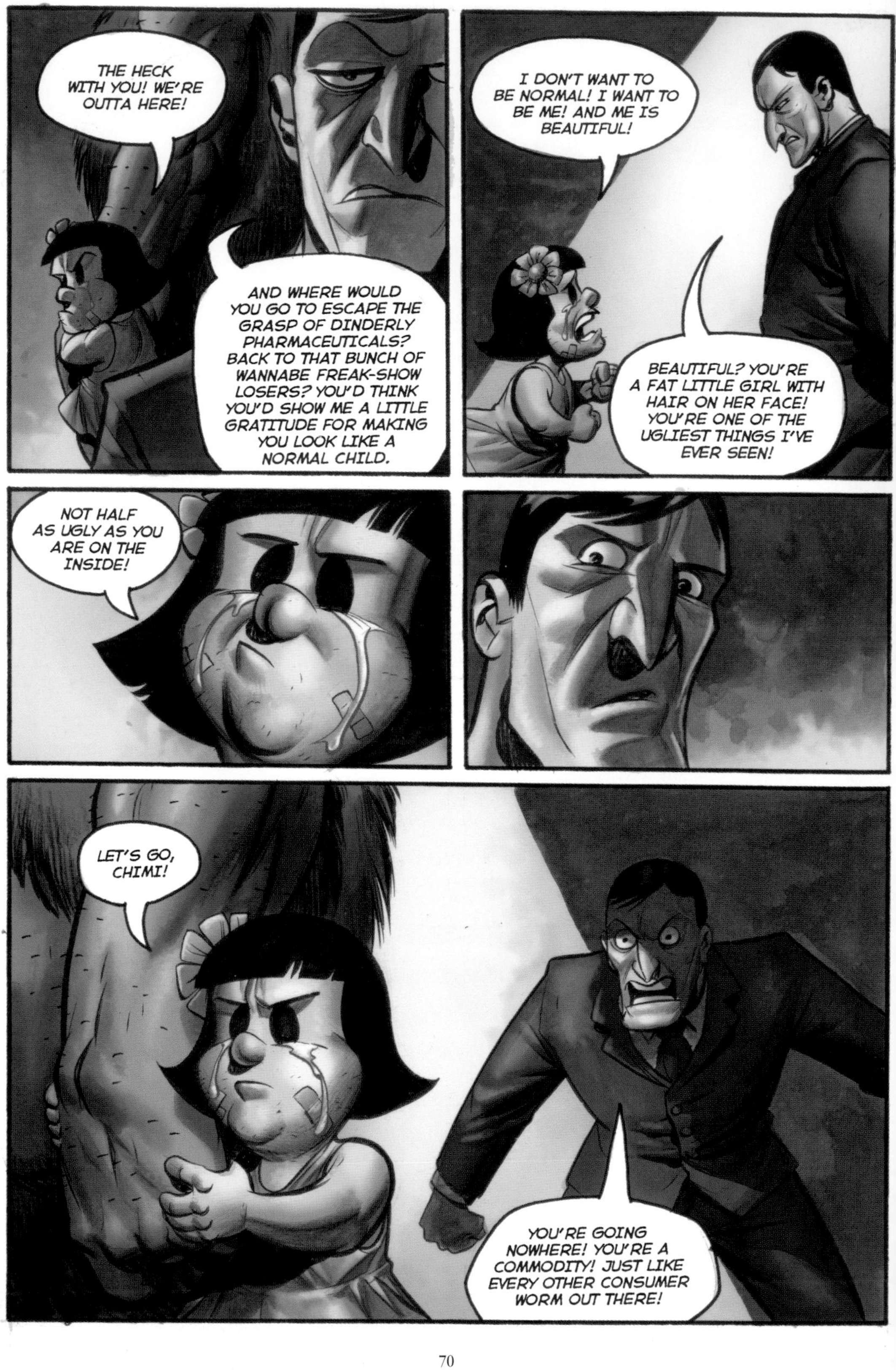
THE HECK WITH YOU! WE'RE OUTTA HERE!
AND WHERE WOULD YOU GO TO ESCAPE THE GRASP OF DINDERLY PHARMACEUTICALS? BACK TO THAT BUNCH OF WANNABE FREAK-SHOW LOSERS? YOU'D THINK YOU'D SHOW ME A LITTLE GRATITUDE FOR MAKING YOU LOOK LIKE A NORMAL CHILD.
I DON'T WANT TO BE NORMAL! I WANT TO BE ME! AND ME IS BEAUTIFUL!
BEAUTIFUL? YOU'RE A FAT LITTLE GIRL WITH HAIR ON HER FACE! YOU'RE ONE OF THE UGLIEST THINGS I'VE EVER SEEN!
NOT HALF AS UGLY AS YOU ARE ON THE INSIDE!
LET'S GO, CHIMI!
YOU'RE GOING NOWHERE! YOU'RE A COMMODITY! JUST LIKE EVERY OTHER CONSUMER WORM OUT THERE!

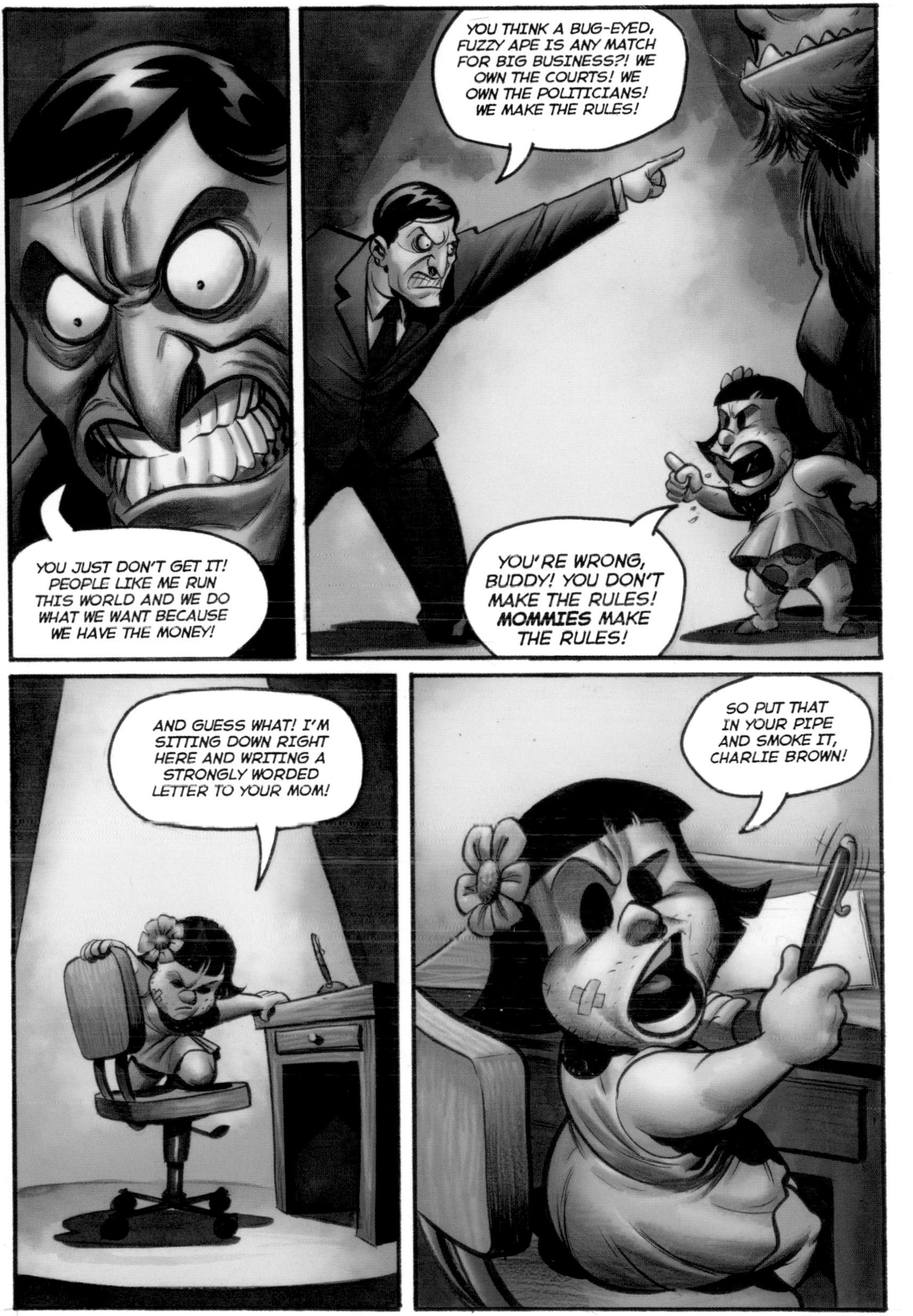
YOU JUST DON'T GET IT! PEOPLE LIKE ME RUN THIS WORLD AND WE DO WHAT WE WANT BECAUSE WE HAVE THE MONEY!
YOU THINK A BUG-EYED, FUZZY APE IS ANY MATCH FOR BIG BUSINESS?! WE OWN THE COURTS! WE OWN THE POLITICIANS! WE MAKE THE RULES!
YOU'RE WRONG, BUDDY! YOU DON'T MAKE THE RULES! MOMMIES MAKE THE RULES!
AND GUESS WHAT! I'M SITTING DOWN RIGHT HERE AND WRITING A STRONGLY WORDED LETTER TO YOUR MOM!
SO PUT THAT IN YOUR PIPE AND SMOKE IT, CHARLIE BROWN!

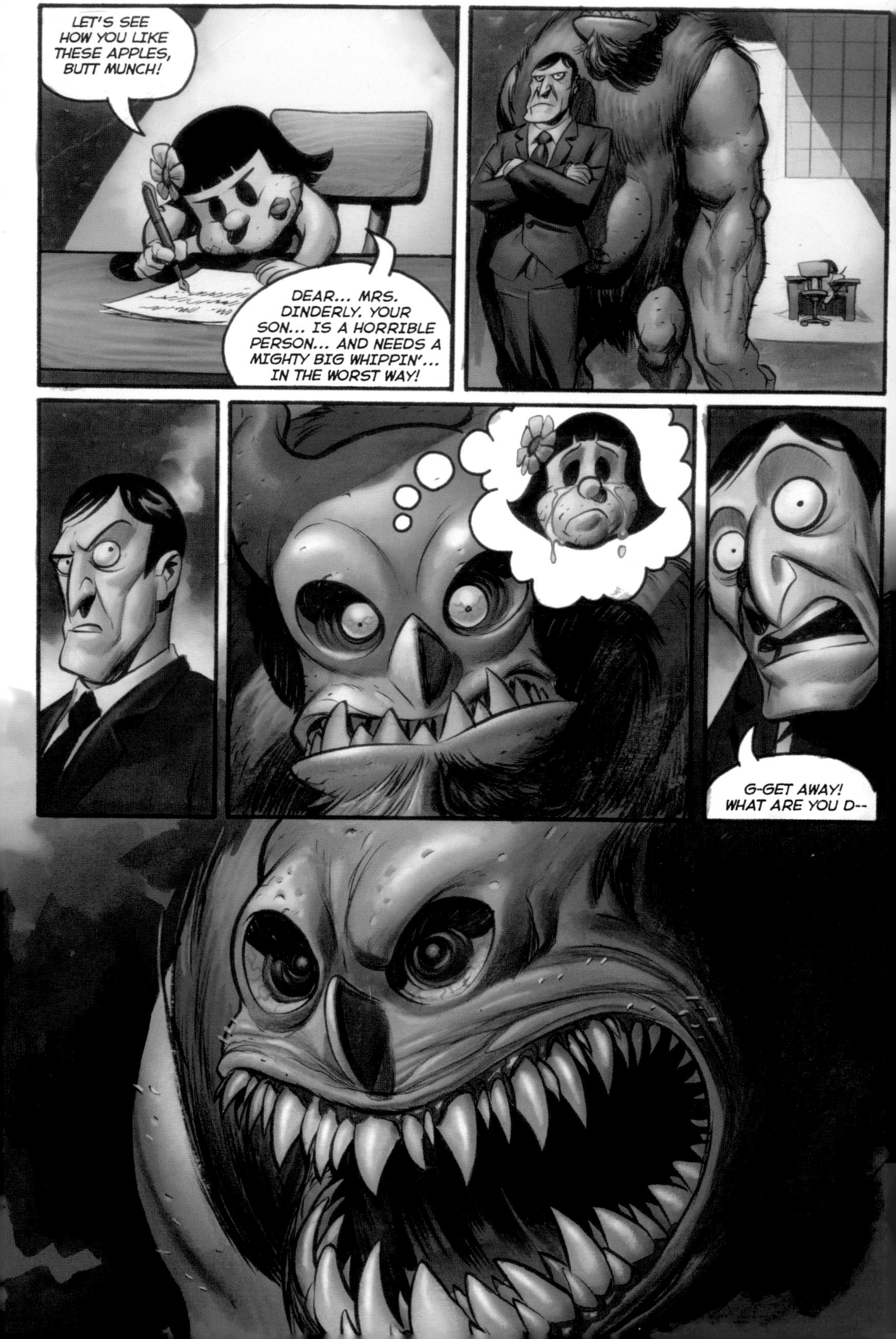
LET'S SEE HOW YOU LIKE THESE APPLES, BUTT MUNCH!
DEAR... MRS. DINDERLY. YOUR SON... IS A HORRIBLE PERSON... AND NEEDS A MIGHTY BIG WHIPPIN'... IN THE WORST WAY!
G-GET AWAY! WHAT ARE YOU D--

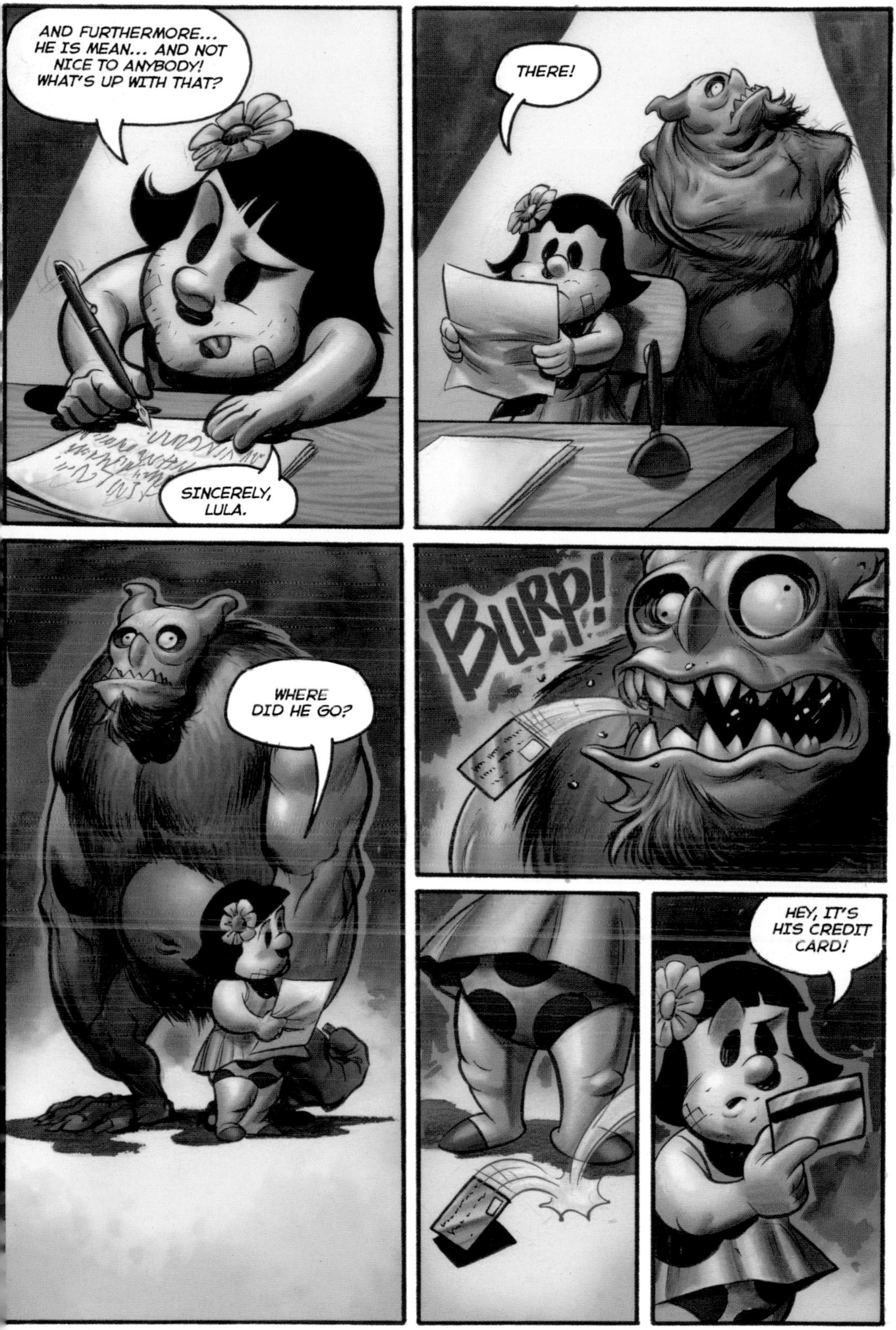
AND FURTHERMORE... HE IS MEAN... AND NOT NICE TO ANYBODY! WHAT'S UP WITH THAT?
SINCERELY, LULA.
THERE!
WHERE DID HE GO?
BURP!
HEY, IT'S HIS CREDIT CARD!

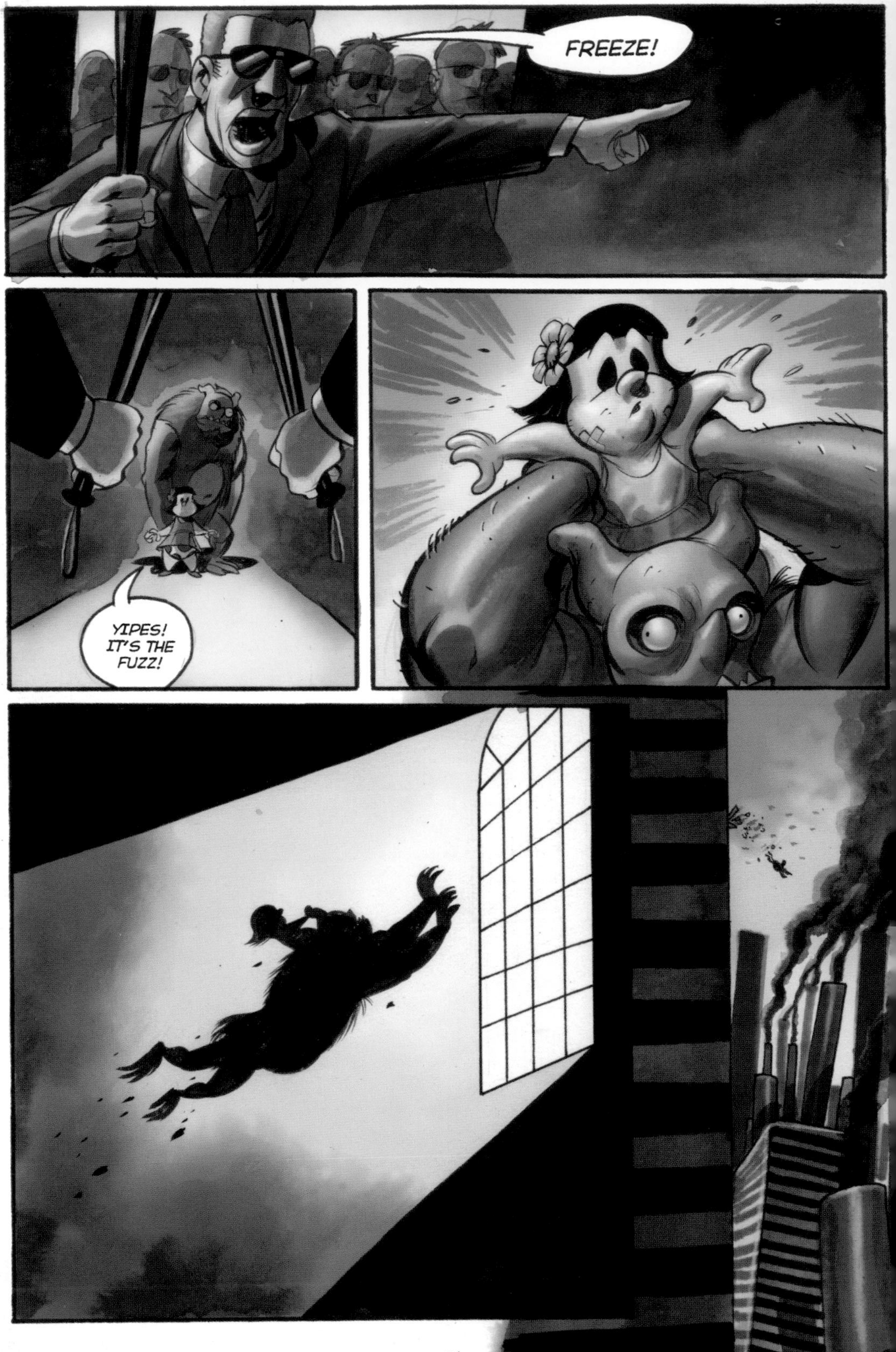
FREEZE!
YIPES! IT'S THE FUZZ!

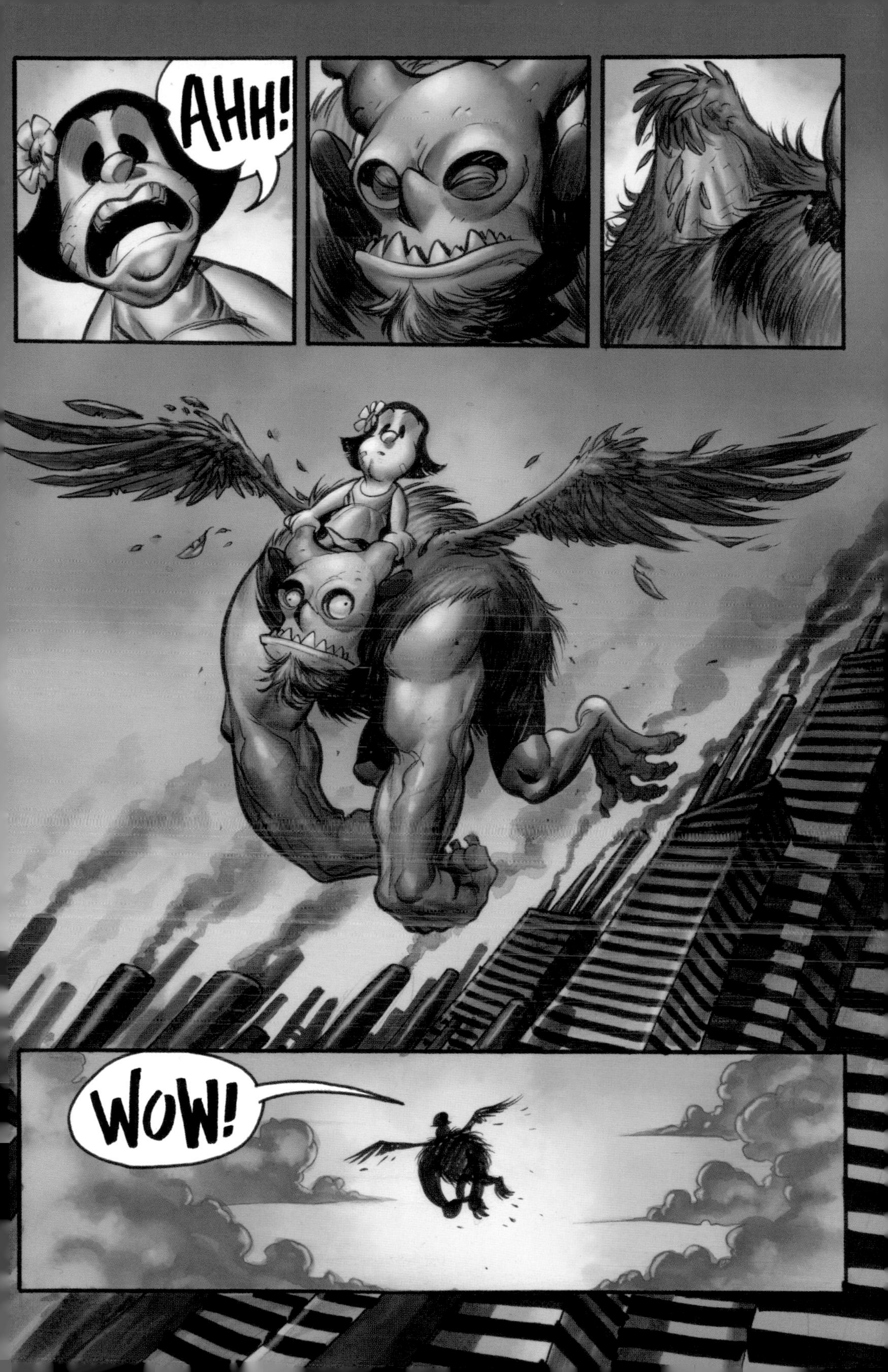
AHH!
WOW!

--THEFT AND BLATANT DESTRUCTION OF PUBLIC PROPERTY! I SENTENCE YOU TO TWO YEARS OF HARD LABOR OR A FIFTY-THOUSAND-DOLLAR FINE EACH!

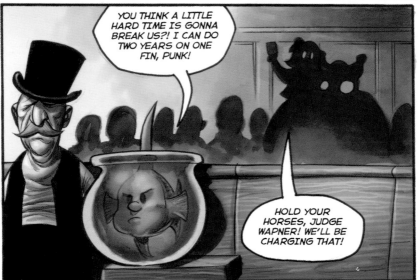

YOU THINK A LITTLE HARD TIME IS GONNA BREAK US?! I CAN DO TWO YEARS ON ONE FIN, PUNK!

HOLD YOUR HORSES, JUDGE WAPNER! WE'LL BE CHARGING THAT!

THEY'RE BACK!

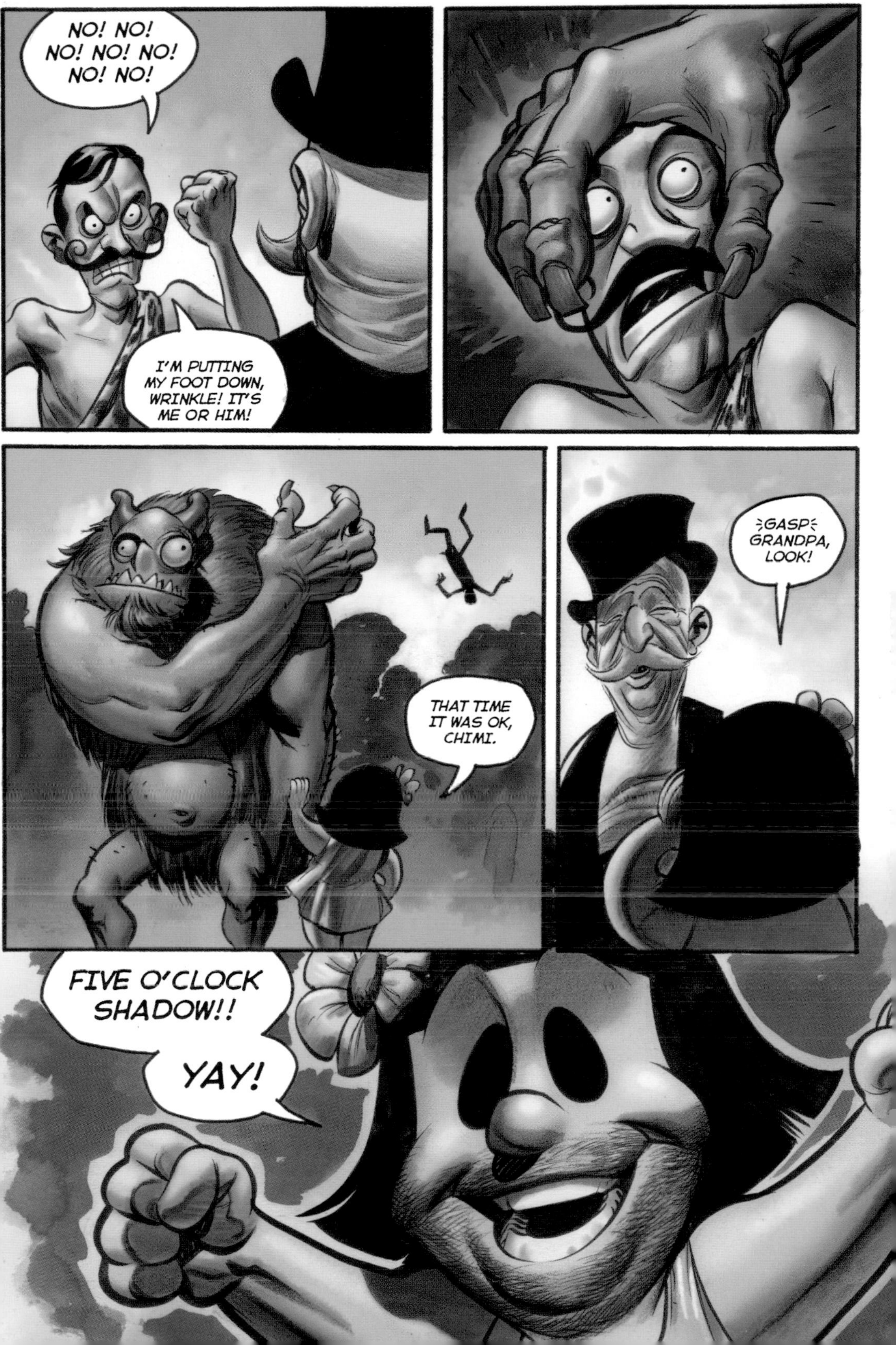
NO! NO! NO! NO! NO! NO! NO!
I'M PUTTING MY FOOT DOWN, WRINKLE! IT'S ME OR HIM!
THAT TIME IT WAS OK, CHIMI.
GASP GRANDPA, LOOK!
FIVE O'CLOCK SHADOW!!
YAY!

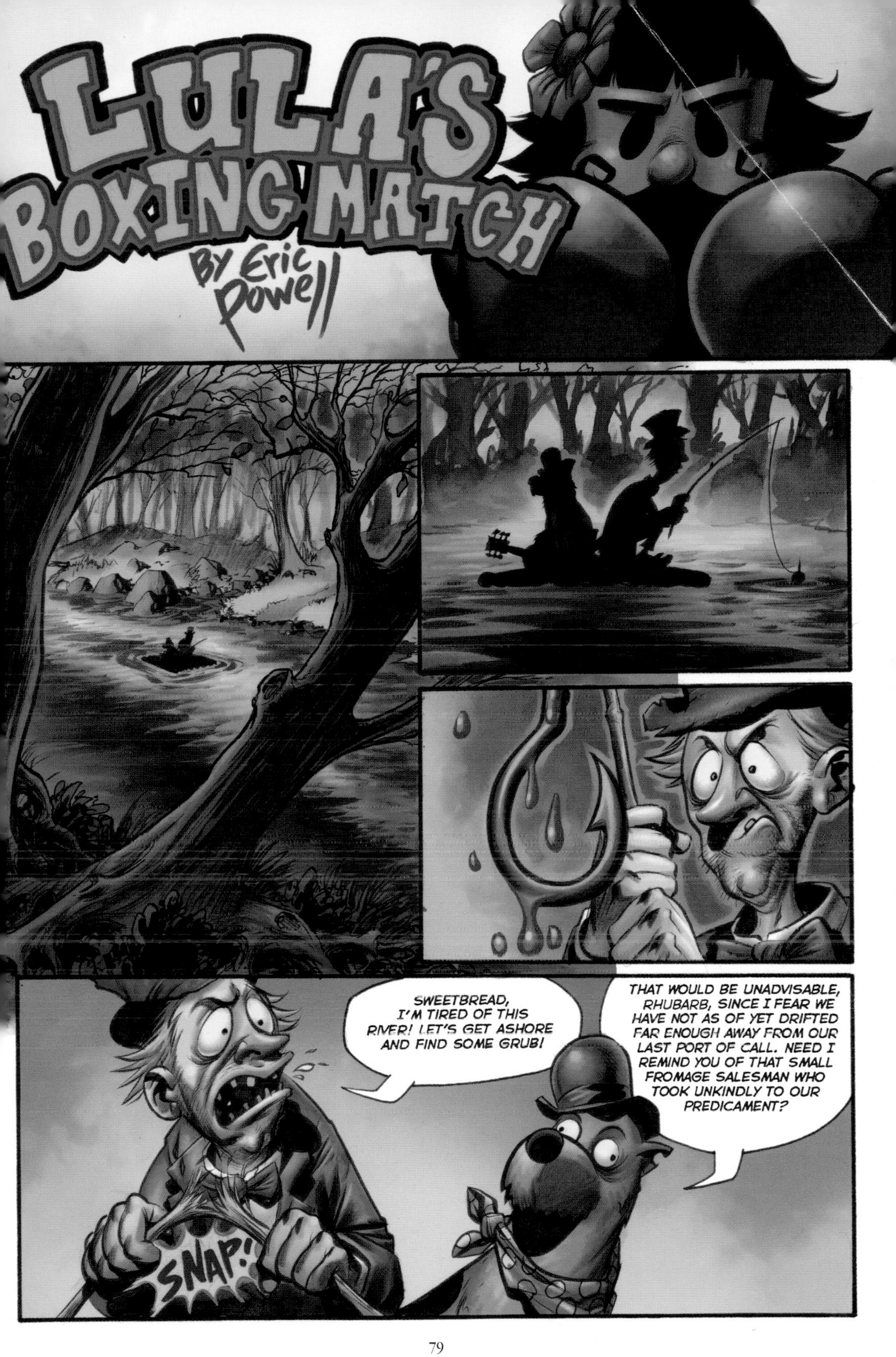
LULA'S BOXING MATCH
By Eric Powell
SWEETBREAD, I'M TIRED OF THIS RIVER! LET'S GET ASHORE AND FIND SOME GRUB!
THAT WOULD BE UNADVISABLE, RHUBARB, SINCE I FEAR WE HAVE NOT AS OF YET DRIFTED FAR ENOUGH AWAY FROM OUR LAST PORT OF CALL. NEED I REMIND YOU OF THAT SMALL FROMAGE SALESMAN WHO TOOK UNKINDLY TO OUR PREDICAMENT?
SNAP!

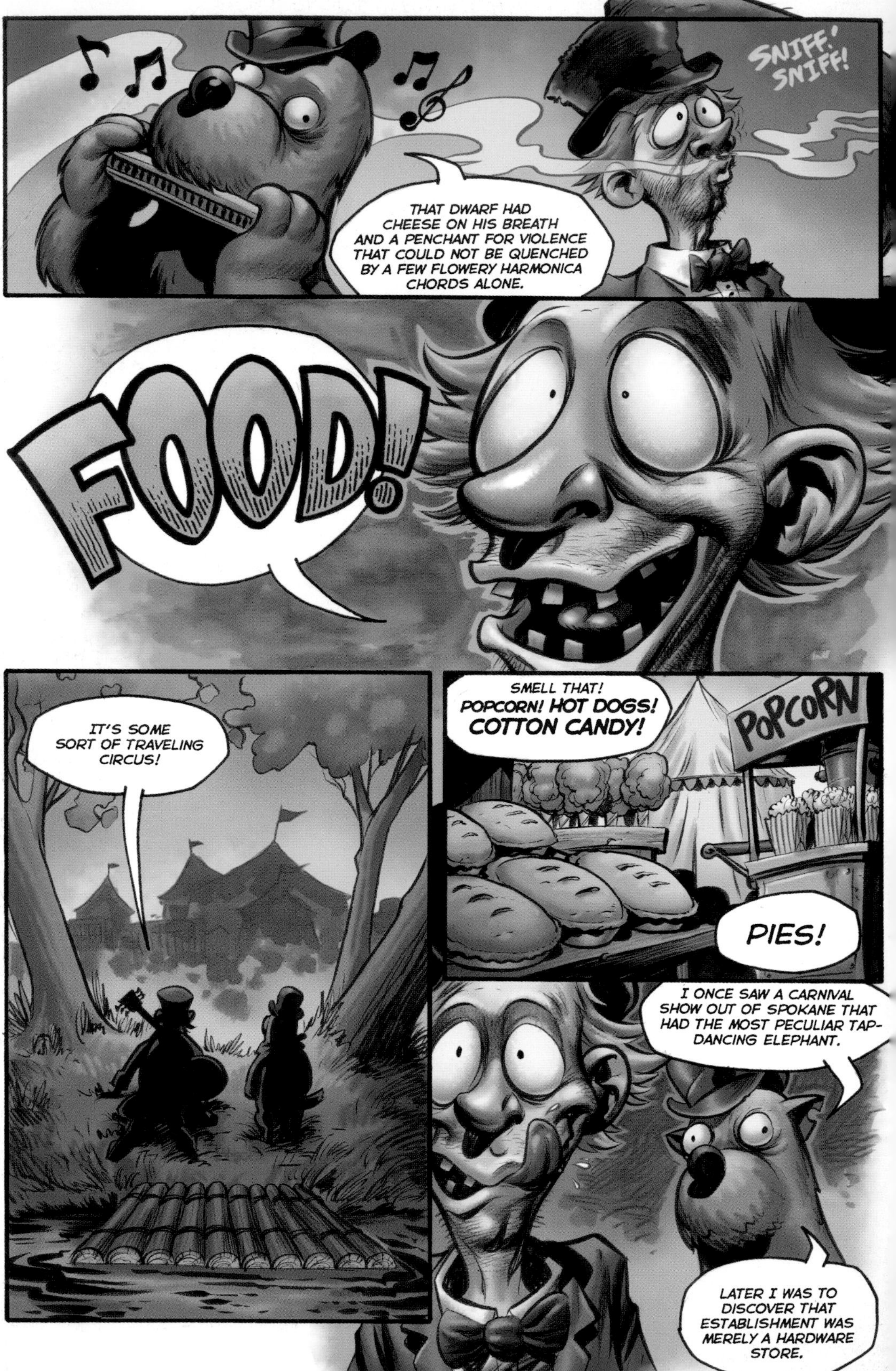
SNIFF! SNIFF!
THAT DWARF HAD CHEESE ON HIS BREATH AND A PENCHANT FOR VIOLENCE THAT COULD NOT BE QUENCHED BY A FEW FLOWERY HARMONICA CHORDS ALONE.
FOOD!
IT'S SOME SORT OF TRAVELING CIRCUS!
SMELL THAT! POPCORN! HOT DOGS! COTTON CANDY!
POPCORN
PIES!
I ONCE SAW A CARNIVAL SHOW OUT OF SPOKANE THAT HAD THE MOST PECULIAR TAP-DANCING ELEPHANT.
LATER I WAS TO DISCOVER THAT ESTABLISHMENT WAS MERELY A HARDWARE STORE.

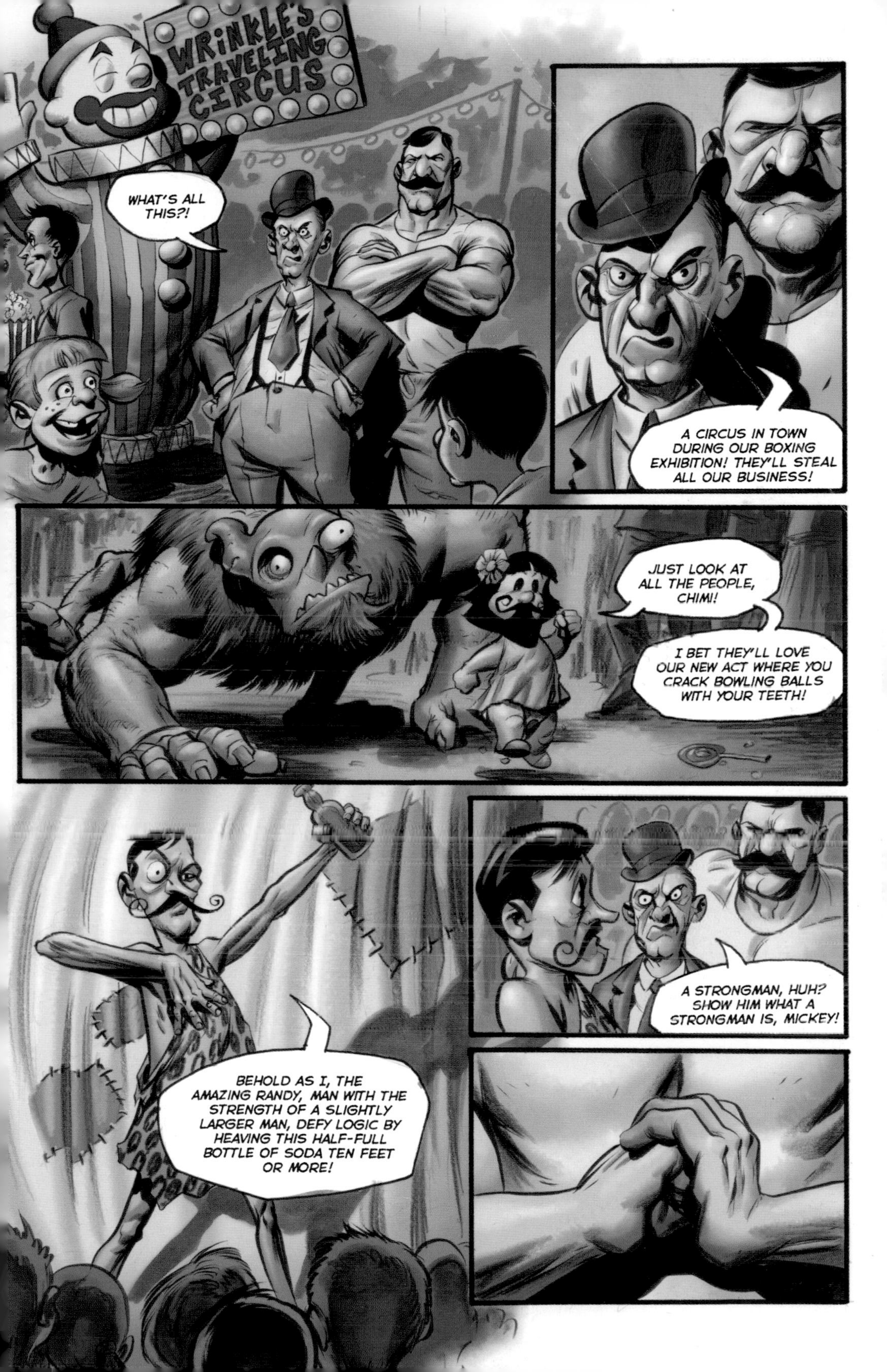
WRINKLE'S TRAVELING CIRCUS
WHAT'S ALL THIS?!
A CIRCUS IN TOWN DURING OUR BOXING EXHIBITION! THEY'LL STEAL ALL OUR BUSINESS!
JUST LOOK AT ALL THE PEOPLE, CHIMI!
I BET THEY'LL LOVE OUR NEW ACT WHERE YOU CRACK BOWLING BALLS WITH YOUR TEETH!
BEHOLD AS I, THE AMAZING RANDY, MAN WITH THE STRENGTH OF A SLIGHTLY LARGER MAN, DEFY LOGIC BY HEAVING THIS HALF-FULL BOTTLE OF SODA TEN FEET OR MORE!
A STRONGMAN, HUH? SHOW HIM WHAT A STRONGMAN IS, MICKEY!

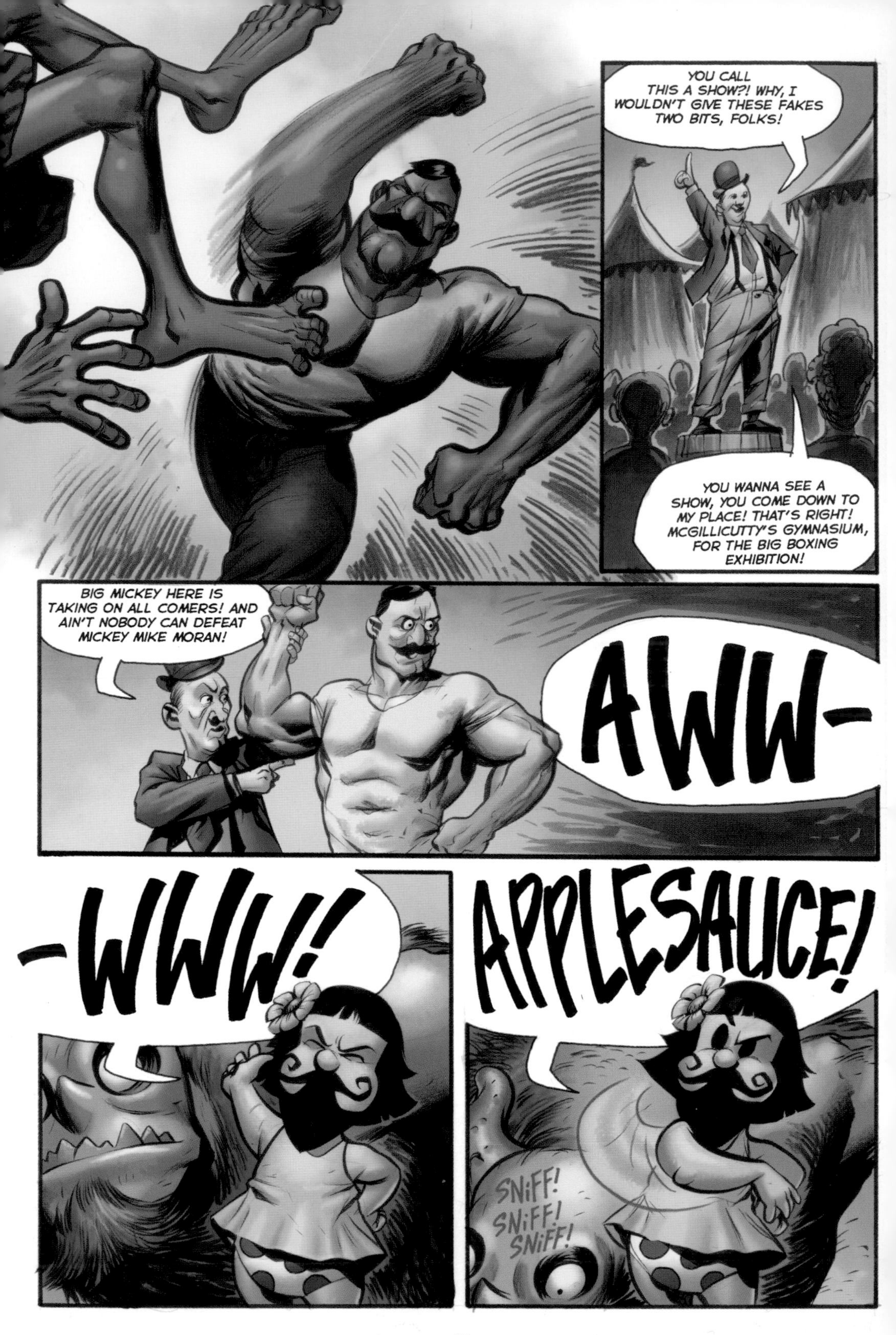
YOU CALL THIS A SHOW?! WHY, I WOULDN'T GIVE THESE FAKES TWO BITS, FOLKS!
YOU WANNA SEE A SHOW, YOU COME DOWN TO MY PLACE! THAT'S RIGHT! McGILLICUTTY'S GYMNASIUM, FOR THE BIG BOXING EXHIBITION!
BIG MICKEY HERE IS TAKING ON ALL COMERS! AND AIN'T NOBODY CAN DEFEAT MICKEY MIKE MORAN!
AWW-
-WWW!
APPLESAUCE!
SNiFF! SNiFF! SNiFF!

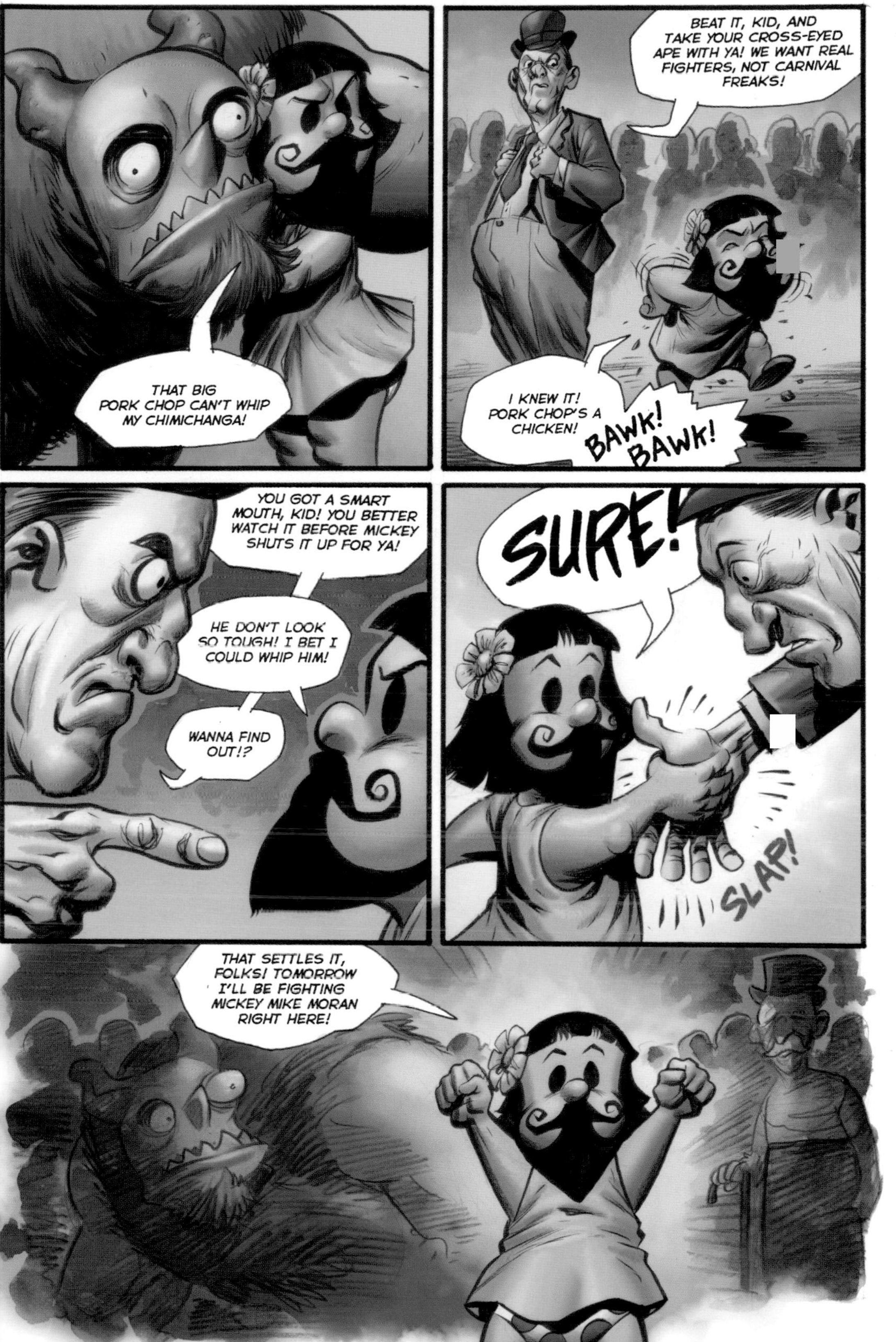
THAT BIG PORK CHOP CAN'T WHIP MY CHIMICHANGA!
BEAT IT, KID, AND TAKE YOUR CROSS-EYED APE WITH YA! WE WANT REAL FIGHTERS, NOT CARNIVAL FREAKS!
I KNEW IT! PORK CHOP'S A CHICKEN!
BAWK! BAWK!
YOU GOT A SMART MOUTH, KID! YOU BETTER WATCH IT BEFORE MICKEY SHUTS IT UP FOR YA!
HE DON'T LOOK SO TOUGH! I BET I COULD WHIP HIM!
WANNA FIND OUT!?
SURE!
SLAP!
THAT SETTLES IT, FOLKS! TOMORROW I'LL BE FIGHTING MICKEY MIKE MORAN RIGHT HERE!

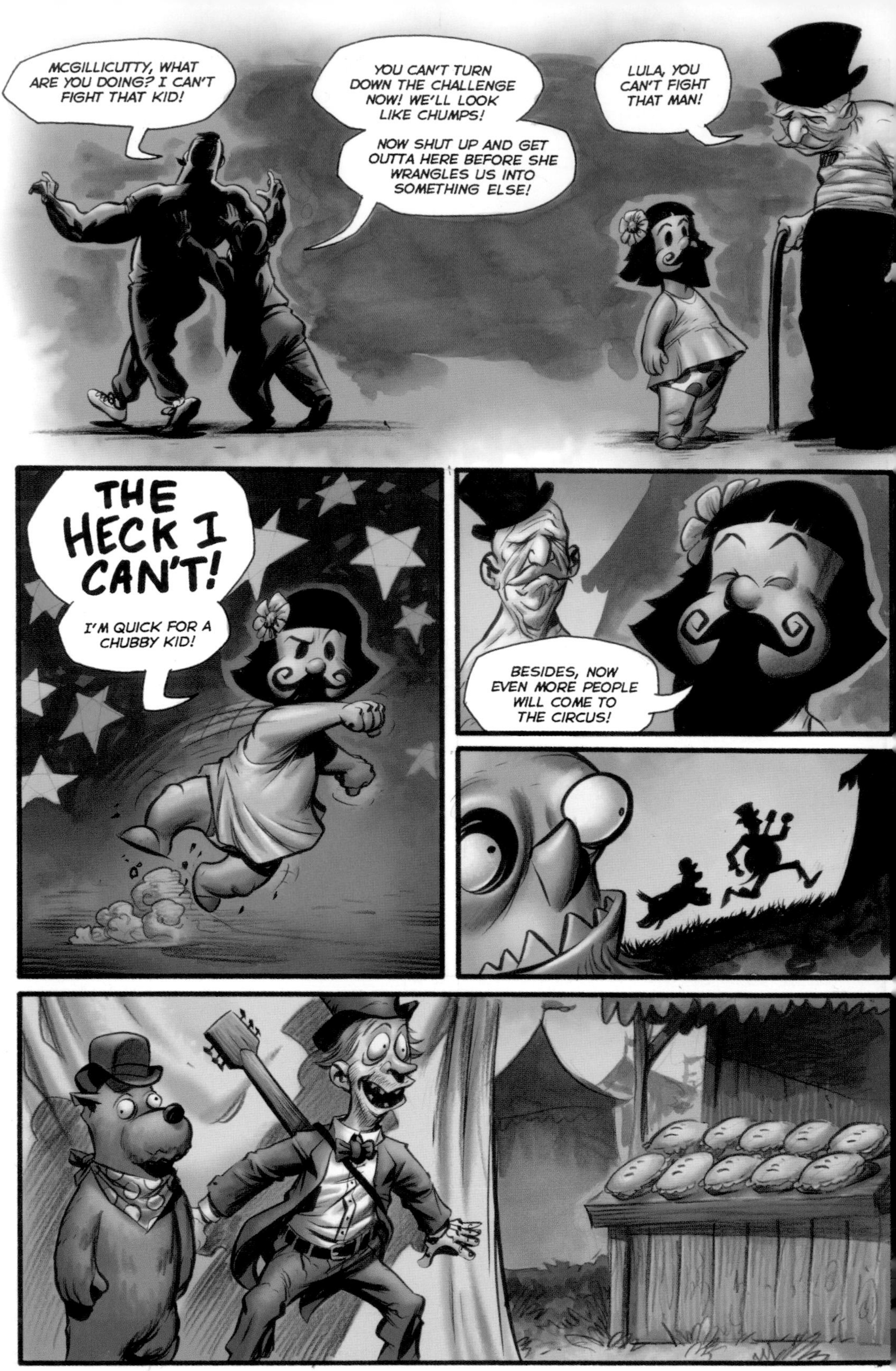
MCGILLICUTTY, WHAT ARE YOU DOING? I CAN'T FIGHT THAT KID!
YOU CAN'T TURN DOWN THE CHALLENGE NOW! WE'LL LOOK LIKE CHUMPS!
NOW SHUT UP AND GET OUTTA HERE BEFORE SHE WRANGLES US INTO SOMETHING ELSE!
LULA, YOU CAN'T FIGHT THAT MAN!
THE HECK I CAN'T!
I'M QUICK FOR A CHUBBY KID!
BESIDES, NOW EVEN MORE PEOPLE WILL COME TO THE CIRCUS!

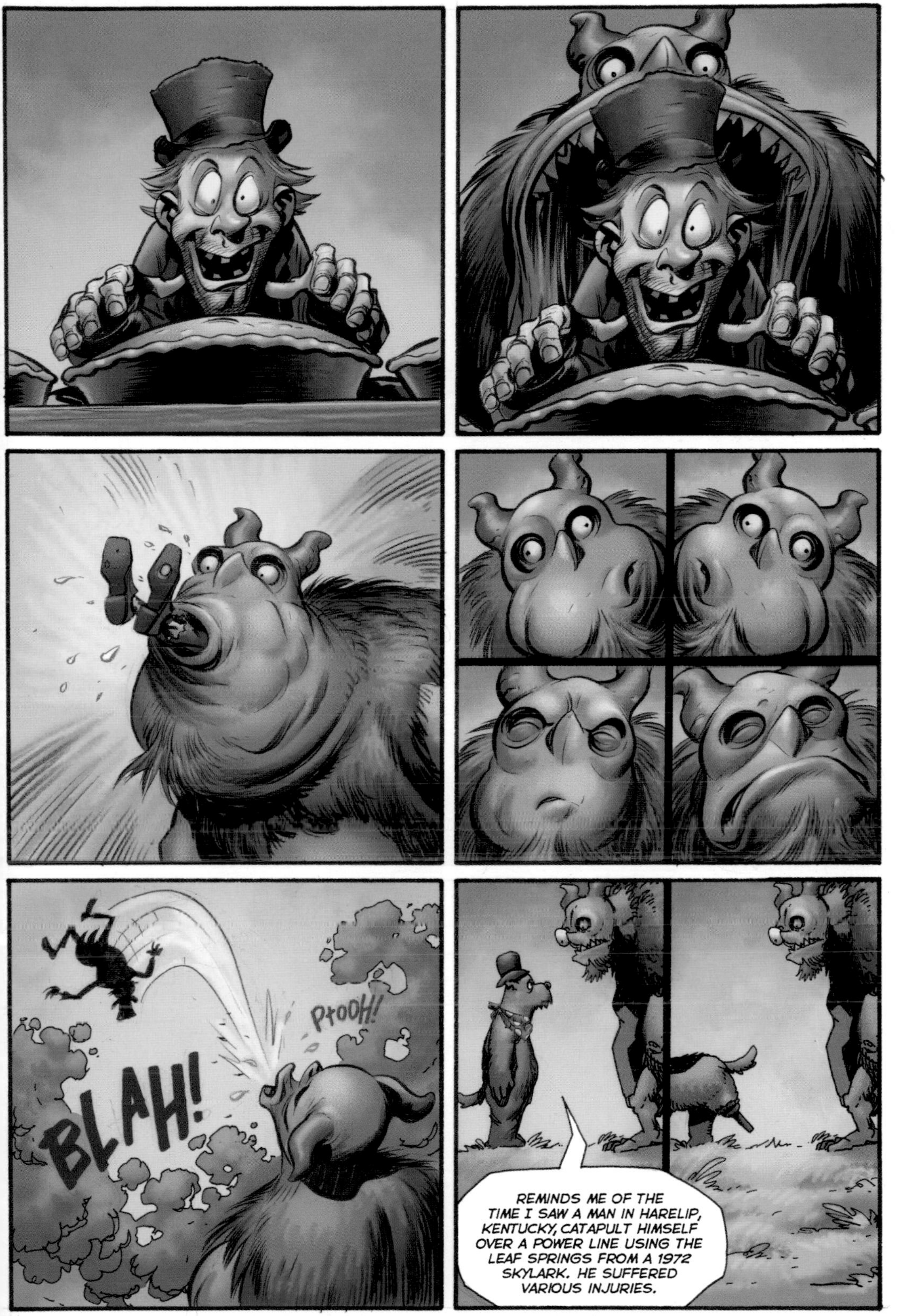
PtooH!
BLAH!
REMINDS ME OF THE TIME I SAW A MAN IN HARELIP, KENTUCKY, CATAPULT HIMSELF OVER A POWER LINE USING THE LEAF SPRINGS FROM A 1972 SKYLARK. HE SUFFERED VARIOUS INJURIES.

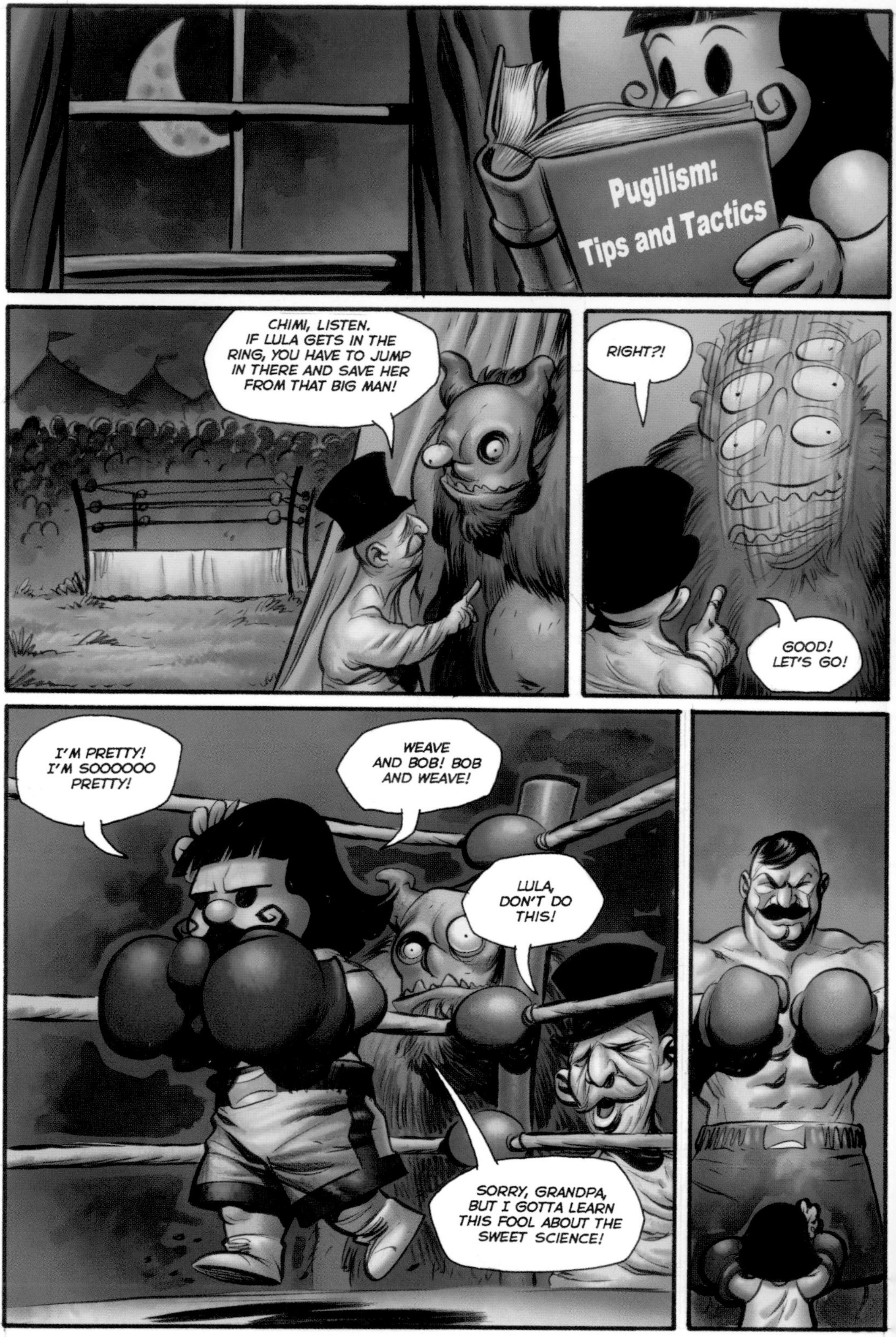
Pugilism: Tips and Tactics
CHIMI, LISTEN. IF LULA GETS IN THE RING, YOU HAVE TO JUMP IN THERE AND SAVE HER FROM THAT BIG MAN!
RIGHT?!
GOOD! LET'S GO!
I'M PRETTY! I'M SOOOOOO PRETTY!
WEAVE AND BOB! BOB AND WEAVE!
LULA, DON'T DO THIS!
SORRY, GRANDPA, BUT I GOTTA LEARN THIS FOOL ABOUT THE SWEET SCIENCE!

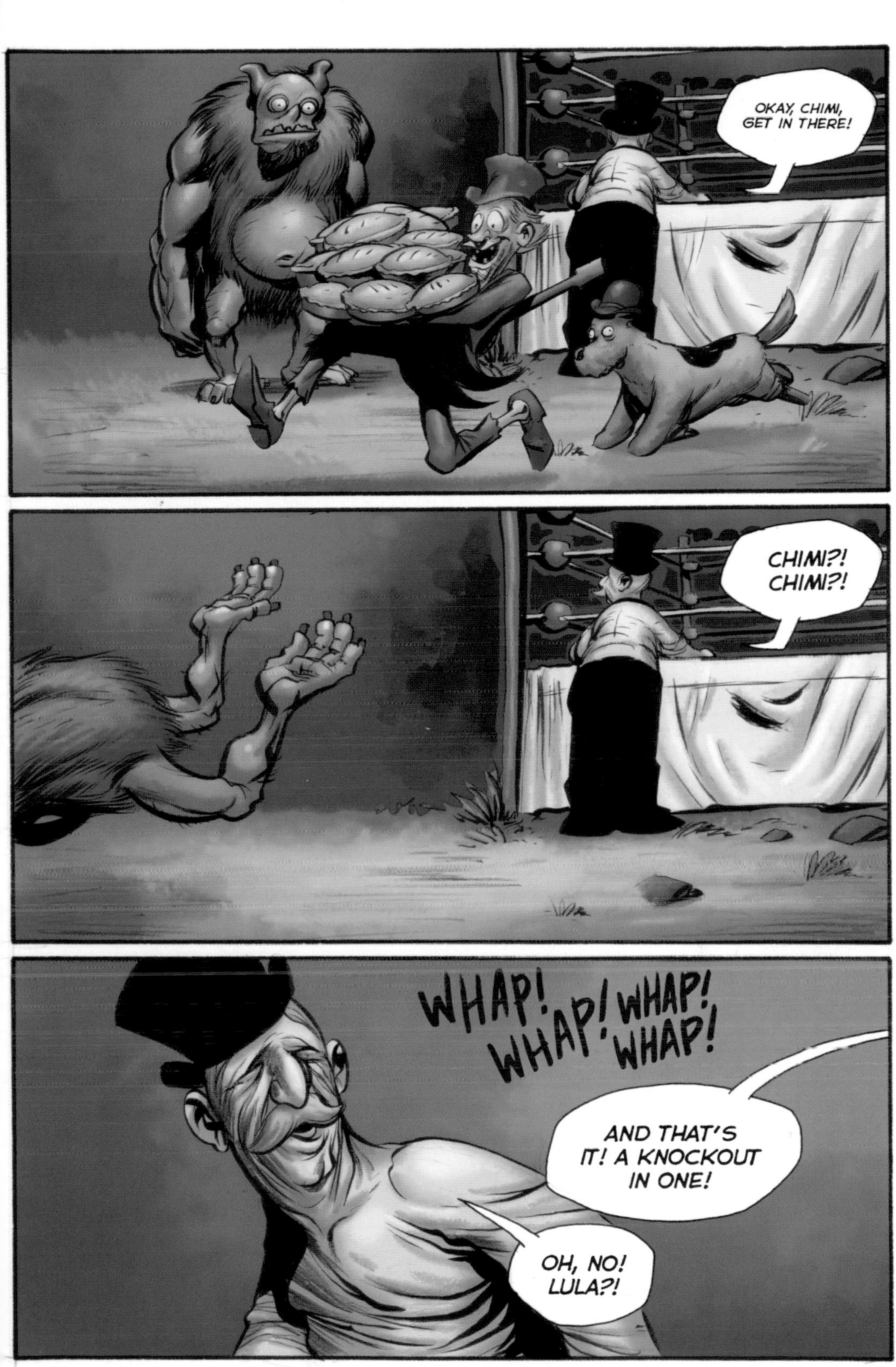
OKAY, CHIMI, GET IN THERE!
CHIMI?! CHIMI?!
WHAP! WHAP! WHAP! WHAP!
AND THAT'S IT! A KNOCKOUT IN ONE!
OH, NO! LULA?!

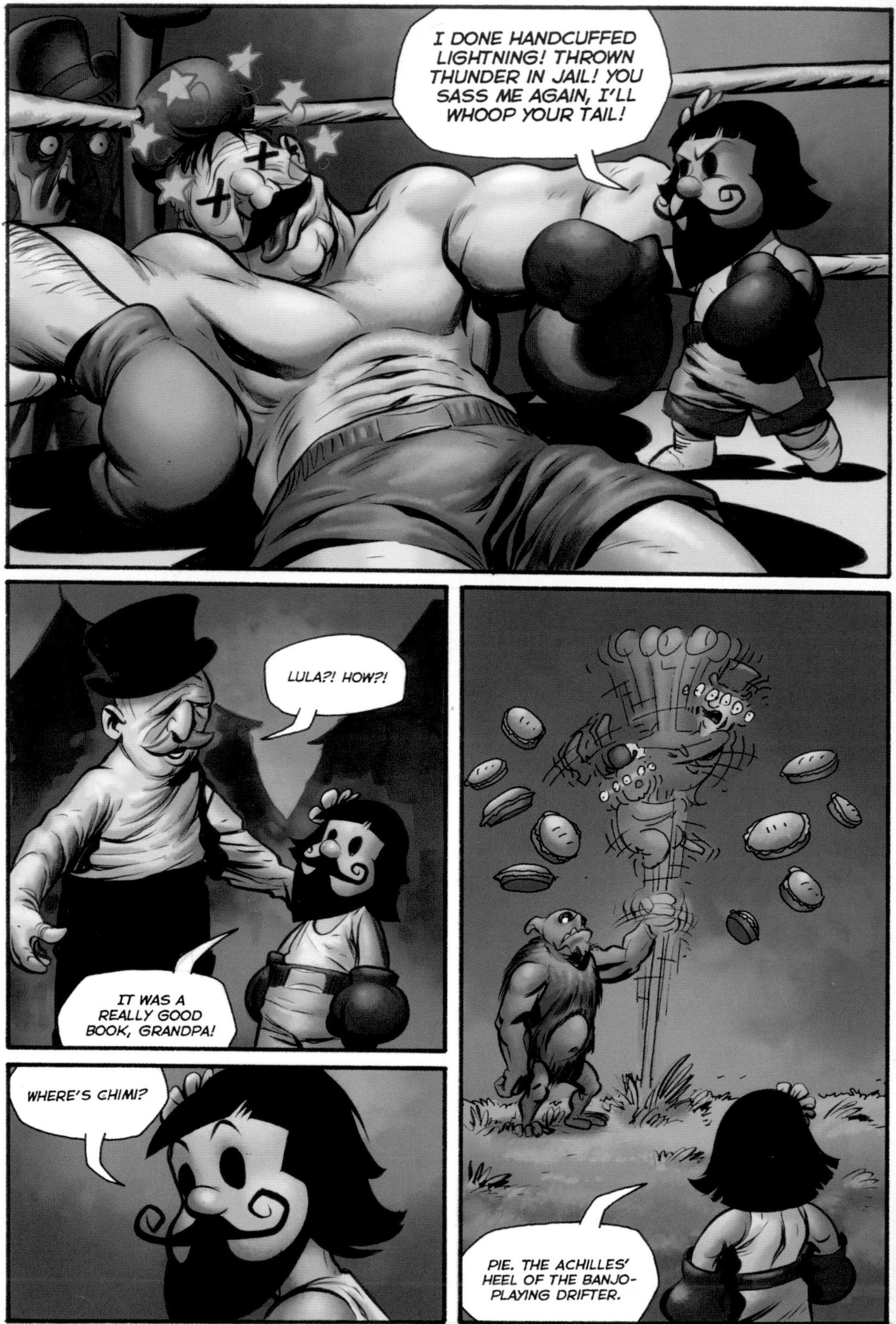
I DONE HANDCUFFED LIGHTNING! THROWN THUNDER IN JAIL! YOU SASS ME AGAIN, I'LL WHOOP YOUR TAIL!
LULA?! HOW?!
IT WAS A REALLY GOOD BOOK, GRANDPA!
WHERE'S CHIMI?
PIE. THE ACHILLES' HEEL OF THE BANJO-PLAYING DRIFTER.
END

Chimichanga Sketchbook

With notes from Mr. Powell

One day I got a call from a cable television network geared toward kids, asking me to pitch them a show. Awesome! I loves me some Hollywood money! I pitched them one thing. They rejected it. I pitched them another (the idea that would become *Chimichanga*). They rejected it. They said the stuff I was pitching them wasn't relatable to children. My first thought was, "And a sponge that talks to a squirrel and wears underwear is?" I finally told them that anything I pitched them was going to be in this vein. This is my style and my voice, and I wasn't the guy they were looking for.

However, my kids saw my sketches of the characters from *Chimichanga*. My youngest son, Cade, in particular, wanted to know all about these guys I'd drawn. I told him what it was about, and he became slightly obsessed with a Chimichanga cartoon. He pestered me about it, asking if it was going to happen and when. This was a new experience for me. I had been working in comics for as long as both my kids could remember. They never cared about anything I was doing. *Goon*, *Batman*, *Hulk*, *The Simpsons*, *Star Wars*. Could care less. But they would not leave me alone about *Chimichanga*. After realizing my sons are probably smarter and have better taste than a TV executive, I decided there was something to this *Chimichanga* idea, and I'd better turn it into a comic.

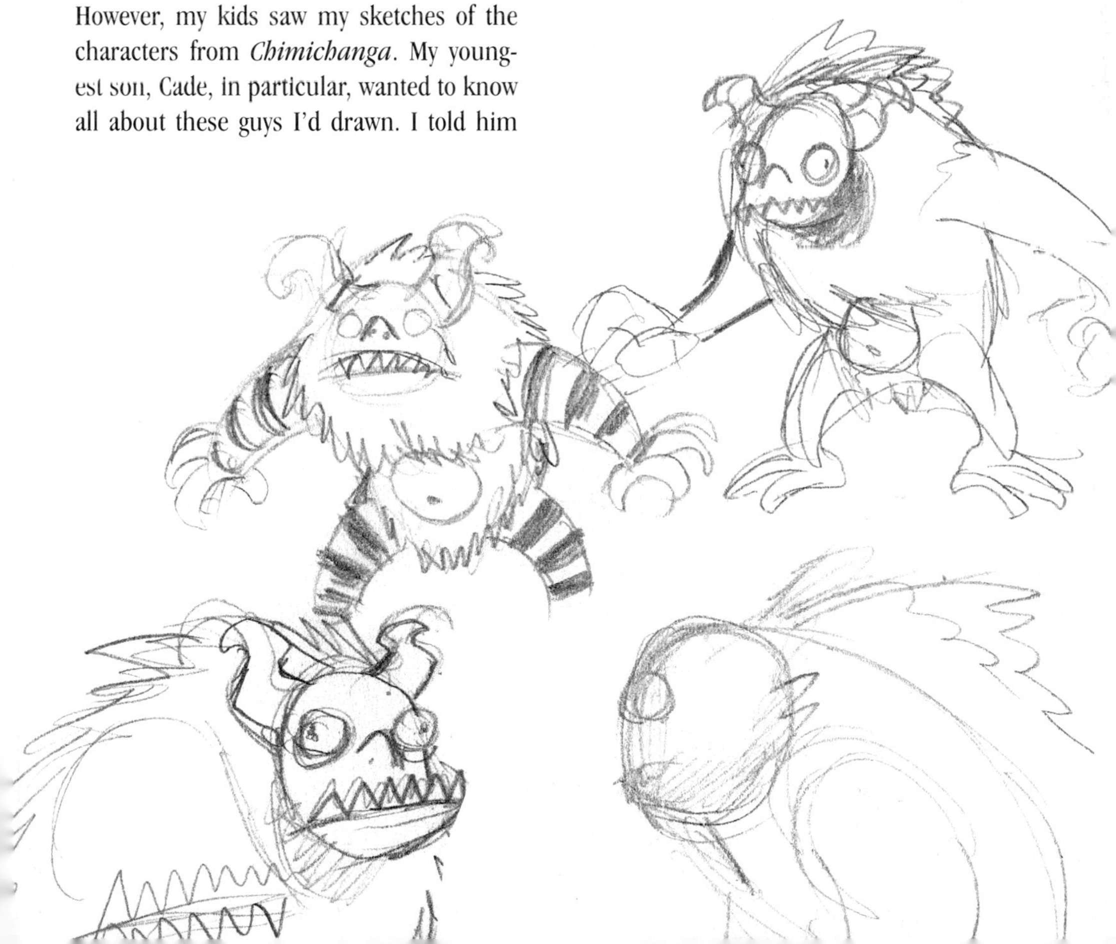

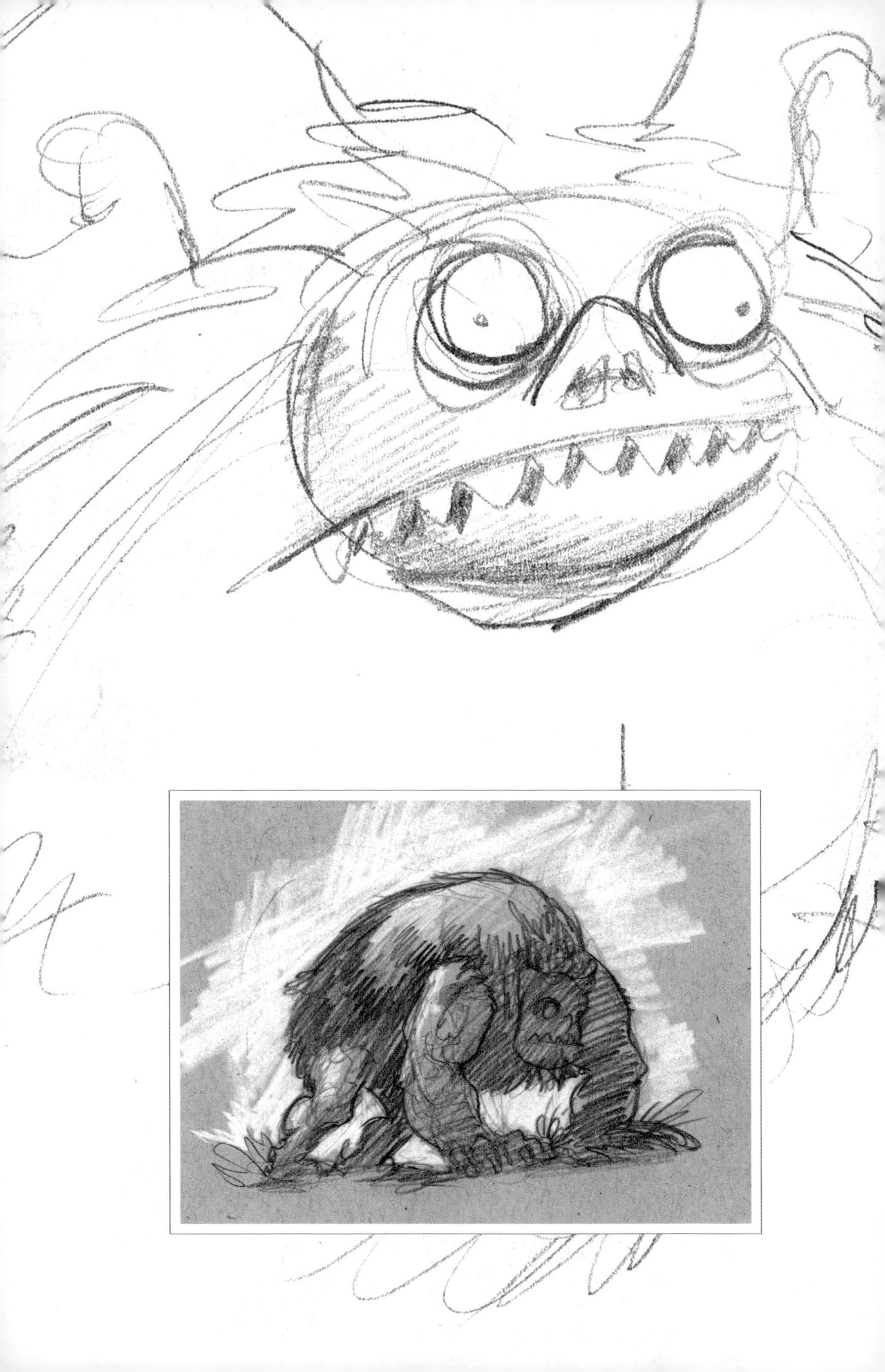

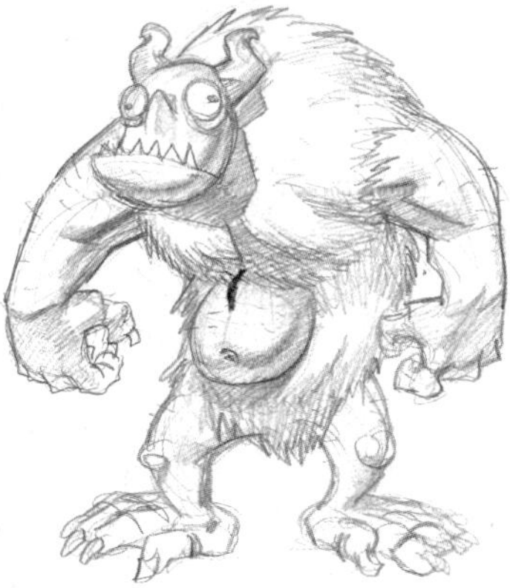

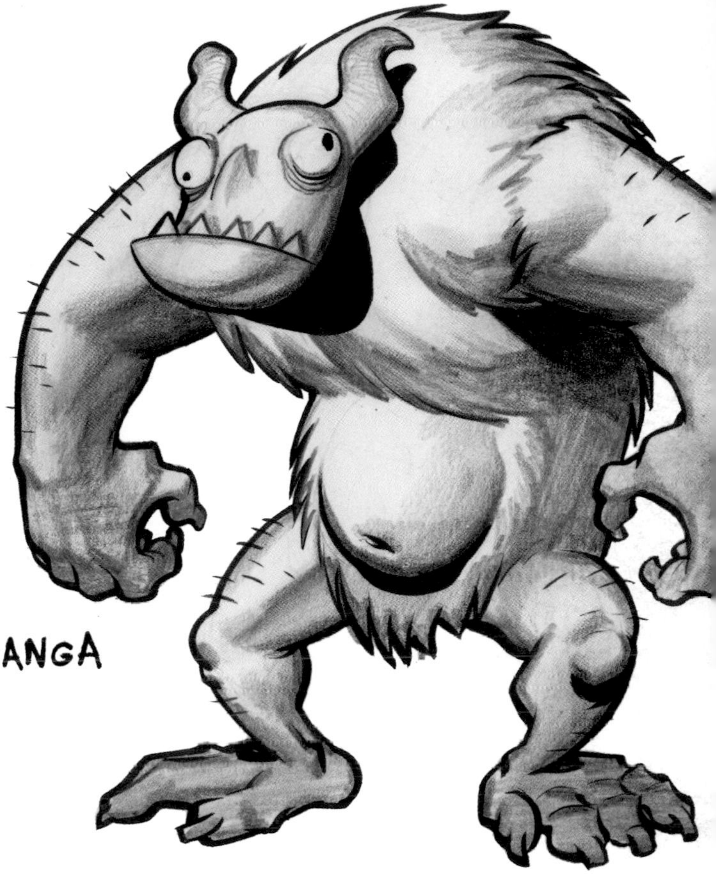

CHIMICHANGA

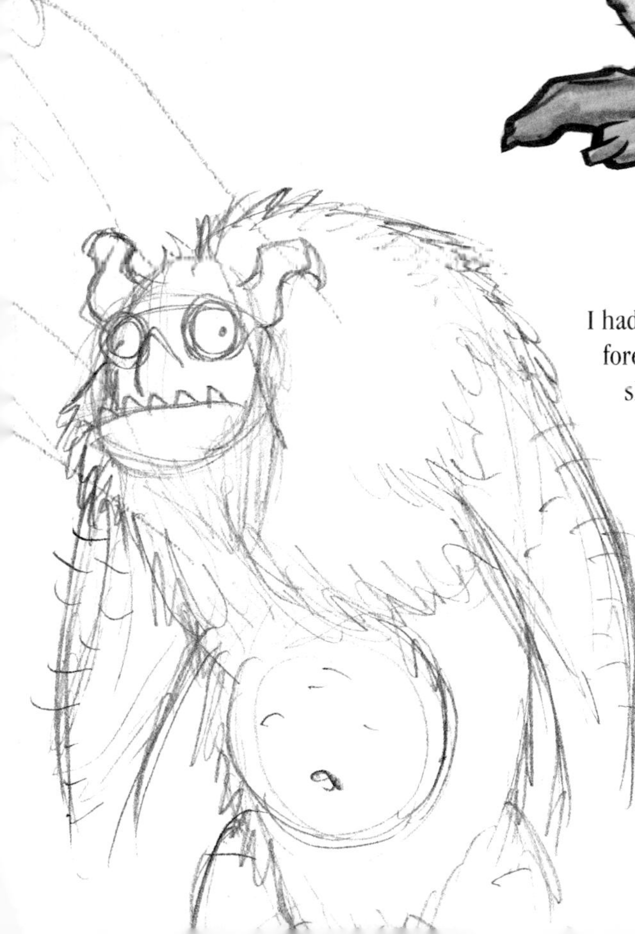

I had the spirit of Chimichanga down before I had his look. He's basically a big, sloppy, spastic dog. I wanted him to be cartoony but not cutesy. I also wanted a vague sense of odd creepiness about him—so you weren't quite sure if he was going be nice to you. I wanted a kind of "You're adorable! Are you gonna bite me?" vibe.

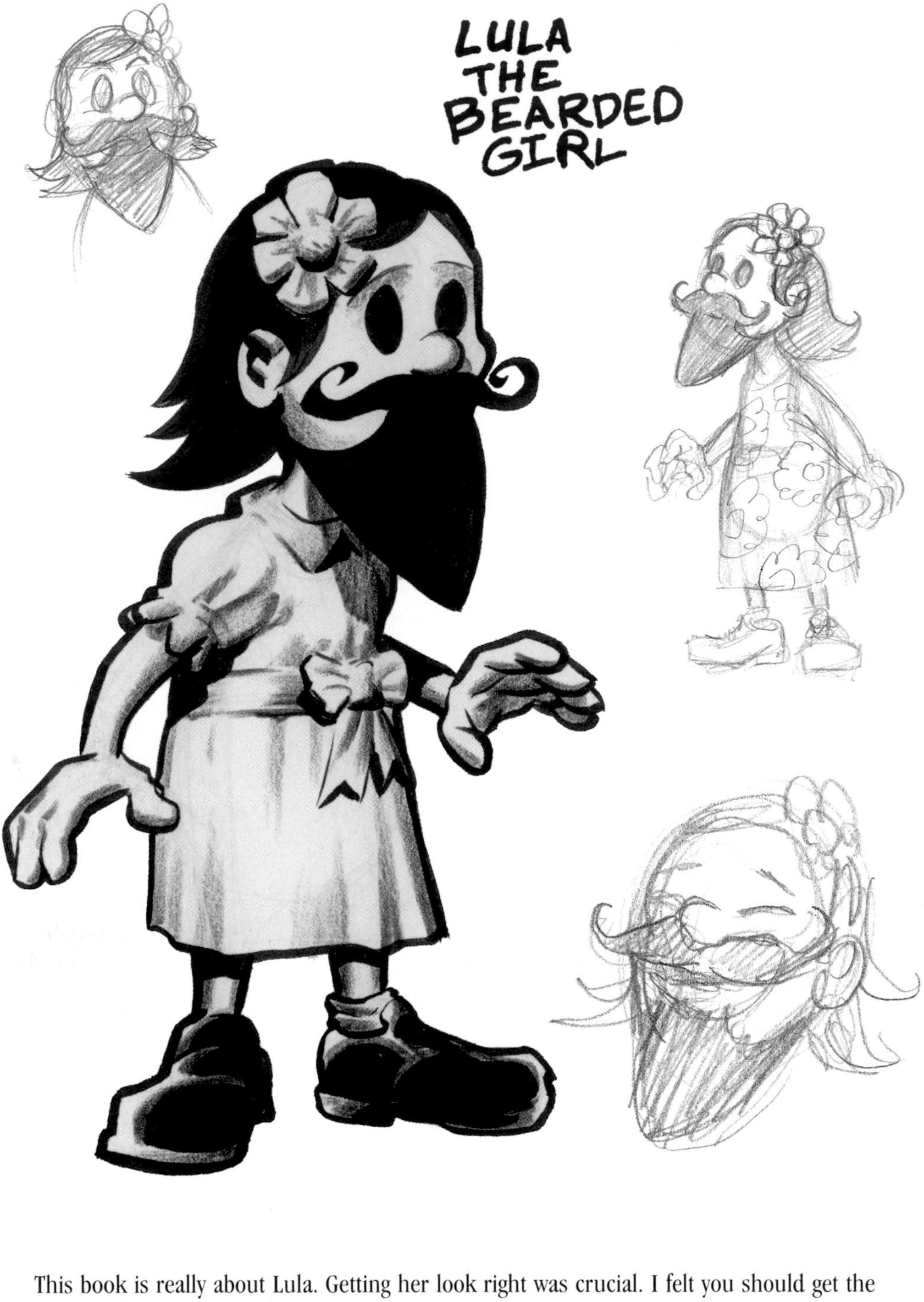
LULA THE BEARDED GIRL

This book is really about Lula. Getting her look right was crucial. I felt you should get the tone of these characters immediately from the visual. In my first sketches of Lula, she was a skinny kid with big, clunky shoes. I liked her. She had a certain nurturing feel to her that fit her story, but she also seemed quiet and meek.

Then I realized the stereotypical bearded lady is also fat. On a whim I scribbled out a chubby version of Lula with meaty little knees. She immediately took on the spunk I was looking for. I loved that her chubbiness, along with her beard, could make her less courageous or outgoing. But with her design and attitude, it seemed to make her more confident.

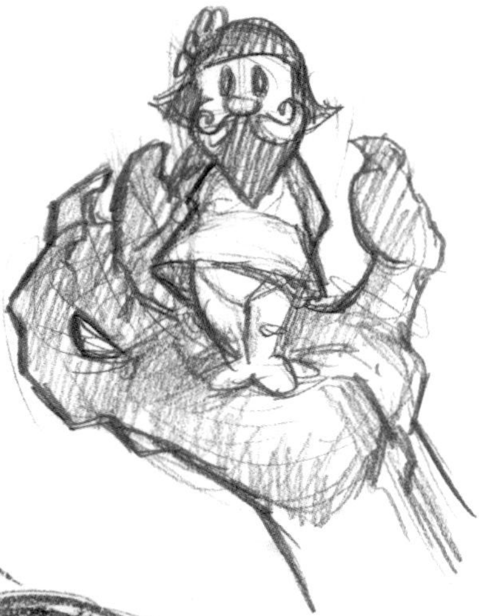

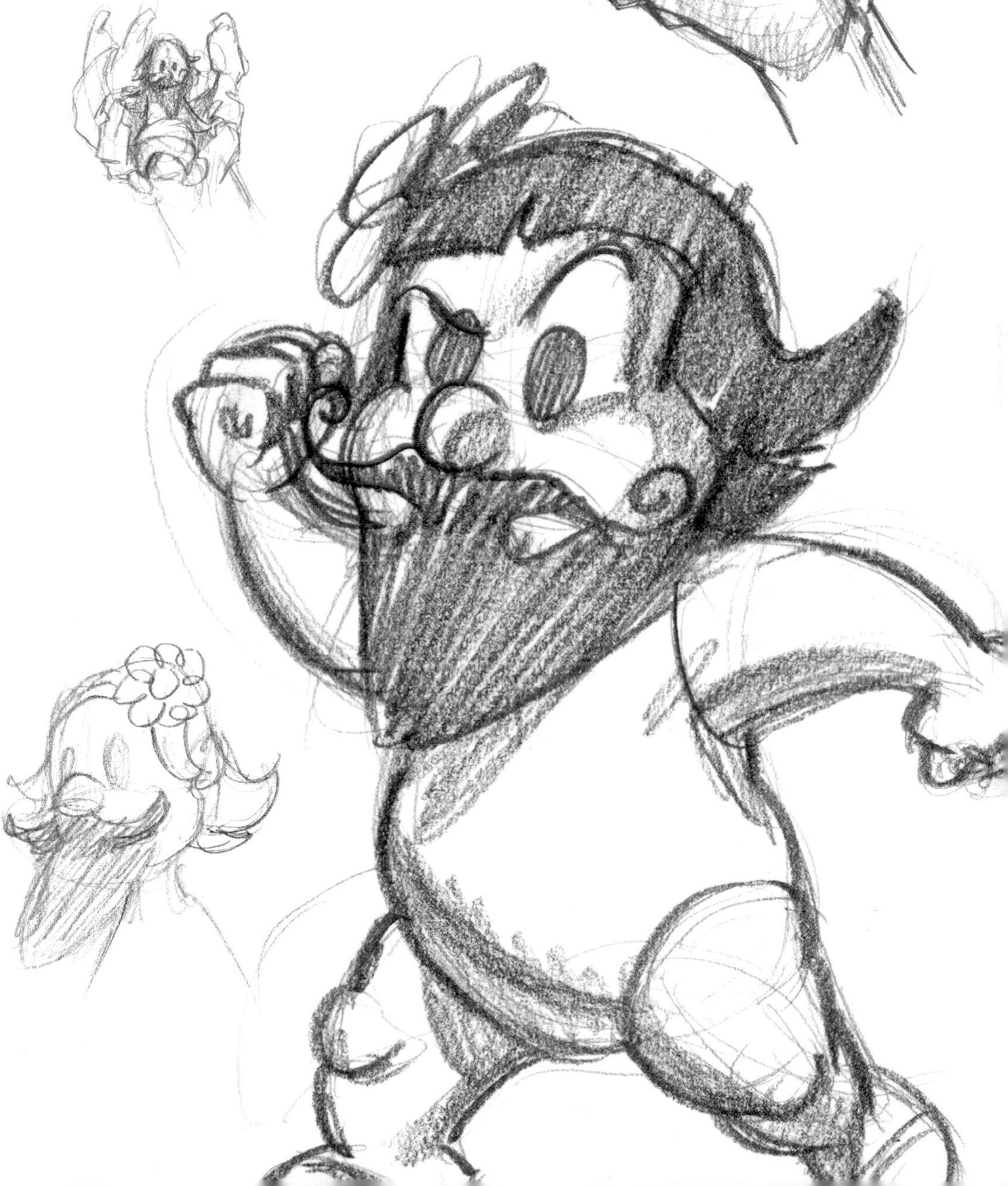

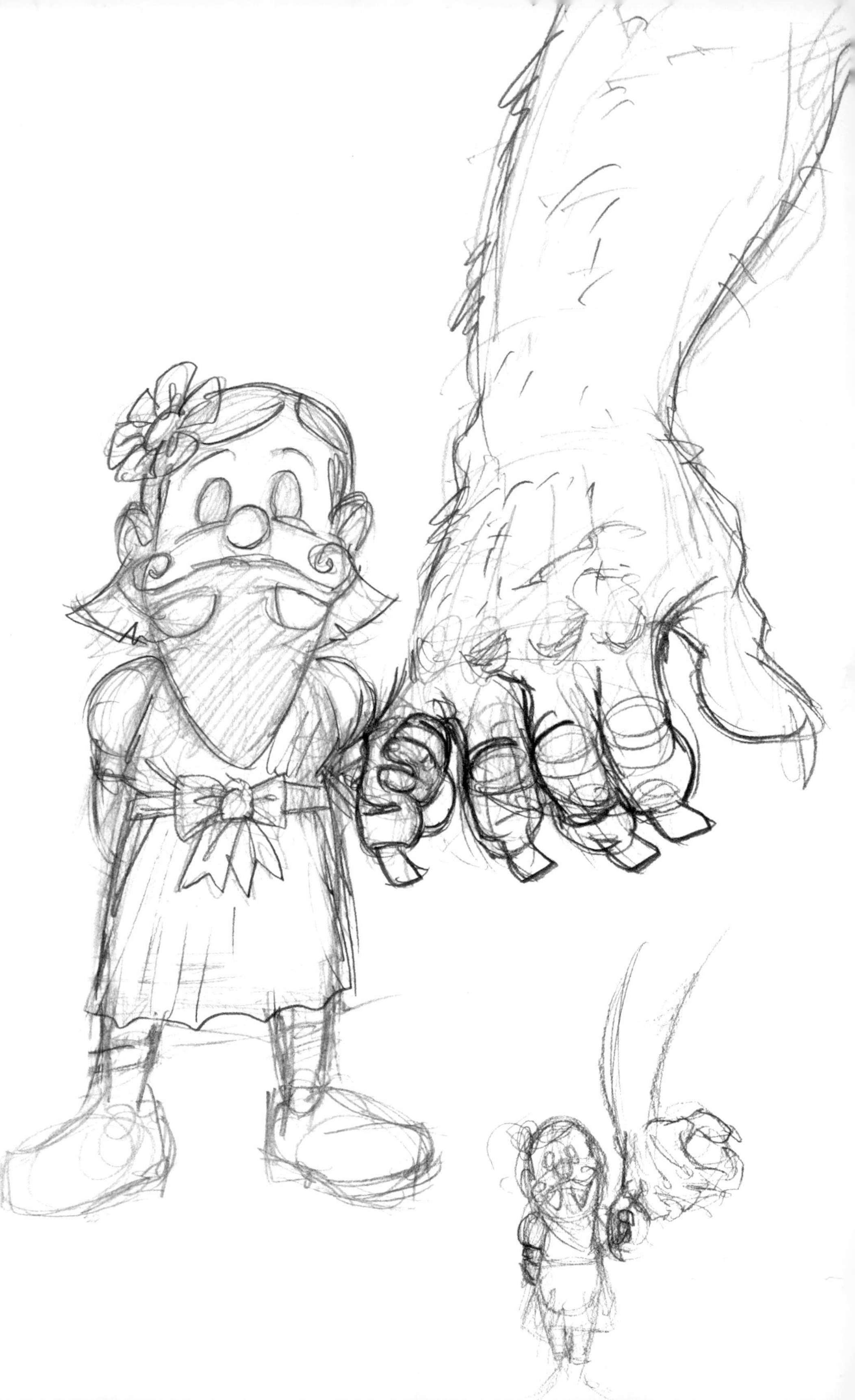

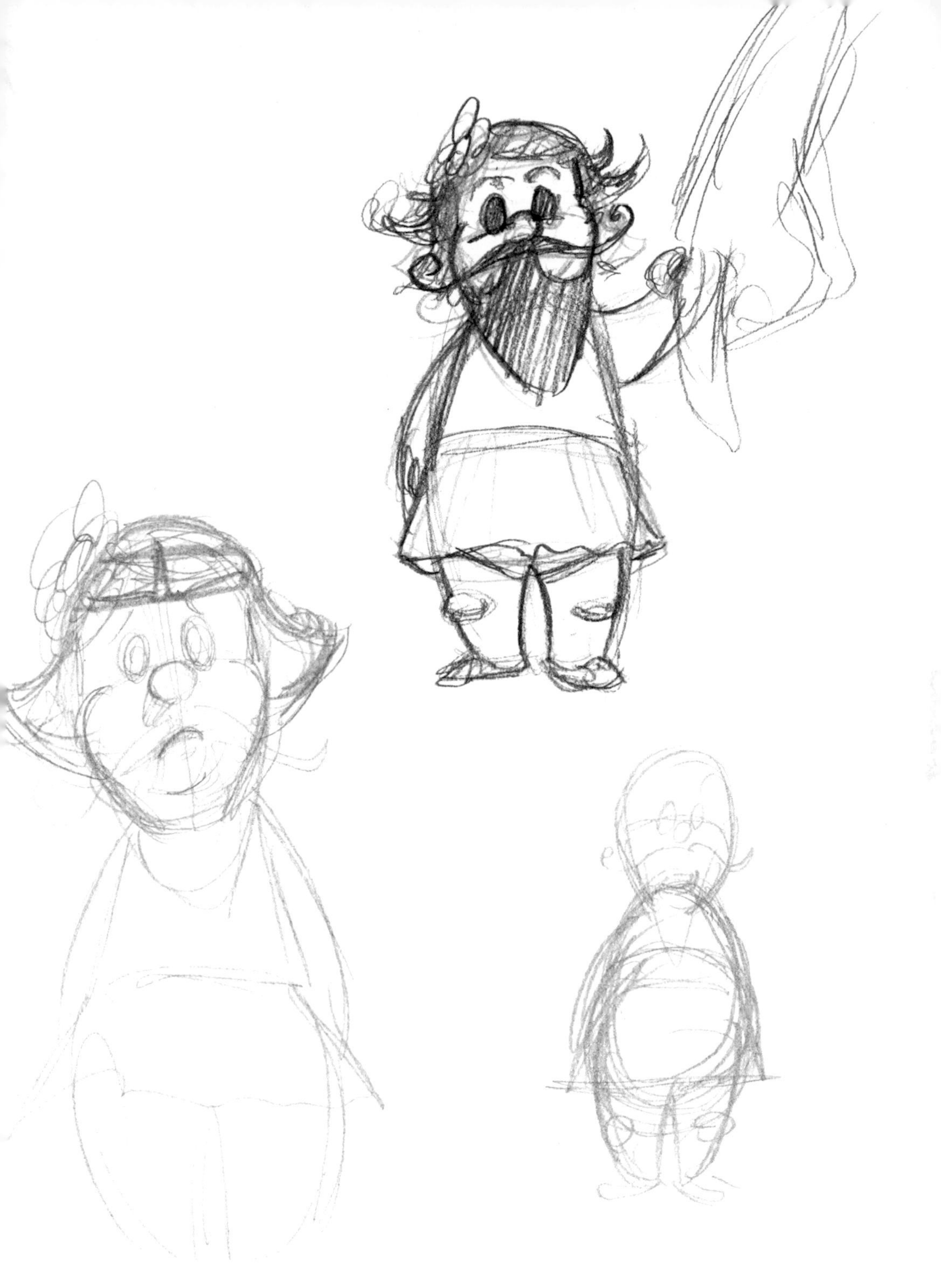

Here are some scribbles for the first cover—the moment I decided to go with a chubby Lula.

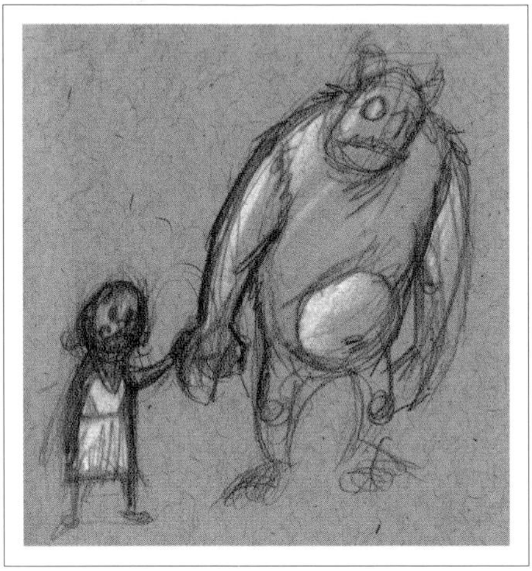

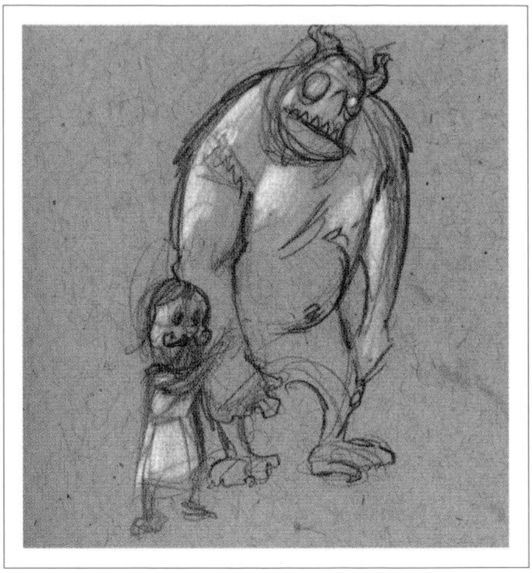

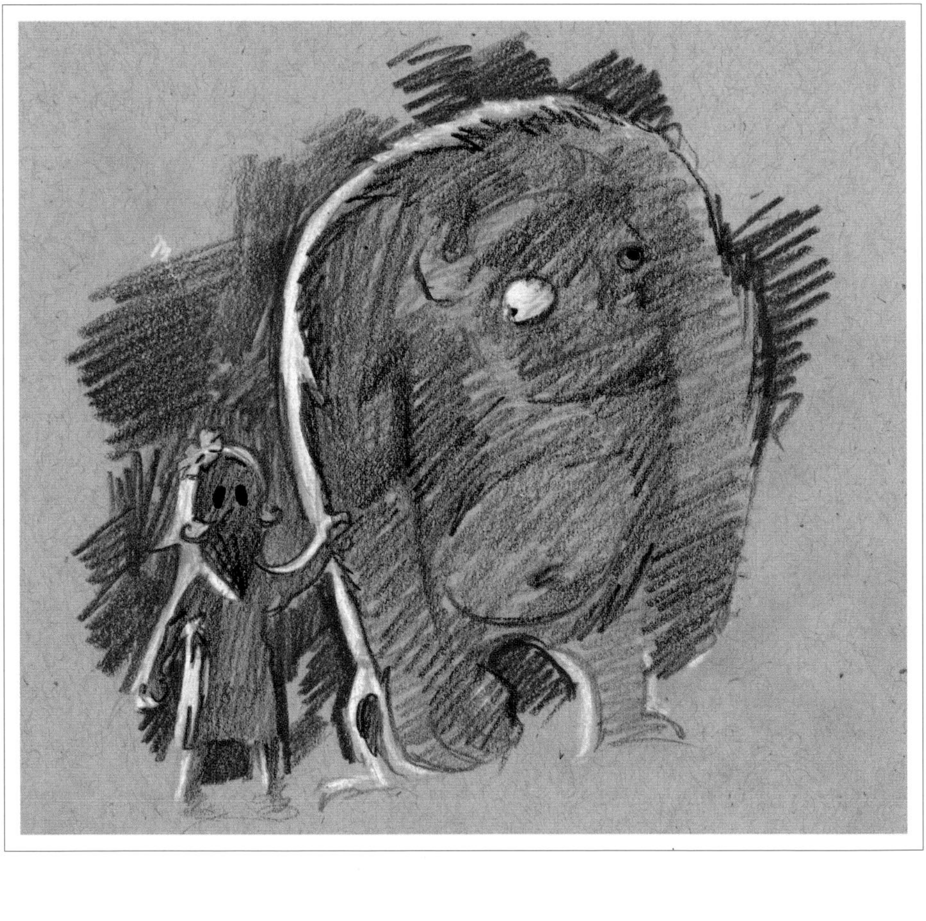

The page to the right is a very early digital painting of skinny Lula. And notice Chimichanga is missing his chin whiskers.

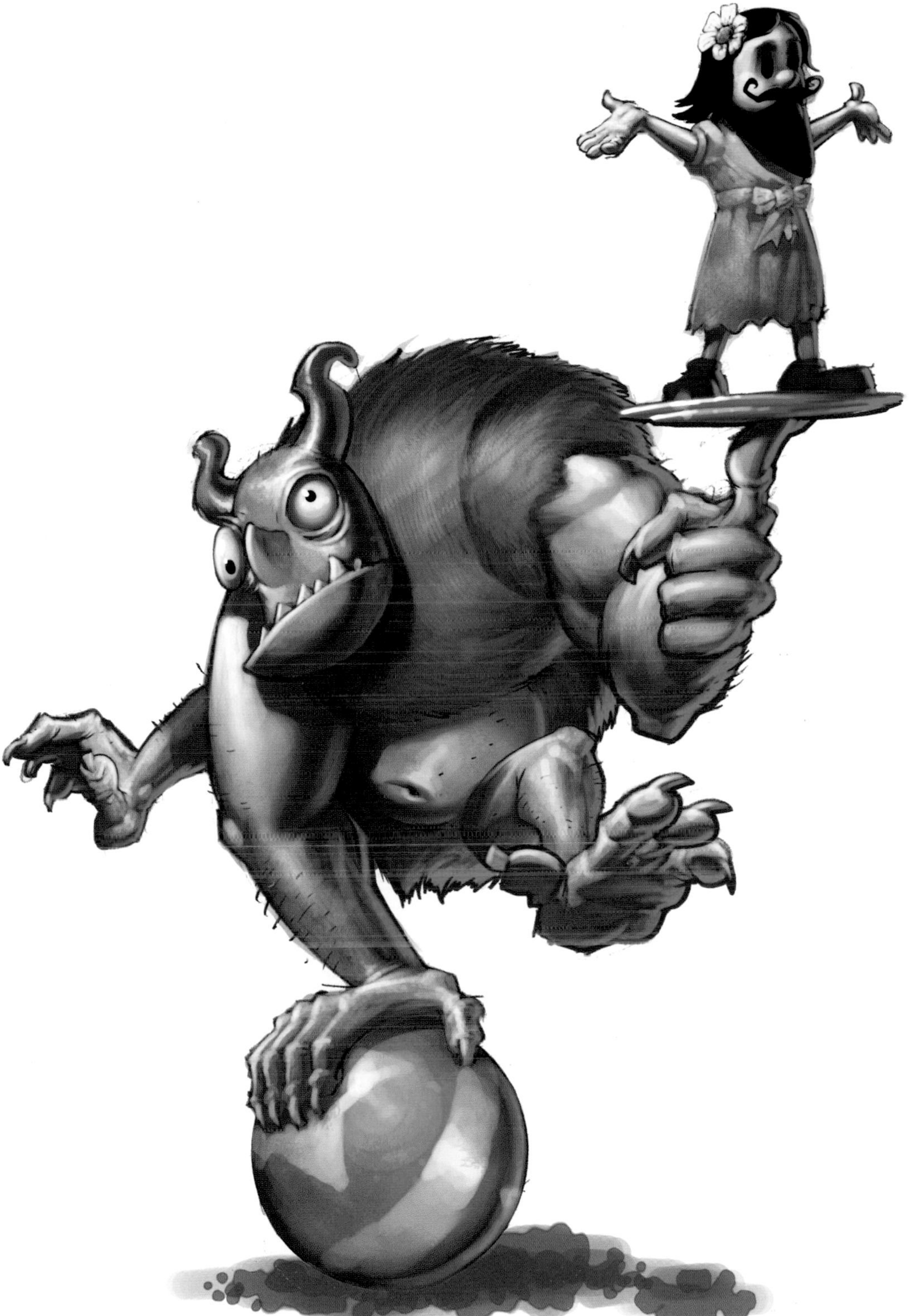

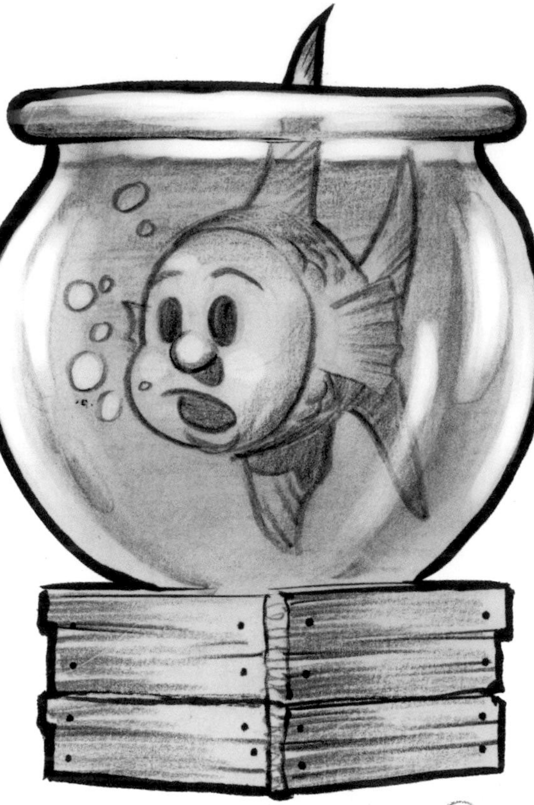

HERATIO THE BOY-FACED FISH

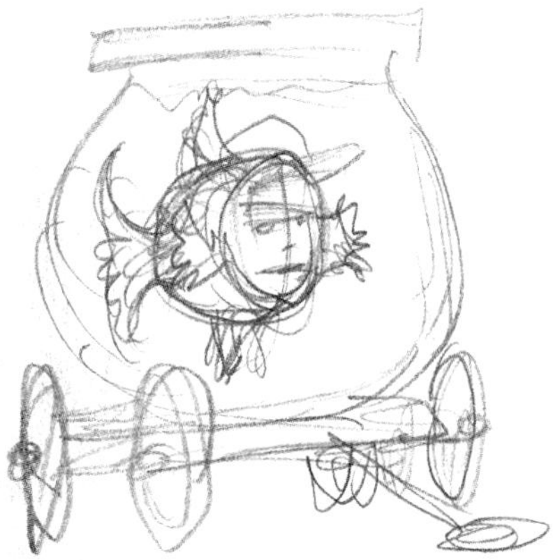

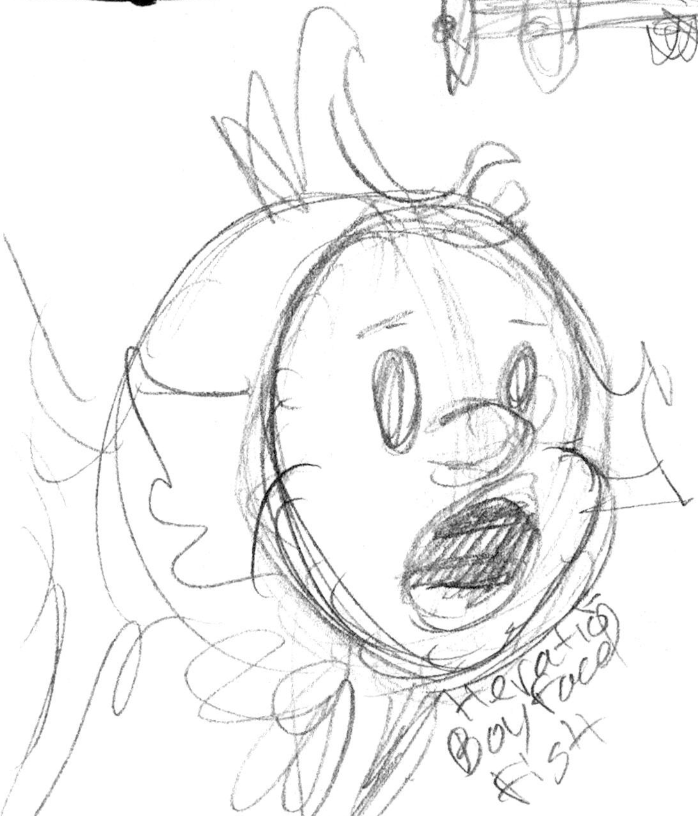
Heratio Boyface Fish

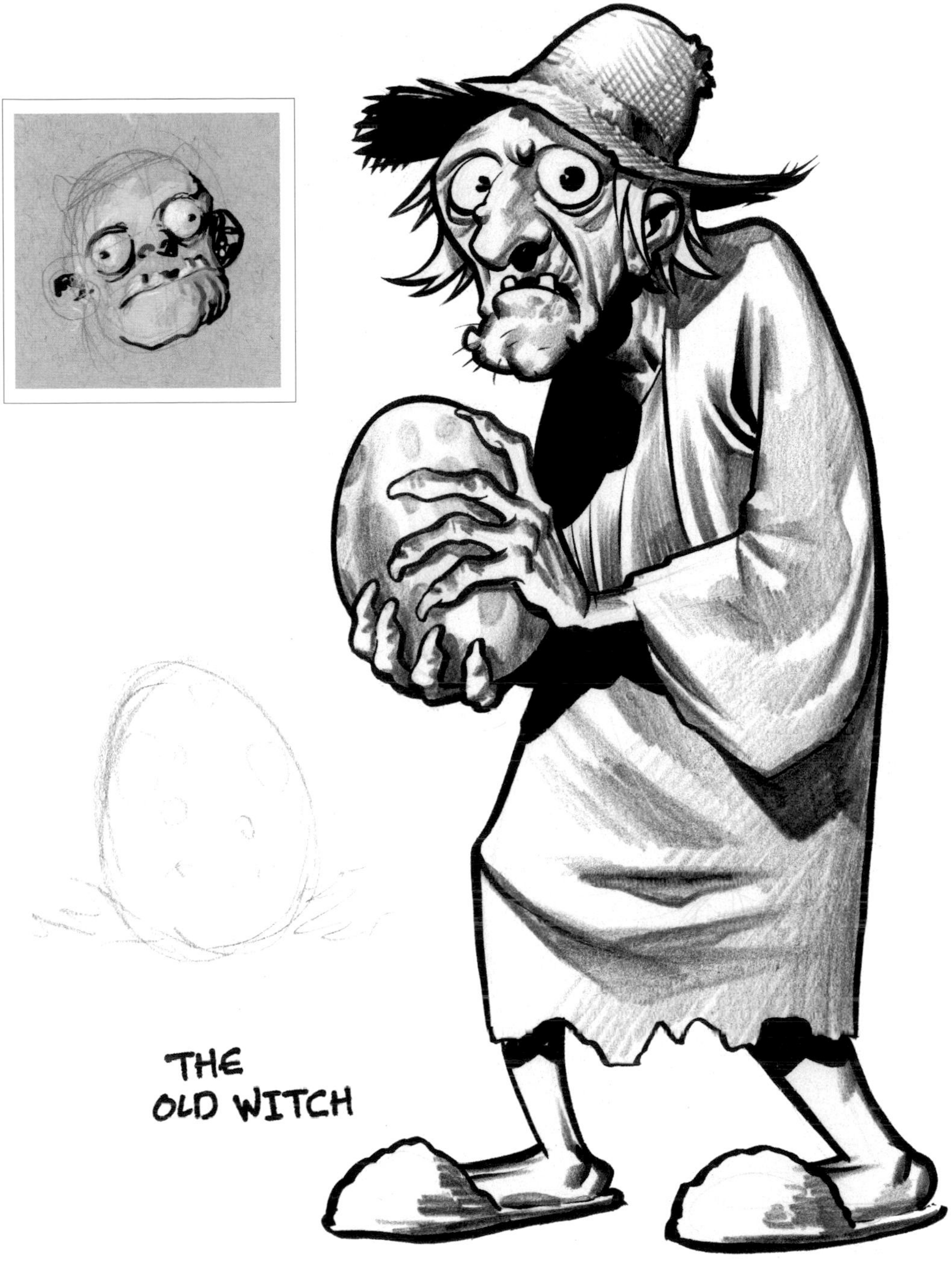
THE
OLD WITCH

There's always a wolf-faced boy or an alligator man in a sideshow. I wanted to flip that idea. That's where Heratio, the Boy-Faced Fish, came from.

I wanted the witch to look like a hobo lady and not a Disney-style villain.

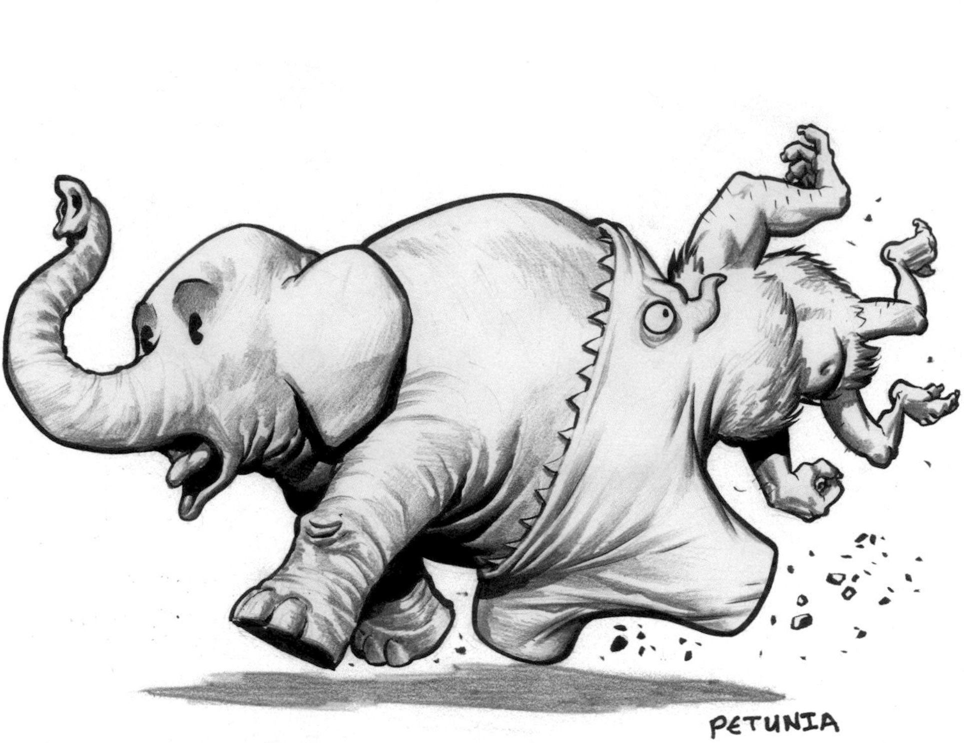
PETUNIA

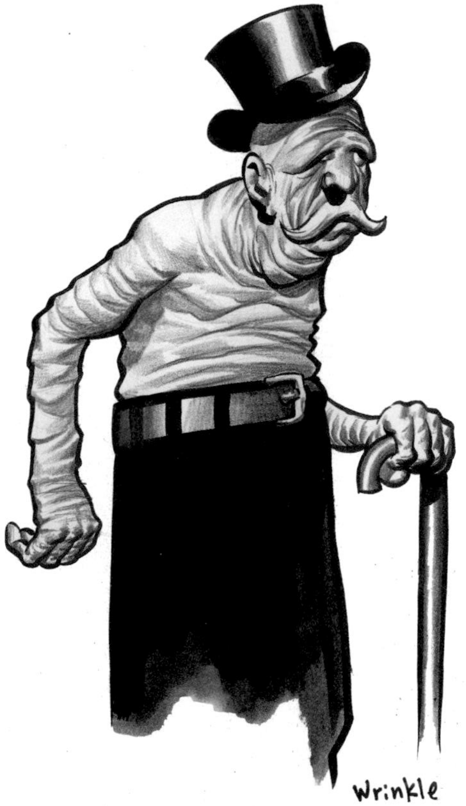
Wrinkle

I really felt the image of Chimichanga with his mouth wrapped around the back end of an elephant was going to sell *Chimichanga* as a TV series. Shows what I know.

The characters of Sweetbread and Rhubarb (opposite page) were in the original cartoon pitch, but they make their first appearance in the bonus story in this collection.

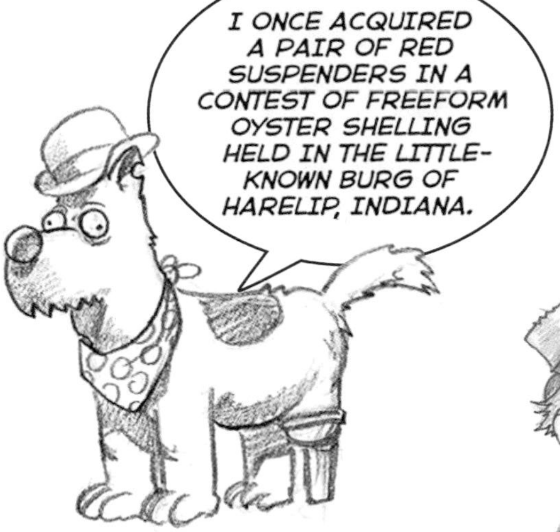
I ONCE ACQUIRED A PAIR OF RED SUSPENDERS IN A CONTEST OF FREEFORM OYSTER SHELLING HELD IN THE LITTLE-KNOWN BURG OF HARELIP, INDIANA.

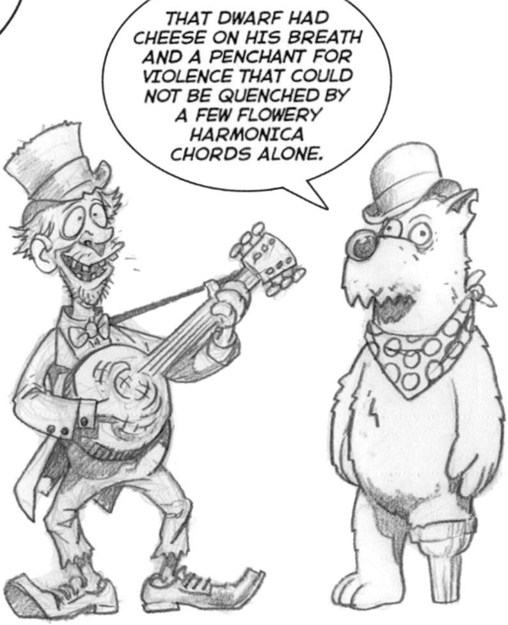
THAT DWARF HAD CHEESE ON HIS BREATH AND A PENCHANT FOR VIOLENCE THAT COULD NOT BE QUENCHED BY A FEW FLOWERY HARMONICA CHORDS ALONE.

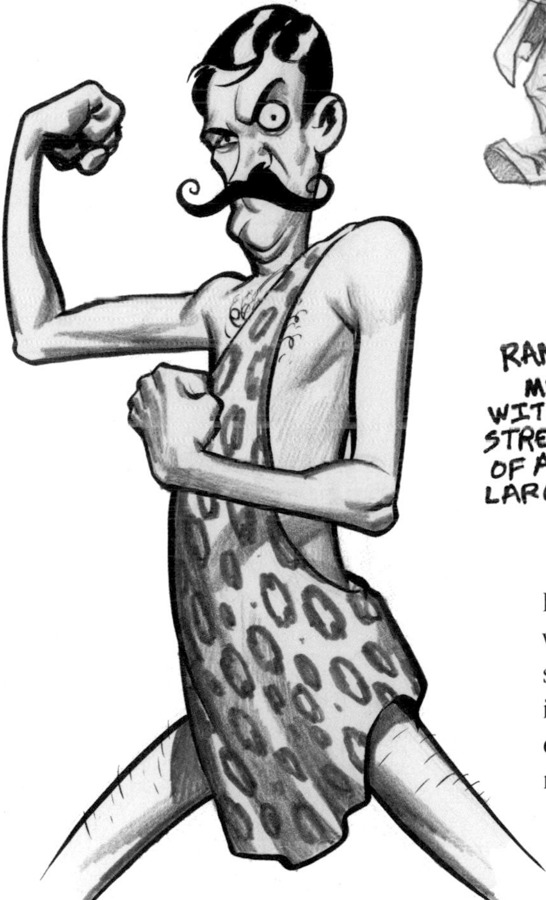
RANDY
MAN
WITH THE
STRENGTH
OF A SLIGHTLY
LARGER MAN

Following page: This strip has nothing to do with *Chimichanga*, but it has a little Lula spunk to it. It's about my son Cade catching the flu when he was four. Without his enthusiasm this book wouldn't have been made. So I'm throwing it in.

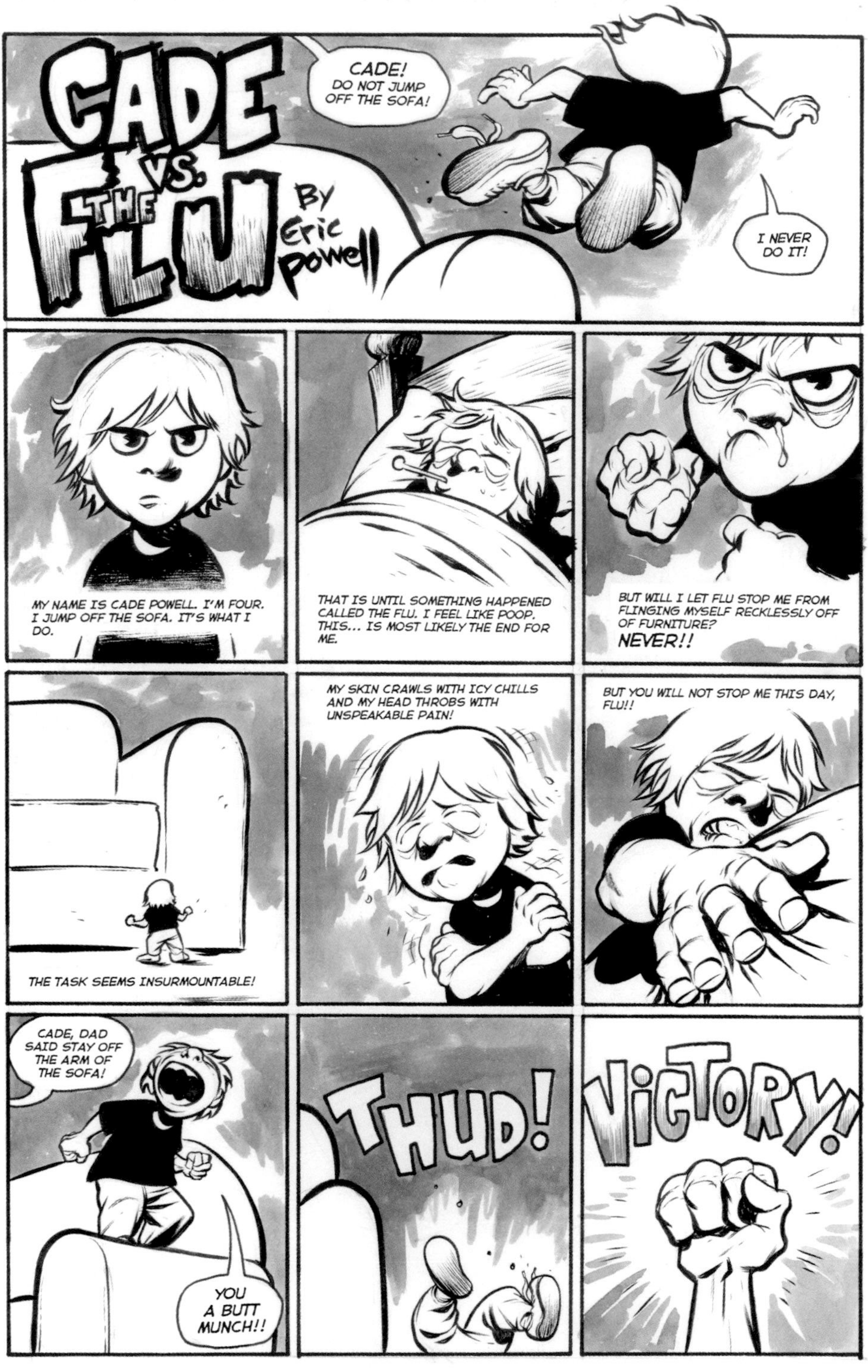
CADE VS. THE FLU
By Eric Powell
CADE! DO NOT JUMP OFF THE SOFA!
I NEVER DO IT!
MY NAME IS CADE POWELL. I'M FOUR. I JUMP OFF THE SOFA. IT'S WHAT I DO.
THAT IS UNTIL SOMETHING HAPPENED CALLED THE FLU. I FEEL LIKE POOP. THIS... IS MOST LIKELY THE END FOR ME.
BUT WILL I LET FLU STOP ME FROM FLINGING MYSELF RECKLESSLY OFF OF FURNITURE? NEVER!!
THE TASK SEEMS INSURMOUNTABLE!
MY SKIN CRAWLS WITH ICY CHILLS AND MY HEAD THROBS WITH UNSPEAKABLE PAIN!
BUT YOU WILL NOT STOP ME THIS DAY, FLU!!
CADE, DAD SAID STAY OFF THE ARM OF THE SOFA!
YOU A BUTT MUNCH!!
THUD!
VICTORY!

THE GOON™

by Eric Powell

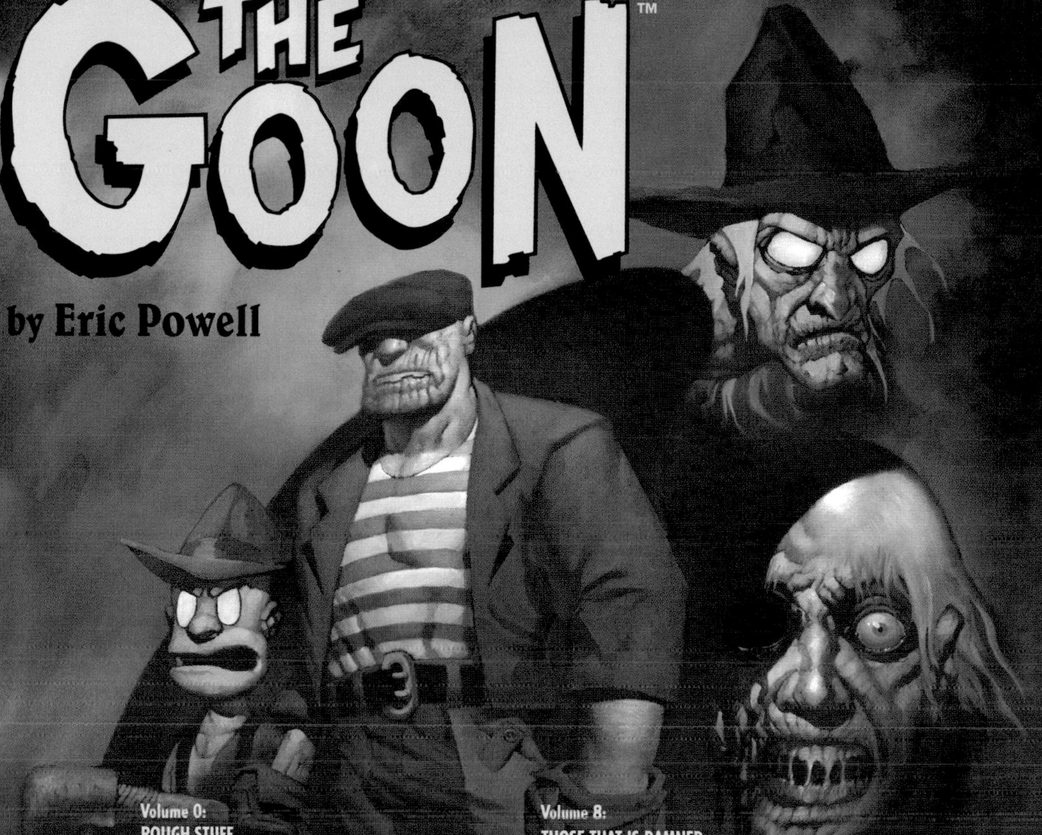

DARK HORSE BOOKS®
DarkHorse.com

To find a comics shop in your area, call 1-888-266-4226 For more information or to
order direct: • On the web: DarkHorse.com • E-mail: mailorder@DarkHorse.com • Phone:
1-800-862-0052 Mon.–Fri. 9 AM to 5 PM Pacific Time

The Goon™ and © 2011 Eric Powell. (BL6053)

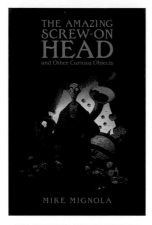

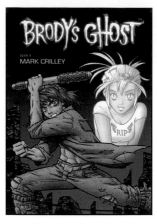

ALSO FROM DARK HORSE BOOKS

THE AMAZING SCREW-ON HEAD
and Other Curious Objects
MIKE MIGNOLA

THE AMAZING SCREW-ON HEAD AND OTHER CURIOUS OBJECTS

Mike Mignola

When Emperor Zombie threatens the safety of all life on earth, President Lincoln enlists the aid of a mechanical head. With the help of associates Mr. Groin (a faithful manservant) and Mr. Dog (a dog), Screw-On Head must brave ancient tombs, a Victorian flying apparatus, and demons from a dimension inside a turnip.

978-1-59582-501-8 | $17.99

BRODY'S GHOST
BOOK 1
MARK CRILLEY
RIP

BRODY'S GHOST BOOK 1

Mark Crilley

Brody hoped it was just a hallucination. But no, the teenaged ghostly girl who'd come face to face with him in the middle of a busy city street was all too real. And now she was back, telling him she needed his help in hunting down a dangerous killer, and that he must undergo training from the spirit of a centuries-old samurai to unlock his hidden supernatural powers. Thirteen-time Eisner nominee Mark Crilley joins Dark Horse to launch his most original and action-packed saga to date in *Brody's Ghost*, the first in a six-volume limited series.

978-1-59582-521-6 | $6.99

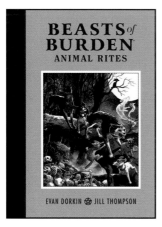

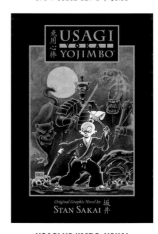

BEASTS of BURDEN
ANIMAL RITES
EVAN DORKIN JILL THOMPSON

BEASTS OF BURDEN: ANIMAL RITES

Evan Dorkin, Jill Thompson

Welcome to Burden Hill—a picturesque little town adorned with white picket fences and green, green grass, home to a unique team of paranormal investigators. Beneath this shiny exterior, Burden Hill harbors dark and sinister secrets, and it's up to a heroic gang of dogs—and one cat—to protect the town from the evil forces at work. These are the beasts of Burden Hill—Pugs, Ace, Jack, Whitey, Red, and the Orphan—whose early experiences with the paranormal have led them to become members of the Wise Dog Society, official animal agents sworn to protect their town from evil.

978-1-59582-513-1 | $19.99

兎用心棒
USAGI
YOKAI
YOJIMBO
Original Graphic Novel by
STAN SAKAI
坂井

USAGI YOJIMBO: YOKAI

Stan Sakai

Yokai are the monsters, demons, and spirits of Japanese folklore, such as the shape-changing *kitsune*, the *obakeneko* demon cats, and the evil *oni* ogres. Usagi faces all these and more when a desperate woman begs for his help in finding her kidnapped daughter. Tracing the abducted girl deep into the forest, Usagi finds it haunted by creatures of Japanese legend and discovers that they are amassing for a great raid on the countryside! Fortunately, Usagi is joined by Sasuke the Demon Queller, who is also fighting to prevent the invasion, but things aren't always as they seem—especially when dealing with the supernatural!

978-1-59582-362-5 | $14.99

AVAILABLE AT YOUR LOCAL COMICS SHOP OR BOOKSTORE · To find a comics shop in your area, call 1-888-266-4226. For more information or to order direct, visit DarkHorse.com or call 1-800-862-0052 Mon.–Fri. 9 a.m. to 5 p.m. Pacific Time. Prices and availability subject to change without notice.

DARK HORSE BOOKS